Readers Love *Dark Hallows*

'Grips you from the beginning… I read it in a few hours'

'Fast paced. Hard to put down… Caught hold of me and had me hooked from the start. I was literally on the edge of my seat reading this book!'

'Enjoyable, mysterious and well written. A great book!'

'A mesmerising read'

'Uniquely perfect'

STEVE FRECH lives in Los Angeles. In addition to writing, he produces and hosts the *Random Awesomeness Podcast*, an improv-comedy quiz show that has been performed at Upright Citizens Brigade, The Improv, iO West, and Nerdist.

Dark Hollows

STEVE FRECH

ONE PLACE. MANY STORIES

HQ
An imprint of HarperCollins*Publishers* Ltd
1 London Bridge Street
London SE1 9GF

First published by HQ Digital 2019

2
This edition published in Great Britain by
HQ, an imprint of HarperCollins*Publishers* Ltd 2020

Copyright © Steve Frech 2020

Steve Frech asserts the moral right to be
identified as the author of this work.
A catalogue record for this book is
available from the British Library.

ISBN: 9780008372170

MIX
Paper from
responsible sources
FSC™ C007454

This book is produced from independently certified FSC™ paper
to ensure responsible forest management.

For more information visit: www.harpercollins.co.uk/green

Printed and bound in Great Britain by
CPI Group (UK) Ltd, Croydon, CR0 4YY

Just close your eyes,
And you and I,
Will brave the dark and go dancing.

The Dreamer's Waltz

Chapter 1

I'm standing in the basement of a run-down, abandoned warehouse, staring at the padlock on a heavy steel door. The walls are coated in grime and there is the sound of dripping water from somewhere in the darkness.

The padlock begins to tremble. It's subtle, at first, but then grows violent, as if some enraged, unseen force is trying to pull it open. The padlock rattles against the door.

"No ... please ... please, hold ..." I whisper, my voice weak in pain and fear.

The shaking intensifies. It begins to infect the door and the walls, filling the basement with a low rumble.

"Don't ... I'm so sorry ... Please ..."

The rumble grows into a deafening roar. It feels like the entire building is going to come down on top of me. Bile rises in my throat.

"No ... no ..."

Everything stops.

I know what's coming. I know what's behind that door.

Oh my God, what have I done?

The lock snaps open.

I bolt upright in bed. Sweat pours down my face and my lungs pull in rapid gulps of air.

In the dawning light of morning, I can see Murphy, my black Lab mutt, lying in his bed in the corner of the room. He cocks his head at me.

I grip my side and hiss through clenched teeth. Sitting up so fast causes the old injury in my side to flare with pain, but it passes. I steady my breath and wipe the sweat from my eyes. I throw off the covers, hop out of bed, and head to the bathroom. The nightmare is nothing new. I've been having it for years, reliving the panic and shock of that night over and over, but I've learned to quickly put it out of my mind.

After throwing some cold water on my face, I pull on a pair of jeans and a shirt and head downstairs to start a pot of coffee. Murphy joins me in the kitchen, but instead of coming over to the counter, he sits next to his food bowl and gives me those big, dinner-plate eyes.

"What? Are you hungry?" I ask.

His tail thumps against the floor.

I feed him a little dry food from the bag in the pantry, and then go to the window over the sink and glance down the drive, past the pond, to the cottage sitting at the edge of the woods.

The Thelsons' car is gone. No surprise there. They said they were getting an early start back to Manhattan.

Coffee in hand, I walk to the front door and pat my leg as I step out onto the porch.

"Let's go, Murph."

Murphy inhales the last of his breakfast and hustles after me. I don't think I've ever seen him chew, even when he was a puppy. He springs off the porch and down the steps. We walk past the pond, towards the cottage. As we pass the truck in the driveway, I make yet another mental note to fix that damn taillight. Somehow, all the mental notes I make about it go unremembered.

I walk around the fire pit and note the wineglasses sitting next to the chairs. I step over to the front door of the cottage, take out my key, and open the door. Before doing anything, I go to the kitchen table and open the guestbook. I flip through the pages until I find the latest entry. The ink is so dark and sharp, it had to have been written not more than an hour ago.

We were in town from Manhattan to do some leaf-peeping and had a wonderful time. The Hollows is a beautiful little town. We loved the shops on Main Street and strolling through the cemetery at the Old Stone Church. What can we say about Jacob's cottage? So amazing! We began every morning with a walk through the woods to check out the hills and always stopped at "The Sanctuary". Jacob is the perfect host. The wine and the s'mores were just the right touch. And then, there's Murphy! Such a sweetie! Can't wait to come back!

~ John & Margaret Thelson

I snap the guestbook closed and look around the cottage. It never fails; whenever someone from Manhattan signs the guestbook, they always have to mention that they're from Manhattan. Hopefully, they'll post the review on Be Our Guest this afternoon, once they get home.

The Thelsons were standard New York City types; taking their yearly fall pilgrimage up north to see some trees. They were a wealthy couple who would call this quaint, one-bedroom cottage "roughing it", even though it had all the amenities, a couple of bottles of wine, and a fire pit outside. Still, they were pleasant, and they've left the cottage in good shape. The turnaround should be quick, and I've got it down to a science.

Murphy walks through the open front door. He's done scouting the fire pit for any stray graham crackers or marshmallows left by the Thelsons, and goes right for the kitchen to see if there are any scraps lying about.

"Happy hunting, Murphy," I say. He deserves it. He's one of my best selling points.

I clap my hands and rub them together. "All right. Time to get to work."

First thing I do is bring in the wineglasses and wash them in the kitchen sink. Then, I collect the bedsheets and towels, put them in a bag, and carry it to the house. Murphy follows close behind. I take the bag down to the basement and pop the contents into the washing machine. Even though we've done this process hundreds of times, Murphy bolts as soon as I open the lid because to him, the washing machine is still some sort of monster. Once I get that going, I head back upstairs. Murphy's on the porch, waiting for me.

"Coward," I say.

He responds by letting his tongue flop out of his mouth and starts panting.

As we begin walking back to the cottage, Murphy spots the ducks that have settled onto the glassy surface of the pond. He pins his ears back and sprints after them.

"Murphy!" I shout.

He stops at the water's edge and looks at me.

"Nope. Come on."

He stares at the pond and then back at me as if to ask, "But do you not see the ducks?"

"Come," I say, with a forceful slap on my leg.

He runs to catch up, but instead of following me into the cottage, he lies down on the cottage porch to enjoy the cool New England morning.

I restock the complimentary toiletries and clean the bathroom. No disasters there. One time, I had a young couple from Los Angeles stay for a weekend and after drinking too much wine, they destroyed the bathroom. I almost left them a bad review, but they were in the "Elite Class" on Be Our Guest, so I held my fire. Thankfully, they left me a glowing review.

I finish scrubbing the tub and stand up a little too quickly. The pain in my side flares again, but it barely registers.

Time to tackle the kitchen. I clean the plates from the s'mores and refill the basket by the coffee maker with packs of Groundworks coffee. I wipe down the counter and sweep the floor. After that, I retrieve the vacuum cleaner from the hall closet. I have my routine down, working my way from the bedroom, then the bathroom, down the hall, and into the living room/kitchen area.

I push the vacuum around the bookcase, which is filled with some of my favorite books—a few thrillers, some Michael Crichtons, *A Christmas Carol*, et cetera. No one reads them while they're here, but they make for good pictures on the Be Our Guest website. There's also a row of DVDs no one watches: *Casablanca*, *When Harry Met Sally*, *Vertigo*, *Roman Holiday*, and *Dead Again*. As I glide the vacuum cleaner over the rug by the fireplace, my eyes catch the stick doll I made years ago, resting on the mantel. It's a crude figure made of twigs tied together with twine. It adds a nice, rugged touch to the place. In Boy Scouts, they taught us to use pine needles instead of twine, but those don't last long—

"For me?" she asked in mock flattery.
"Just something I learned in Boy Scouts."
She saw right through my bullshit.
"Well, I shall treasure it always," she said, clutching the doll to her chest, toying with me …

I'm pulled from my memory by Murphy whining.

He's sitting in the doorway. His expression is a perfect balance of wanting to enter the cottage but respecting the vacuum cleaner.

I flip the switch, and the vacuum engine whirrs to a stop.

"Done," I tell him, and put the vacuum back in the closet.

While in the closet, I rotate the stacks of towels, and accidentally knock over the small dish hidden on the top shelf, which contains a spare key to the house and the coffee shop. I keep a spare key for both out here because I learned the hard way that I should when I locked myself out of the house about a year ago.

I put the keys back in the dish, tuck it all the way back on the shelf, and close the door. I pull out my phone and take a series of pictures of the cottage. It's been a while, and I need to change the photos on the Be Our Guest website.

I head back to the house and transfer the sheets and towels to the dryer. Once again, Murphy stays by my side until I get to the basement stairs, because the dryer is the washer's evil twin. That accomplished, I head back down to the cottage to do one last spot check to make sure everything is perfect.

I normally wouldn't do an extra check, but tonight, I'm breaking a rule.

Here's the deal—a few years ago, my parents died. We weren't particularly close. In fact, we weren't close at all, which is strange for an only child, but there was history. They were the successful, wealthy, married couple who had done everything right, while I was nothing but one dumb decision after another. I could never get my feet under me and it was my own fault. I squandered every chance they gave me.

It got so bad that they finally cut me off after I screwed around my sophomore year in college. I had to find another way to pay my tuition, which I did. I told them I got a job, but not the whole story about what the job was. They were pleased that I had finally taken responsibility for myself and tried to reconnect but for me, the damage had been done. I wanted nothing to do with them. There were obligatory phone calls on Christmas and birthdays, filled with awkward conversations. I was living in Portland, Maine, while they had moved to Hilton Head, South Carolina.

Their passing was quick. Mom became ill. I offered to come down and help out, because that's what an only child does, right, even if we hadn't really spoken in years? Dad declined my offer, claiming he could handle it. Well, he couldn't. The stress got to him and he had a heart attack. It was over before he hit the floor. I got the call from the nurse Dad had hired to look after Mom. On my way down to the funeral, Mom passed away. The nurse said it was from a broken heart. I didn't know how to feel. They hadn't been a part of my life for so long, it felt like they were already gone, but I did wish that I had maybe tried to patch things up.

The dual funeral was surreal. There were a lot of people there, and I didn't know any of them. When they found out who I was, they came up and commented on how painful and sad it must be for me, and what wonderful people my parents had been. I tried to be sympathetic, but I worried that they would be able to tell that I really didn't know my parents. The worst was having to give a speech. I felt like a fraud. No, I *was* a fraud. Thankfully, any question of my sincerity could be chalked up to shock and grief. I felt guilty for not knowing them. All those people were moved by their passing, and I was ashamed of myself. I pictured what my funeral would look like, and it was not a well-attended affair.

Then came the will.

My parents left me everything. There was no personal declaration in it—no directions as to what I was supposed to do with their life's savings. There was only the simple instruction that I was to receive everything. I assumed that it was their way of saying that I had shown myself worthy after making my own way. Maybe they were saying that they were sorry. Maybe they thought that some day, we really would be a family again. I don't know, but that's when I made the decision. I had made so many mistakes—the worst of which were only known to me. I decided then and there—no more messing around. It was time to straighten out my life.

I grew up in Vermont, and since I was looking at this as a reset, I decided to go back. I did my research, found The Hollows, and bought the property on the outskirts of town. The nearest neighbor was a half a mile away. The property was secluded, but not isolated. I loved the plot of land, which was nestled up against the woods. There was the main house, the pond, and the cottage. The cottage had been the main house when the land had been a farm, but around a hundred and fifty years ago, the land had

7

been sold, the new house built, the pond dug, and the cottage was abandoned. The fact that the main house was old gave it a sense of maturity and responsibility that I now craved.

I also loved The Hollows. It had originally been settled by two French explorers in the early 1600s, who named it "Chavelle's Hollow". Then came the British, and after the French-Indian War, they decided to change the name to "Sommerton's Hollow", in honor of the British General, Edward Sommerton. The problem was that the town was so small and located right on the border between the French and British territories, people called it by both names. Then the American Revolution happened, and Sommerton served in the British Army. After the war, the citizens of the newly formed country didn't want to have a town honoring their recently vanquished enemy, so they changed the name to "Putnam's Hollow", in honor of Rufus Putnam of the Continental Army.

This all happened so fast, relatively speaking, that people were calling the town by all three names at the same time, depending on if they were French, British, or American. When the town finally got a post office, which is what makes a place an official town in the eyes of the government, the surveyor was so fed up with trying to determine the correct name for such a small town, he simply wrote down "The Hollows", and it stuck. The Hollows became one of those towns you see on travel websites—a charming New England town with a Main Street comprised of three-hundred-year-old, colonial-style buildings, a town green, an old stone church, and winding roads, hidden among the rolling hills and forests.

After purchasing the house, I moved on to the next phase of my plan—opening my own business.

I rented a storefront on Main Street and opened a coffee shop. Like the rest of the town, Main Street was a postcard. The centuries-old buildings that line the street each have a plaque identifying the year they were built and for whom. Instead of switching to electric lights, the town kept its old gas lamps. At night, it was a fairy tale.

My shop was a small, single-story structure just down and across from the church, which everyone called the Old Stone Church. My coffee shop's large front window gave the perfect view with the town green across the street, and the old cemetery next to the church, to the south. I named the place "Groundworks" and began my little endeavor. I quickly realized that I had bitten off way more than I could chew, but since there was no Plan B, I had put nearly all of my inheritance into the house and the shop, so I had to stick it out.

Little by little, I got it under control. I started by giving out free samples of Groundworks' signature coffee to the local hotels and B&Bs to put in their guestrooms. They jumped on it as a way to promote local business. That's what the fall tourist season is all about. The Hollows is a cottage industry. It also paid off in that everyone staying at the hotels and B&Bs came to the shop during their exploration of the surrounding hills and countryside. I slowly fought my way out of the red, and while things were looking up financially, it was really hard work.

One downside of moving to a new town and putting in so many hours was that I was lonely. On an impulse, I took a trip to the local animal shelter. Behind the shelter was a pen where they allowed the dogs to run and play. I told myself I was going to adopt the first dog who came up to me. I stepped through the gate and this little black ball of fur with oversized paws broke from the pack and came flying at me, ears and jowls flapping wildly. He charged and didn't stop. He simply plowed into my shins and careened across the ground. He instantly sprang up and repeated the process. After the third time of tumbling over my feet, he was going to try again but was so dizzy, he fell over.

I was laughing so hard, tears poured down my cheeks, and I had to sit down. The mutt leapt at me and attempted to lick my face off. That was that. I named him Murphy, and we've been inseparable ever since. I'm not exaggerating about that. In four years, we've rarely left each other's side. With the long hours I was putting in at the shop, I couldn't leave him at home, alone, so I brought him with me. Before long, Murphy was Groundworks' unofficial mascot.

I remodeled Groundworks to give it an "old-timey" feel and it started to pick up steam. I was there almost fourteen hours a day, seven days a week. Business continued to grow.

One morning two years ago, Maggie Vaughn, who runs the Elmwood Hotel a block away, stopped by to pick up her supply of coffee, and remarked that her hotel was so full, she was turning people away.

That sparked an idea to give myself a side project and make a little extra coin.

By that time, I had hired some staff to lighten the load and had some time for myself.

I had been using the cottage as storage for Groundworks, but I took out some money, and renovated it as a place to stay. I fixed it up into a charming, one-bedroom affair with a remodeled kitchen and bathroom. I even added the fire pit out front. At the time, Airbnb was starting to take off. I thought they might be too crowded, so I went with a rival start-up called "Be Our Guest". It marketed itself as a more selective and upscale version of Airbnb. They weren't going after people looking to save a buck. They were after wealthy people wanting a different experience. These were exactly the tourists who were coming to The Hollows.

Since Be Our Guest was new, they wanted unique properties. I contacted them with photos of the cottage, and they went berserk. A representative from Be Our Guest came out to inspect the cottage and loved it. We went through the formalities. I had to sign a bunch of papers, promising to comply with their policies, one of which was that I wouldn't become involved "physically or otherwise" with a guest during their stay at my property. I had to submit to a background check, which always makes me nervous. I was confident they wouldn't find anything, but still, I worry.

Once that was done, I was cleared for takeoff, and take off, it did. Be Our Guest ran the cottage as a featured property and immediately, the reservations filled up. It was great. I was charging $200 a night in the off-season and $300 a night in the fall. If I wanted to, I could have booked the cottage every night. It's the easiest money I've ever made. I usually only saw my guests once or twice. They were always polite—well, most of the time, and all it took was an hour or two, at most, to clean and reset the place after they left.

Some of the hotel owners in town were upset that I had gotten into the game, but not too upset. They were still operating at capacity. I think they were more worried that other residents with extra bedrooms might try to go the Airbnb route. Anyway, like I said—easiest money I ever made. I could set my own dates, and if I wanted to take a break from keeping up the cottage, I just blocked out a week or two here and there. People enjoyed their stay. I made sure to keep the cottage stocked with wine from local wineries and coffee—only Groundworks, of course. Once I put in the fire pit, I also made sure to have the stuff to make s'mores in the kitchen. Everyone took advantage of it.

And everyone loved Murphy.

I did have some rules, though. I didn't allow anyone to stay at the cottage who hadn't already written at least three reviews on Be Our Guest. That's one of the beauties of the site. Hotels have to let anyone stay at their place, so long as they have a credit card. With Be Our Guest, I get to vet who stays at my place. I can see what they've said about other places, and you can tell who's going to be a problem by their reviews. They're the people who are determined to have a bad time, no matter what. That's my rule—three reviews to prove that you are a reasonable person. It's my most sacred rule.

And tonight, I'm breaking it.

Two months ago, I received a request from a woman named Rebecca Lowden to stay in the cottage for one night, only. I was going to reject the reservation request when I saw that she had no previous reviews, but I always check the reservation request to see where they heard about me to stay informed about where Be Our Guest is advertising. I clicked on her request, which took me to her profile page. She was undeniably beautiful, with brunette hair and blue eyes, but it was her bio that caught me.

In the bio sections, Be Our Guest encourages you to list things, like your hobbies, favorite books, and favorite movies. As one of her favorite books, she listed *A Christmas Carol*. And in the "favorite movies" section? *Dead Again*, which is in my top five. Also, she had grown up in a town not too far from where I grew up.

So, out of simple curiosity, I broke my rule and accepted the reservation.

*

I pull the sheets and towels from the dryer, and head back to the cottage. I make the bed, pulling the sheets tight and tucking the corners securely under the mattress. I never made my bed until the cottage. Now, I can't sleep in a bed that's not made. I hang fresh towels in the bathroom, and stack the rest on the top shelf in the hall closet.

And with that, I'm done. The cottage is ready to go. Check-in time is three o'clock and right now, it's noon. She could be here in three hours, or she might not arrive until tonight, but it's a safe guess that she'll be here closer to three. Most people treat arrangements like this as though they're arriving at someone's house, rather than a hotel. So, like I said, she'll probably be here closer to three. I kind of want to be here when she arrives.

Again, it's only curiosity. Don't look at me like that.

I put the key in the lockbox next to the front door, and reset the passcode for the four digits I sent Rebecca in the confirmation email.

I have to head to Groundworks in a few hours, but until then, I can kill time in the hopes of meeting her.

I head back to the main house, and walk into my office on the first floor. The floorboards in the hall squeak in a familiar sound that I've grown to relish. It reminds me of the sense of responsibility for the aged house. It's seen the very end of a Civil War, a World War, a Great Depression, another World War, the Seventies, the turn of the millennium, and I'm the one to make sure it sees the next milestone. I spin into the swivel chair at the desk and fire up the computer.

I check my emails and see that Sandy Bellhurst, the manager I hired to help me at Groundworks, has sent me the receipts from yesterday. I enter them into my accounting software and take care of some more emails. When I'm done, I look over to the door and see Murphy's half in and half out of the room.

"What? Are you hungry, again?"

Murphy's tail starts wagging so furiously, it causes his butt to oscillate.

"All right. Fine."

He turns and runs to the kitchen. I get up and follow.

I feed Murphy a little more food from the bag in the pantry. I heard somewhere that you should give dogs a little food at a time rather than full meals to keep them from getting overweight. It's healthier and I want Murphy at my side for as long as I can keep him.

After I feed him, I set up on the porch. I think about taking Murphy on a walk to The Sanctuary, but decide to play it cool and drop into a chair with a paperback to enjoy the autumn afternoon in case Rebecca arrives early.

It's really beautiful. The breeze carries the scent of dead leaves from the forest to the porch. The colors are at their peak. The cotton-ball clouds race through the sky overhead. It's that perfect temperature where I need a jacket, but not a coat. There's only a few more days until Halloween, which is The Hollows' time to shine.

Murphy comes out, pushing open the unlatched screen door with his nose, and plops down with a contented sigh next to my chair.

Rebecca Lowden can take her time.

I'm perfectly fine.

*

Hours later, I'm still on the porch, but I need to get going.

I'm meeting at Groundworks with a rep from Alliance Capital. It's a company that's interested in turning Groundworks into a franchise.

Murphy's still here on the porch with me, thrashing around on his back, trying to get an itch on his spine. He snorts as he writhes back and forth. I decide it's a great pic, and take out my phone. I get out of my chair and crouch down near his head. Still on his back, he looks at me as if to ask, "What the hell are you doing?"

I get low, right by his nose, and snap a photo. I know right away I can't use it for the Be Our Guest website because the cottage is framed between his open hind legs. It's hysterical, but probably not appropriate. Also, as I hit the shutter button, a Ford Focus pulls into frame, and parks next to the cottage. I take another picture, for my own collection, and tuck the phone into my pocket. Murphy rolls over, taking note of the new arrival.

I stand up and move to the steps, ready to greet Rebecca Lowden, but stop. It's not her. It can't be. Someone has taken a wrong turn. The woman getting out of the Focus has red hair. Rebecca is a brunette.

Murphy takes off towards her. I follow. He pulls up a few yards short, and strikes a submissive pose. She crouches down, and pats her knees in encouragement.

Wait. I'm wrong. It is Rebecca Lowden. She's dyed her hair a deep red.

Murphy gets closer and playfully rolls onto his back for a tummy rub. She obliges.

I keep walking forward. Yes, it is indeed Rebecca Lowden. She's still a knockout, but that red hair isn't working for her.

"Hi," she says to me, while patting Murphy's stomach. "Are you Jacob?"

"Yep. You Rebecca?"

"That's me."

"Sorry. I didn't recognize you with the hair. It's different from your profile pic."

She stands. "Yeah. Just something I'm trying."

Murphy gets up, and spins his hindquarters into her for a butt-scratch.

"And you must be Murphy!" she says in baby talk, running her nails across his hips. Murphy is in heaven. "Sorry I'm late."

"No, no. You're not late. You can check in whenever you want. The key is in the lockbox next to the door."

"Great. Thank you."

"I'd offer to show you around, but Murphy and I have to run into town for a little business meeting."

She lightheartedly slaps Murphy's butt. "No worries."

"I don't know what your plans are, but there's coffee and wine in the cottage, and stuff to make s'mores. If you want to use the fire pit, there are some logs around the back."

"Great."

"If there's anything else you need, you've got my number, right?"

"Yep."

There's this weird pause where I feel like she's waiting for me to leave.

"Okay," I say. "Come on, Murph."

He hesitates, but then comes to my side, and follows me to the truck. I glance over my shoulder and watch as she goes to the lockbox and punches in the code.

By the time Murphy and I reach the truck, she's already entering the cottage. She goes in and closes the door.

I open the truck, and Murphy leaps in. He loves car rides. I climb into the cabin and turn the key in the ignition. As the truck roars to life, the light goes on in the cottage.

"Murphy, is it just me or was that a little weird?" I ask.

I look over and see his tongue lolling out the side of his mouth.

"Oh, yeah. You're a dog."

I pop the truck into gear and roll down the driveway. I turn onto Normandy Lane, take one last look at the cottage in the rearview mirror, and head towards town.

*

Groundworks is busy, which is good. Aside from the revenue, I want it busy so the Alliance Capital rep can see that it's a thriving business.

Heads turn at the sound of the jingling bells on the door when Murphy and I walk in. There are a few regulars I recognize, like Reverend Williams from the Old Stone Church. He usually drops by once a month, but most of the customers are tourists I've never seen before. They may not know who I am, but Murphy is the ultimate kryptonite, and everyone is instantly enamored.

I'll share a little secret with you; at first, I hated this place. From the moment it opened, I regretted staking everything I had on it. I felt like I had thrown all my money away on something I could never get off the ground. Now, I love it. The smell of fresh coffee penetrates every surface. The constant hiss of the cappuccino maker. The perfect view of The Hollows' main thoroughfare,

16

capped by the Old Stone Church at the end of the street. The location had been expensive, but it paid off.

Sandy is manning the register, while Tom and Sheila, two local high school kids, race back and forth, concocting drinks. The line is sizable, but not unreasonable.

"Hey, Sandy," I say, stepping behind the counter.

"Hey, boss," she tosses over her shoulder, and redirects her attention to the man at the counter. "That'll be $18.47."

The man hands her a twenty. Sandy makes the change.

Sandy's a bit younger than me, and has a single-mindedness in her pursuits. She wants to be successful in business, and she will be if I have any say in it. When Groundworks started to take off, it was too much for me. I didn't know how to keep the momentum going. Sandy did.

"We'll call your name when it's ready."

The man turns, and goes to wait by the creamer station.

"How's it been today?" I ask.

She multi-tasks as she answers. "Good. I've placed the orders. The new napkins with the logos arrive next week. Colton's Bakery is late with the brownies, again. Other than that, it's a good day."

"What would I do without you, Sandy?"

She turns to me with all seriousness. "Two stores when the franchise kicks in. That's the deal."

"Done. Is he here?"

She nods over to the corner of the restaurant.

"Yep. Over in the booth."

I follow the gesture, and see a bald guy with glasses sitting in the corner booth, next to the window. He's got a laptop and a latte in front of him. He's thumbing through his phone, and occasionally glances out the window to the shops and the town green across the street.

"You didn't charge him, did you?"

Sandy comically rolls her eyes.

"Good," I reply, and head towards the booth.

17

"Two stores," she calls after me.

"Yeah, yeah, yeah."

Murphy gets up and follows me.

The man looks up as I slide into the opposite seat across the table.

"Hi. I'm Jacob Reese."

"Gregory Tiller. Alliance Capital. Pleased to meet you," he says and extends his hand.

We shake.

"Good to meet you. This is Murphy," I say, with a flick of the wrist in Murphy's direction.

Tiller nods at him. "Hi, Murphy."

"So," I begin. "What do you think of the place?"

"Well, as you know, this is just a preliminary scouting trip. I'm pretty low on the totem pole, and have to report back my initial findings, but I have to tell you, I love it—the décor, the themes, the menu. It's really impressive and your associate … ummm …"

"Sandy."

"Yes. Sandy. She and I went over a lot of the finances before you got here and, I don't mean to sound rude, but you could be making so much more with this place."

"Well, I hope that's where you come in."

He smiles. "Good answer." He consults his laptop. "Now, I believe I have everything I need to set up a meeting with Helen Trifauni. She's one of our brand developers. She's tough, but fair, and I think she'll really go for this place."

"Perfect."

"Great. How does next week sound?"

"Fine with me, but it's getting really close to Halloween, and it might be a little chaotic here in The Hollows. We tend to go all out. There's the parade and everyone dresses up. It's kind of a madhouse."

"That's what we want. It will add to the charm of Groundworks."

"Then next week is perfect."

He looks out the window to the green, where preliminary decorations are starting to take shape for the celebration. "Everyone dresses up?"

"Yeah. There's a costume contest that some of us business owners take pretty seriously."

"How seriously?"

"That seriously," I say, pointing to the trophy sitting on a shelf on the wall near the door.

He laughs. "There's a trophy?"

I nod.

"And last year, you won?"

"And the year before that and the year before that and the year before that," I answer.

"What's your costume for this year?"

I good-naturedly shake my head. "Everyone keeps their costume a secret."

It's true. None of us who enter the competition want to tip our hand. My costume was delivered over a month ago. It's sitting on a shelf in my hall closet. Tiller's question reminds me to talk to the post office, because the box was partially open when it was delivered.

"Will you win?" Tiller asks.

"Yep."

"Love it. Well then, we're on."

We shake hands, again.

"If this works out," he says, sitting back and gazing out the window, "there could be a Groundworks Coffee in dozens of towns in two years, and in five years, who knows?" He takes a sideways glance at me. "And that could potentially mean a couple million for you."

"I can live with that."

Tiller and I trade some more polite conversation. He starts talking about working Murphy into the logo. I tell him it's all great, and of course, acting as his agent, Murphy would love to do it.

By the time we wrap up, it's dark, and it's close to closing time. We shake hands one last time, and agree to set up a meeting next week, based on Mrs Trifauni's schedule.

Once he's gone, I check in with the staff, and Murphy and I head towards the door.

"Email me the day's receipts," I call over my shoulder to Sandy.

"Two stores!" she reminds me.

I stop and turn. "If this works out the way these people are planning, you can have more than that."

She gets thoughtful, and nervously glances around. "Three stores?"

"Done."

"Seriously?"

"Yep." I turn back to the door. "Email me the reports."

"Could I have gotten more?"

"You said three!"

I push open the door, and am greeted by a blast of cold air.

"Good night, boss!" I hear her call out.

"Good night!"

*

I'm buzzing the entire ride through the woods and farmland back to the house. I pull into the driveway, and see that there's a fire in the fire pit outside the cottage. Rebecca is sitting in one of the chairs next to it. I park and hop out, followed by Murphy.

As I start walking towards her, I'm suddenly filled with an overwhelming sense of dread. Something's off, but I can't put my finger on it. I'm not sure if Murphy's reading my body language or what, but even he seems cautious.

Rebecca is watching me as I approach.

I stop next to the fire pit, which is directly between us. The flickering light plays across her darkened features and red hair.

20

"Hi," she says.

"Hi."

"You know the taillight on your truck is out?"

"Yeah. I've been meaning to fix it."

"How did your business meeting go?"

"Good …"

Why am I so uncomfortable? I've come home to this scene many times. It's always ended with pleasantries and, sometimes, inebriated conversation. Why does this feel so different?

"Is something wrong?" Rebecca asks.

I try to shake it off. "No. Sorry. The meeting gave me a lot to think about. That's all."

"Oh."

"How do you like the cottage?"

"I love it. It's perfect."

"Good."

That's when I see it—the stick doll. She's holding it in her hands. My mouth goes dry and my knees soften. The image in front of me is paralyzing—her smile, that red hair, her holding that doll.

For a split second, she's someone she can't possibly be.

"Are you sure you're okay?"

"W—what?"

She notices that I'm looking at the doll. Her eyes drift down to it and back up to me. Maybe it's just a trick of the dancing glow of the fire, but I catch something accusatory, something righteous in her gaze.

"I'm sorry," she says. "I was just admiring it inside, and I had it in my hands when I came out here to start the fire."

"No. No reason to be sorry."

It has to be a coincidence. It has to be.

This afternoon, I had wanted to talk to her, to get to know her. Now, I want to get away from her. I *need* to get away from her.

I finally find my voice. "Well, I'm going to head inside. If there's anything you need, let me know."

She cocks her head. "Are you sure you don't want to hang out?"

She's being deliberate. That smile. The doll. The red hair. All she needs is the scar. This can't be a coincidence, can it?

"I—I'd love to," I stammer. "But that business thing I was just at …"

She nods, sympathetically. "A lot on your mind?"

"Yeah."

I feel like a wounded mouse staring up at a grinning cat.

"So, if you need anything …" I weakly offer.

"I'll call you."

"… great."

I turn and begin walking away.

"Good night," she calls out.

"Good night," I say over my shoulder.

Murphy follows me up the gently sloping lawn to the house. All the while, I'm fighting the urge to look back.

Once inside, I stand with my back to the door, trying to catch my breath. I go to the kitchen and pour myself a cup of water. I down it in one gulp, pour another one, and repeat the process. After standing there for I don't know how long, I go to the cabinet over the fridge. I pull out a bottle of bourbon, pour myself a healthy dose, and down that as well. I wrangle my nerves and head into the living room, keeping the lights off. I go to the window, and peer through the curtains.

The fire pit glows but she's no longer there. The light in the cottage is on. There are instructions as part of the rental agreement that you are not to leave a fire in the fire pit unattended, but I'm not going back down there. I want to stay in here, and convince myself that I'm being paranoid.

It was a coincidence. It has to be.

I pull the chair over to the window, sit down, and watch through the small space in the curtains.

There is no movement from the cottage. Only the single, solitary light.

*

I've been sitting here for hours, watching. Murphy's curled up in his bed with his favorite red tennis ball. It's midnight, and I'm slowly coming to my senses.

Of course, I'm being stupid. I'm seeing things that aren't there. Yes, it was uncanny. All she needed was the scar above her eye, and that would have settled it, but she didn't have one. It was a bunch of little coincidences that my mind assembled into an impossible conclusion.

Finally, the light in the cottage goes dark. The fire has long since burned out.

I'm an idiot.

I rise from the chair, joints aching, and head upstairs to my bedroom.

"Ridiculous," I say aloud as I crawl into bed.

Murphy pads into the room. He comes around to the side of the bed, rests his snout on the mattress right in front of my face, and looks at me.

"Yeah. Fine. All right. Just for tonight. Up-up."

He leaps onto the bed, and curls into a ball near my feet. He's not supposed to do this. He's got his own bed in the corner, but I've got too much on my mind to argue with him.

"You're going to feel so stupid in the morning," I tell myself and turn off the light.

The lock snaps open.

I continue to stare at it, immobilized with fear. I'm sweating. I can taste the bile in my throat. I know what's coming. I know what's behind that door.

"No … no …"

The handle turns with a groan that echoes through the base-ment.

I open my eyes.

The sun is coming up.

I go through the process of catching my breath and remembering where I am. That's two nights in a row. That never happens. Not since they first started. It's usually once every few weeks. The most troubling thing about this time is that the nightmare was slightly different. It always ends with the lock popping open. This time, the nightmare kept going, and the handle turned. That was new.

I roll over and glance at Murphy, who is taking up more than half of the bed. He's lying on his back with his legs splayed out in what I callously call his "highway dog" pose.

I shake the image of the dream from my head and play the events of last night over in my mind.

I was right. I was seeing things that weren't there. I'm also right about feeling stupid.

I take a shower and absent-mindedly run my finger over the two dime-sized scars in my side, while I think about Rebecca. I'm going to apologize to her for being so awkward last night. I want that positive review and the curiosity about who she is has come back.

I go down to the kitchen and put on a pot of coffee. I look out the window above the sink at the sun peeking over the hills. My gaze drifts down to the cottage.

I stop.

The car is gone.

That's not unheard of. Some people head out early to catch the sunrise or to make good time to their next destination. What makes me stop is that the door to the cottage is open.

Coffee in hand and Murphy close behind, I head out the door, step off the porch, and start walking towards the cottage. The woods are playing their early chorus of birdsong. A morning mist hangs a few feet above the ground. As I get closer, I realize that no, my eyes are not playing tricks on me. The front door is wide open.

I stop outside the door, and peer into the cottage.

"Miss Lowden?"

The sound of my voice stops the nearby birds, leaving the air filled with an unnerving silence. There's no hint of a reply from inside.

Murphy waits by my side, sensing my tension.

"Rebecca?"

Nothing.

I step through the door. The air inside the cottage is cold, meaning the door has been open for hours. Nothing's been touched. The coffee packets wait in the basket by the coffee maker. There are no water droplets in the sink. The throw pillows on the couch are exactly where I left them yesterday.

"Hello?"

I start walking down the short hall to the bedroom. Halfway down, I turn my head to look into the bathroom. The towels and toiletries are undisturbed.

I continue to the end of the hall. The bedroom door is closed. I stop next to the door and stand motionless, listening for any sound from within. I glance back down the hall. Murphy is waiting anxiously in the living room, prepared to flee at any moment.

I tap the door.

"Rebecca?"

There's no response, which means either she's not in there, or she is in there, and there's something really wrong. I gently grasp the knob, turn, and slowly open the door.

The stick doll is on the bed, propped up on the pillows. The guestbook is lying open before it. Angry red letters are carved across the pages. The coffee cup slips from my hand, and falls to the floor.

I step closer, and a name stares back at me from the pages of the guestbook.

LAURA AISLING

The dread of last night comes crashing back, tenfold. My mind was not playing tricks on me. It wasn't a coincidence.

That wasn't Laura Aisling. It can't be, because Laura Aisling is dead, and I thought I was the only one who knew that.

So this means someone knows my secret.

Chapter 2

"Yes, I know the account was deleted this morning. I'm trying to figure out who she was."

"I don't understand. Was there a problem with her payment?"

"No. That's not—"

"Was there damage to your property?"

"No."

"Then, I don't see the—"

"You said the account was created two months ago. She made one reservation request. My place. Right?"

"Let me see … Yes. That appears to be correct."

"And then, when she left my place this morning, she deleted the account?"

"Yes."

"And I'm saying that I'm trying to figure out who the hell Rebecca Lowden really was. I've tried online searches, and I can't find anything about her. Nothing on Facebook or LinkedIn, nothing on Google. It's like she never existed."

"Sir, at Be Our Guest, we strongly discourage any attempt to contact a guest outside of your transaction on our site. Besides, I'm still not seeing the problem. It is unusual, but I don't see anything to be concerned about. I'm sorry that you might not get the review, but your property is one of our most popular spots. I can see that you've already had two reservation requests yesterday for December."

"That's not the point."

This has been my entire morning. I immediately tried to find out who Rebecca Lowden was on my own so that I wouldn't have to contact Be Our Guest and I could avoid these questions, but my search came up empty. So here I am, arguing on the phone with a rep from Be Our Guest.

"I'm still trying to understand this," the representative continues. "You're saying that there was no damage to your property?"

"No, dammit. I told you that already—"

"Did you try contacting her through her contact info?"

"Yes. The number is disconnected, and I'm not crossing my fingers on the email I sent."

"Okay. Yes, I admit, that's odd."

"Do you?" I reply with maximum snark. "Do you admit that?"

"Sir—"

"Look, she deleted the account, but you guys still have her information, right? You have a copy of her driver's license?" I know they do. Owners and renters alike have to submit to a background check when they sign up. I had to email a scanned copy of my license to set up my account. So did she.

"Yes."

"Do you have it pulled up, right now?"

"Sir, I'm not going to give you any information from her—"

"I don't want you to, but do me a favor and do a search for the address on her driver's license. I want to know if the address is real."

"Mr Reese, that would be highly irregular."

"I'm not asking you to tell me where she lives. Just tell me if it's a real address. If it is, I'll hang up, and you and I can go about our day."

He sighs. "One moment …"

I hear the clicking of his keyboard through the phone. It stops, as does his breath.

"You still with me?" I ask.

"Well … yes, there does seem to be an issue with the address."

"Where did it put you; the middle of the ocean?"

"It might just be a problem with the—"

I shake my head. "It's gotta be a fake ID."

"Well, that is a possibility. I'll be sure to make a note of it in the—"

"Let me ask you something: just how thorough are those background checks you do over there at Be Our Guest? I know they cost money. You guys cutting corners?"

"Mr Reese," he answers with a new note of concern in his voice, "I'll pass this along to my supervisor, and they'll get back to you once we've resolved the issue."

"Like you said, the account's deleted, so there's nothing you can really resolve, but sure, you let me know."

I hang up the phone.

Whoever Rebecca Lowden is or was, she went to great lengths to mess with me, and I want to know why.

*

There's another couple checking in this afternoon. I've got a few hours until they arrive, and since she didn't touch anything, the cottage is ready to go. I rip the pages out of the guestbook, and burn them in the fire pit, destroying the only tangible evidence I have of her existence.

I need to think. I need a trip to The Sanctuary.

Behind the cottage is a path leading into the woods. About half a mile in, over some ridges and across a stream, is a dense area of pine trees. For the life of me, I can't figure out why it's there. When I first came across it while scouting the property, I thought

29

it might be a man-made pine farm that had been forgotten, but the trees aren't in rows. It's just a fluke, I guess.

I reset the passcode on the key lockbox for the cottage, grab Murphy's favorite red tennis ball, and we head off into the woods. Murphy knows the route, and darts back and forth across the path, going from smell to smell. We take this walk three or four times a week. Today, he strays a little further from the path than usual, but I don't bother with his leash. My thoughts are too tangled.

Birds chirp from the trees as we make our way further and further into the forest. Normally, I would be drinking it in, but I can't. I keep going over last night in my mind—the hair, the doll, the name nearly carved into the guestbook. We arrive at the stream. There's almost no water in it, but sure enough, Murphy finds a puddle to splash in.

We crest the final ridge and the path slopes down to the right, leading to the opening of The Sanctuary.

The thick, interwoven pine branches that form the opening look like the mouth of a cave. Murphy runs ahead and plunges through. I follow a few seconds behind.

Stepping through the opening, I'm wrapped in almost total silence. The soft breeze can't penetrate the needles overhead. The sun's light is scattered, casting the area into an even shade. Murphy barks at a fleeing squirrel and there's not even an echo. About fifty yards in, amongst the massive trunks, is a clearing. There's a downed tree off to the side, like it was purposefully placed there to serve as a bench. You can sit on it and look up at the sky through the hole in the trees, like you're staring out of a well.

I love this place. The outside world doesn't exist here. It was in this spot, sitting on this log, that I made the decision to buy the house and start the coffee shop. For a while, I didn't tell my guests about it because I didn't want to share it, but one day, a guy from Tulsa who was staying at the cottage found it, raved about it in his review, and I figured since the secret was out, I'd use it as a selling point.

I take a seat on the log. Murphy gives up on the squirrel and runs over to me. He sits and waits.

"What?" I ask, with an exaggerated shrug.

Murphy's tail begins to thump on the ground.

"I don't know what you want," I say, shaking my head.

He yaps, and lowers his head.

"Okay, fine."

I take the red tennis ball out of my pocket and begin throwing it for him. He darts after it, brings it back, and we repeat the process over and over. My mind begins to drift, and I start thinking of *her*.

She's always there, in the back of my mind, the pangs of guilt, and the dreams. After so many years, I've buried it in the recesses of my mind, but after the events of this morning, I'm pulled back to the party where *we first met—*

—at a party at a frat house at Wilton University in Rutland. It was a Christian college, but even some Christian colleges have frat houses. Our introduction happened where a lot of college introductions happen—over a keg of Bud Lite.

The party had spilled into the yard. She was sticking close to a group of girlfriends while us guys circled like sharks, waiting for the opportunity to pick them off. The problem was that all the sharks wanted the same fish. She had light blue eyes, pale skin, high cheekbones, a strong chin, and gorgeous, flowing red hair that cascaded over her shoulders in waves. In all this perfection, there was the small scar over her right eye that added an air of mystery.

While other guys looked for an opening, I watched her beer. Once it got low, I made my way to the almost forgotten keg in the corner of the yard.

My strategy paid off when she came over for a refill.

"Let me get that for you," I said, as only a smooth twenty-four-year-old would say.

"Thanks." She smiled.

"I'm Jacob. Jacob Reese."

"Laura Aisling."

"Nice to meet you, Laura Aisling. Who are you here with?"

"Just some friends. You?"

"Just some friends." That was my first of what would be many lies to her.

We made small talk and drifted over to a picnic table near the edge of the yard, away from the crowd. I tried to be clever and used pick-up lines that had been successful on countless other girls on countless other campuses. She was amused, but not taken by them. As we spoke, I began to fiddle with some sticks and long pine needles that I picked up off the ground.

"What are you doing?" she asked.

"You'll see."

We continued talking. She was a political science major who had transferred from New Hampshire University her sophomore year.

"Why did you transfer? Couldn't cut it at UNH?"

She rolled her eyes. "Yeah. Something like that."

"I hope you don't mind me asking, but that scar?"

She touched the scar with her fingers. "Childhood injury. Fell out of a tree."

"Really?"

"Yeah. I wish there was a better story behind it."

"Well, maybe this will make it better." I handed her the stick doll I had been working on. The sticks formed the torso, arms, and legs, while the pine needles had been tied to hold it all together.

"For me?" she asked in mock flattery.

"Just something I learned in Boy Scouts."

She saw right through my bullshit.

"Well, I shall treasure it always," she said, clutching it to her chest, toying with me.

She paused, contemplated the doll, and looked at me.

"How many girls has this little trick worked on?"

My confidence rushed out of me like a deflating balloon. She had called me out and made me feel like an idiot, which made her all the more enticing, but I took it that the chase was over.

"It works on most girls, but obviously, you are not most girls," I said.

She started laughing, which drew the attention of some of the party attendees around the yard.

"All right, all right. I'll take it back," I said, holding out my hand.

She held it closer to her chest, and twisted her torso away from me. "No, no, no. I'm keeping it." There was that playful smile, and those eyes shone as she held the doll against her perfect breasts. She was something and she knew it.

"Okay," I said, my confidence returning. "What do I get?"

"For what?"

"For the stick doll."

"That's rude," she said, feigning insult. "He has a name."

"Oh, yeah? What is it?"

She looked down at the doll and then smiled at me. "Duh. His name is 'Woody.'"

Man, she was good.

"Okay. What do I get for Woody?"

She shrugged. "What do you want?"

"I'll settle for a phone number."

She bit her bottom lip, reached into her pocket, and pulled out her phone. "Tell you what—how about you give me your number, and I'll think about it?"

"Deal."

I gave it to her, and she typed it into her phone. Once she was finished, she tucked the phone back into her pocket, and hopped off the picnic table.

"I'm gonna get back to my friends. We'll see you around, Jacob Reese." She began walking back to the group of girls at the other end of the yard.

33

"Just be careful with the doll. They're pretty flimsy," I called after her.

She turned to me while continuing to walk backwards towards her friends. "Don't worry. I won't play too hard with your Woody."

Every conversation around the yard stopped. The only sound was the music playing from the open window of the frat house. My cheeks burned, but I wasn't mad. I liked being recognized as the target of her flirtations.

Laura and her friends gathered and left. She gave me one final glance as they headed off down the street. I relaxed on the picnic table and sipped my beer, basking in the glow of our conversation, but after a few minutes, it was time to attend to business.

I hopped off the picnic table and headed inside the frat house.

Loud music thumped from the first floor as I climbed the stairs. The place stunk of beer.

At the landing to the second floor, I headed down the hall, past closed bedroom doors, and the occasional pair of people talking or drinking. The closer I got to the door at the end of the hall, the stronger the smell of weed became, along with incense that was trying mightily to mask it.

I stopped at the end of the hall and listened. I could hear voices, laughter, and music coming from inside. I rapped on the door and it opened a few inches. A face peered through the crack and gave me the once-over.

He turned to the interior of the room. "It's Jacob."

"Let him in," a voice answered.

The door swung open. I stepped in, and it was quickly shut behind me.

I was greeted with a chorus of "Jacob!"

It was the fraternity's recreational room. There was a pool table in one corner, a ping-pong table in the other. There were couches situated around a TV, where guys were playing video games. The room was thick with haze, and I was sure that I was already getting a contact buzz. These were all the seniors—the cool guys. There were some girls there too, taking hits from the water bong on the table in front of the TV. There were also copious beer bottles and a few handles of Jack Daniel's and Jägermeister scattered around the room.

Jeremy Massi, the fraternity's president, got up and gave me a bro hug.

"What's up, Jacob? How you been?"

"Good."

"You want a beer or something?"

"No, thanks. Just doing my regular pickup, and I'll be on my way."

"Got it."

He went over to a shelf, took down a book, opened it, and pulled out an envelope. He walked over and handed it to me.

"There you go."

I took out the wad of cash from inside and began counting the assortment of hundreds, twenties, tens, and fives.

"Sure you don't want to hang out?" Jeremy asked. "It's a party."

"Nah. I'm good," I said.

It took me a while to count the cash, given that it was a couple thousand dollars in small bills.

"It's all there, man. Two grand from all the frats on campus."

"Just covering my ass," I reassured him.

He patiently waited as I finished counting.

"All right," I said, tucking the envelope into my jacket. "Jimmy will be by later with the delivery."

"Tell him to hurry. We're running low and the party is just getting started."

"Will do. Pleasure doing business with you."

We bro hugged again. I had been doing the job for a little over a year and Jeremy and I had gotten to know each other—not well, but well enough.

I turned to leave when one of the guys on the couch, I think his name was Dustin, sat up.

"Hey, Jacob?" he asked, stoned out of his mind.

"Yeah?"

"So, like, do you carry a gun when you do these deals?"

Jeremy sighed. "Dustin, come on, man."

"No, I don't carry a gun. I just handle the cash," I answered.

Dustin smiled and slowly blinked his eyes. "That's cool, man. Your life is like *Scarface*, right?"

"Shut up, Dustin," one of the other seniors said.

Dustin turned to him. "What? *Scarface* is cool."

"See you later, Jacob," Jeremy said, waving me out the door.

"Later." I waved back.

I walked out the door, back into the relatively cleaner air of the hallway, and headed downstairs.

No, I didn't carry a gun.

This was the job I had turned to after my parents cut me off.

I had worked odd jobs to try to pay my tuition but it wasn't cutting it. I needed to finish school, or so I thought, and took on massive amounts of debt. I think my parents were waiting for me to ask for help, but I was an arrogant twenty-something who felt that he had been wronged. So, no. I was going to do it myself, no matter how it wrecked my financial future.

I did a little better in my classes, now that I was paying for them myself, but the stress was too much. I started slipping, again. I'd blow off class and hang with an acquaintance of mine named Mattie, who had transferred to Lyndon University.

We'd smoke at his place. He bought it from a guy named Reggie, who sold to all the frat houses and college campuses in a ninety-mile radius. It was a nice little operation Reggie had going, but he used idiots to do his deals. They were guys who stuck out like sore thumbs on campuses, and they carried the cash and the drugs at the same time, which was flat-out stupid.

I saw a chance to make a little money, and asked Mattie if I could talk to Reggie. Mattie said I was nuts, and he was right, but I got the meeting. I laid it out for him. I explained that I was someone who didn't look out of place on a college campus, and if you separated the money from the weed he was selling, it made it harder for the police. If someone was caught with a ton of money and a ton of weed, that was the ball game. If someone only had weed, it was harder to prove intent to sell. I learned that years ago from another friend who had gone into criminal law. I told Reggie that I would be his bagman. I would collect the cash and take a small cut that we would both agree to.

Looking back on it, yeah, it was insane, but Reggie went for it. The money was good and the work was incredibly easy. I was dealing with frat boys. This was nothing like *Scarface*. I graduated and decided to keep going, just until I paid off my loans. I knew I couldn't do it forever, but at the time, it was the perfect way to pay off my student debts, which at that rate, would only take two or three more years.

I had just stepped out the front door of the frat house when my phone pinged with a text message.

Thanks for the Woody. I've never had one before and they're fun to play with. Oh shit! I just sent you my number, didn't I? Dammit. I guess you'll have to call me sometime.

My night was now complete. I went back to the yard, found the almost empty keg, downed another beer, and tossed the cup into the bushes. *Time to—*

"—go, Murphy," I say aloud, and get up from the log.

Murphy, who's been lying on the soft needles trying to chew his red tennis ball into oblivion, jumps up to join me.

We need to get back. I want to double check that there's nothing suspicious at the cottage before the next guests arrive.

*

We arrive back at the cottage and everything is as it should be.

Since he's already wet from our hike, I throw Murphy's ball into the pond a couple of times. He gleefully plunges into the water after it. Soon, it'll be too cold but for now, he doesn't seem to mind. I throw it one more time. When he brings it back to the shore, he signals that he's done with our game by ignoring my requests to bring the ball to me, and carries it up to the porch, where he goes back to work trying to destroy it.

*

The Shermans arrive at three on the dot.

They park their Buick in front of the cottage and get out. They're an older, retired couple and present quite the picture. She's tiny. I'm guessing not more than five feet tall, with unnaturally brown hair with gray roots, and bright red lipstick. Mr Sherman is six foot four, with tired eyes and a drooping neck. She's full of energy. He's decidedly not.

She starts walking towards me, all smiles and a slight limp.

"Are you Jacob?" she asks.

"That would be me. You must be Linda."

"Yes, indeed, and this is my husband Franklin." She gestures to him with a flash of her hand.

I nod. "Pleased to meet you both. Any problems finding the place?"

"Oh, no. I'm the navigator for our little trip, and I got us here without a hitch, didn't I, Franklin?"

"Yes, you di—"

"Yep, without a hitch."

I glance over at Franklin. He may have had more to say, but his expression lets me know that this is probably the way of their conversations.

Linda turns slowly, I assume on account of a bum hip, and takes a deep breath. "Well, this really is beautiful."

Murphy awakes from his nap on the porch and comes down to join us.

"And there's Murphy!" she exclaims.

Murphy approaches, and she gives his head a good scratch. I'm glad he's tired. His standard energetic greeting would have been too much for her.

"So, I read in your reservation that you two were doing a little Haunted New England tour?" I ask.

"Oh, yes. We're hitting all the haunted sites, aren't we, Franklin?"

"Yep. We came fro—"

"We came from Salem," she quickly interjects. "Spent a few days there, hoping to see some ghosts."

"Any luck?"

"No. Beautiful town, but a little bit of a let-down. Too touristy, right, Franklin?"

"It was a little crowd—"

"So many people. *Too* many people, and they were dressed up in costumes. We may have seen a ghost. Who knows? But I don't think we did. I have to confess, I'm psychic about such things."

"Really?" I ask, playing along.

"Oh, yes."

"Well, I also saw in your reservation request that you were heading over to Maine after this, so maybe you'll have better luck there."

"We're hoping to find some ghosts here in The Hollows." She gets a giddy smile. "Oh, I love that name. The Hollows." She savors the words. I don't have the heart to tell her that the name was the result of a frustrated surveyor. "We stopped in Tarrytown, too. That's the real name of Sleepy Hollow. Nice place, but too modern. No luck with any ghosts there, either. But maybe here in The Hollows. I mean, there are ghosts everywhere you know, and I have to tell you, I'm getting a strong sensation from this place. So, you *have* to have some ghosts, here."

I shrug. "Not that I know of. We had our own little witch trial way back in the sixteen hundreds, where three women were hung from a tree in the Old Stone Church cemetery, but nothing else."

She waves me off. "We'll find 'em. Won't we, Franklin?"

"We'll look for—"

"Yep. We'll find 'em."

"Well, I certainly wish you happy hunting, and even if you don't, you'll still love the cottage. Do you need help with your luggage?"

"No, thank you, dear. Franklin can handle the bags, can't you, Franklin?"

This time, Franklin only grunts an affirmation.

"Great. Well, the key is in the lockbox. I have to head into town. If you're out tonight, you can come see me at the coffee shop on Main Street. It's called Groundworks, and you can tell me how your ghost hunt went."

"Sounds wonderful."

"If you need anything, you have my number?"

"Sure do."

"All right, then. Welcome to The Hollows."

"Mmmmm, The Hollows," she says once again, relishing in the words.

"Come on, Murphy," I say, and start walking towards the truck. He follows, and a few moments later, we pull out of the drive and head towards town.

*

They've finally started bringing in the tents on the green for the Halloween celebration. Extra picnic tables have also started appearing for the face-painting, pumpkin-carving classes, and food stalls that will arrive soon. More decorations are going up along Main Street. Orange and black ribbons adorn the gas lamps,

40

and jack-o'-lanterns are popping up in the shop windows. The Hollows does not mess around when it comes to Halloween. It prepares the same way New York might prepare for New Year's, or Boston for St. Patrick's Day.

Groundworks is already jumping by the time I get there. Todd and Sheila are in the weeds, trying to keep up with the ever-growing line that is almost to the door. I hop behind the counter and go into machine mode, cranking out drinks left and right. Murphy finds his bed by the register and sinks in. Just his presence soothes some of the nerves of the customers who have been waiting for their lattes, coffees, and cappuccinos.

For the next few hours, it's turn and burn. I try to stay three steps ahead. Organize, prioritize, move, and above all, smile.

I need this.

The constant movement and concentration send the thoughts of last night and this morning further and further from my mind.

Eight o'clock rolls around.

Sheila flips the sign on the door to state that we're closed, even though there are still people in the shop. We'll let them finish their drinks, but no one else can come in. This leads to the nightly ritual of having to turn away some disappointed people. Most accept it and move on. Others plead. Some of them are belligerent. It's the same every night.

When the last of the customers leave, I tell Shelia and Todd that they can head home. I'll finish up on my own. I thank them for their hard work, and give them their paychecks. When the franchise deal works out, I'm giving them big, fat bonuses. They don't know that, yet.

Finally, Murphy and I have the store to ourselves. I sweep and mop the floor, restock the stations, and wipe down the machines. I take the garbage to the dumpster in the parking lot out back. Once all the grunt work is done, Murphy and I go to the office. I slip into the swivel chair at the cluttered desk. I bring up the accounting software and get ready for the tedium of running the reports and processing *all the credit card—*

"*—payments?*"

"Yeah, Reggie. I got the payments," I said, taking the envelope out of my jacket and handing it to him.

He painstakingly started to count it by the headlights of his Dodge Challenger, seemingly oblivious to the fact that if a cop drove by, he'd ask what we were doing parked on the side of the road in the woods, counting a stack of money.

"It's all there, Reggie."

He glared down the cigarette that was clamped in his lips at me. "Why the fuck would I trust you?"

I decided to keep my mouth shut.

As he hunched over the hood to count the cash, I caught a glimpse of the grip of the massive gun he had tucked into the waistband of his jeans, hidden under his jacket.

He finished counting.

"We happy?" I asked.

"Yeah, we happy."

He shuffled the large stack of bills, and hit them on the hood of the car to line them up with a *tap, tap—*

—tap.

The tap on the shop window startles me.

Murphy barks.

I walk out of the office and into the restaurant to see a young couple standing at the door.

"Are you open?" the girl asks in exaggerated tones, as if the glass is soundproof. She also apparently can't read the sign, or notice the fact that no one is in here.

Still, gotta keep that smile.

"Sorry. We're closed," I say.

They move on.

I hit the lights to make sure anyone else who can't read knows that we're closed.

*

When I arrive home, the lights are on in the cottage. From the porch, I can see into the living room. Linda Sherman is talking on her phone. Franklin is sitting on the couch, watching TV. I have a feeling this is reminiscent of a lot of their nights at home.

Maybe I should go down there, play the cheerful host, and see how their day went …

Nah. It's been a long day. I'm going to bed.

*

I wake up early, shower, and brew some coffee. I look out the kitchen window and see the Shermans are packing up the car. I'll go ask them about their stay and wish them safe travels.

I step onto the porch. Murphy's right there beside me. I walk past the truck and make another mental note about fixing that stupid taillight.

Linda sees me, waves, and starts walking towards me. She's excited. Even from this distance, I see Franklin roll his eyes and begin to follow. The walking takes a little bit of effort for her, so I go to meet her halfway. She must be really excited, because her limp is less pronounced than yesterday.

"Good morning!" she calls.

"Good morning, Mrs Sherman. How was your stay?"

"Wonderful! Such a perfect little town."

"Did you do some exploring?"

"We sure did. We saw so many old houses, and we stopped by the 'Hanging Tree' in the church cemetery. So creepy."

"Great," I say because apparently "creepy" is good.

Why is she looking at me so strangely? Like we have some sort of inside joke?

I glance over to Franklin. He looks tired and, if I'm not mistaken, apologetic. She's still waiting.

"Well, how does our little town compare to Salem?" I ask. "Did you see any ghosts?"

"Not in town," she replies with a wink, and waits.

"I ... I'm sorry. I don't understand."

"I said not *in town*."

"So ... you're saying you did see a ghost?"

She nods, downright giddy, but says nothing.

"I'm still not— Well, where did you see one?"

"We saw one here!" she says with a clap of her hands. "I told you! This place is so old and the town has history and ghosts are everywhere! I said that, didn't I, Franklin? Didn't I say that ghosts were everywhere?"

"Yes, you d—"

"And I was right! I just knew it!"

"I'm sorry. I'm still confused. You're saying you saw a ghost ... *here*?"

She playfully slaps my wrist. "Oh, don't sound so surprised. You knew. I could tell you knew there was a ghost here when we met, yesterday."

I glance at Franklin. He shrugs, indicating that I should play along.

"Really? So, uh, what happened?" I ask.

"Well, in the middle of the night, I thought I heard something outside by the door. Franklin heard it, too. Didn't you, Franklin?"

"Yes, but I—"

"He thought it was deer or something, so he didn't get up, but I knew. I told you, I have a psychic feel for these things." She taps her temple for emphasis. "So, I got up and went to the living room, and there she was, standing just off the porch by the front door! She was looking right at me!"

My mouth is dry. My lungs aren't working properly, and I'm trying desperately to hide it from her.

"*She?*" I ask.

"Yes! It was a woman ghost!"

"That's—that's incredible."

"I know! Incredible! She was right there!" she says, pointing to a spot near the fire pit.

"So, um, wh—what happened?"

"Well, we stared at one another for a few seconds, and then she smiled at me, and started walking towards the woods. I yelled at Franklin to get up. I yelled, 'Franklin, get up! You need to see this!' Didn't I, Franklin? Didn't I yell for you to get up?"

"Yes, you did—"

"But he didn't get up, did you, Franklin?"

"No, I d—"

"He didn't get up. So, I ran outside and, well, I don't run so fast," she says, patting her hip, "and by the time I got out onto the porch, I just caught a glimpse of her as she walked into the trees." She points again, this time to the path behind the cottage, leading off into the woods to The Sanctuary.

"That's amazing," I croak. My throat feels like sandpaper. "What did she look like?"

"Oh, she was beautiful. She was tall, with long red hair, and these really blue eyes. She wore a cloak. And, I'm not sure, but it looked like she had a scar, here, just above her eye."

Chapter 3

"Hello?"

"Maggie, it's Jacob Reese."

"Ah, Mr Coffee! How's it going? Calling to talk smack about the costume contest?"

"Actually, I called to see if you've got any rooms available over there at the Elmwood Hotel."

There's an understandable pause before she replies. "Seriously?"

"Yeah. I had a pipe burst in the cottage, and I need to redirect some guests for a few nights."

"Well, the only thing I have available is the Rose Suite."

"The Rose Suite?"

"Yeah."

"Come on, Maggie. When I need a room, the only one available happens to be the most expensive room in your hotel?"

"You think I'm lying?"

"No. Sorry. That came out way too— I'm really sorry, Maggie. It's been a long couple of days, and I'm on edge."

"Listen," she says, her tone softening not one bit, "normally I wouldn't have anything available, but that rent-a-room bullshit is creeping into The Hollows. You've got people staying at your place all the time. Now, other people are renting out their spare

46

rooms. So, yeah, I have a room available, but only because of people like you. The Rose Suite is all I've got. Take it or leave it."

She's right, and I feel like a jerk. "Maggie, I'm sorry. I didn't mean to insinuate that you were lying. Of course, I'll take the Rose Suite. How many consecutive nights can I get?"

Now, her tone softens. "Wow. That must be some burst pipe. You call Stuart yet?"

Stuart Delholm is the local plumber. If I say I called Stuart, she might run into him, and ask about the cottage. I want to keep everything under wraps.

"No. It's too big a job for Stuart. I called a bigger operation out of Burlington."

"Jeez. That's rough. Let me see how many nights I've got ..."

I hear her typing. I can just imagine her at the front desk of the Elmwood, back perfectly straight, smile plastered on her cheeks as she greets incoming guests.

"I've got twelve consecutive nights, starting tonight."

"I'll take ten."

Ten nights is the minimum cancellation notice policy for Be Our Guest.

Maggie lets out a light whistle. "Damn, Jacob."

I'm sure she feels bad for me, but won't have a problem pocketing the three grand I'm giving her.

"Do you want my credit card?" I ask.

"Nah. I know you're good for it. You can drop by the hotel whenever you want."

"Thanks."

"Jacob?"

"Yeah?"

"Listen, despite what I said a little bit ago, I really am sorry. I know that it's going to be a hard hit for your place's reputation."

"Thanks. I'll be back up in no time."

*

After hanging up with Maggie, I call Be Our Guest and give them the lie about the burst pipe, but reassure them that I've found comparable accommodations for my guests. I also cancel all reservations for the next three months. The representative on the other end of the line is dumbfounded. I keep getting passed up the ladder until I'm talking to a regional executive who says that Be Our Guest will send a plumber and an inspector to get me back up in three days. That's how important my place is to them. I turn him down.

Then, the strong-arming attempts begin. He starts talking about Be Our Guest's policies and that I may be in violation, but I'm ready for it. I'm doing everything by the book. He points out that I'm turning down thousands of dollars. I tell him I'm aware of that, as well. He argues that even if I do get back up after three months, my reputation might be permanently damaged unless I can get everything repaired as soon as possible. I'm not swayed. I'm going dark for three months.

Hopefully, this will all be sorted by then … whatever "this" is.

*

It's not my day to be at the shop, but I want the distraction. I can't sit at the house, staring out the window, waiting for Laura to wander out of the forest.

Sandy lights up when she sees Murphy and I walk in.

"What are you doing here?" she asks, steaming a cappuccino.

"Wanted to help out."

She motions to the growing line of customers. "Have at it."

I hop behind the counter. Murphy retreats to his bed near the register. Instantly, he starts to receive the fawning attention he is accustomed to. I always know when someone is petting him because I can hear his tail thumping on the floor.

I go about taking orders, changing filters, and unloading the small dishwasher behind the counter. I'm good for a while, but as the day drags on, it becomes painfully obvious that I'm off my game. I can't keep the image of Laura out of my head.

It can't be her. It's not possible.

"So, that was one chai latte, a caramel mocha, and an iced tea?" I ask, repeating an order to a customer.

The old lady blinks at me from behind her thick glasses. "No. It was a regular latte for me, and a hot chocolate for my husband."

"I had the chai latte," the guy in front of her says.

"I had a hot tea, but not an iced tea," the lady behind the old woman chimes in.

I shake my head. "Right, right, right. Sorry. My bad."

I turn to start correcting my mistakes and notice that Sandy is looking at me.

"You all right, boss?"

"Yeah. I'm fine. Just not firing on all cylinders today."

She's slow to look away, but is forced to when she hands change to a customer.

I whip up the latte, steam the milk for the hot chocolate, and hand it to the guy.

"Here you go," I say. "Latte and a hot chocolate."

"Nope," he says, and points to the old lady behind him, who's looking at me like I'm crazy.

I curse under my breath. "Sorry. Here's your latte *and your hot—*

"—*chocolate*," the barista said, handing the Styrofoam cup to Laura. I was already putting cream and sugar in my coffee at the station next to the counter.

We found a small table at the back of the coffee shop, which was located on Franklin Street, next to Wilton University's campus.

"I can't believe you're drinking coffee at eight o'clock in the evening," Laura said, sliding into the seat. "You're gonna be up all night."

"Then so will you," I replied with my best roguish smile.

She blushed, and took a long sip from her hot chocolate.

Afterwards, we took our time and simply wandered through Rutland. We strolled down Merchants Row, laughing at the drunken students staggering out of the different bars. The conversation flowed, but there was the tension of who would be the first to say it—a tension that grew as it got later.

"So, where to?" I asked.

"My roommate is visiting her parents. Sooooo … back to my place?"

From that moment on, we knew where the evening was heading. We didn't say much else, and I tried to not quicken my stride in anticipation. It was a little corny going back to her dorm room, but those blue eyes and red hair wiped away any reservations I had.

We arrived at the door to her dorm, and she swiped the key card over the sensor. There was a buzzing and the lock clicked. She pulled the door open, and we entered the foyer. She quickly led me off to the right, down a short hallway, and into the stairwell. As we reached the first landing, I wrapped my arm around her waist. She turned to face me and we kissed. We staggered against the wall. Our hands were everywhere, and we fought to balance our kissing with the need to breathe. A door opened somewhere above us. We tried to separate, but it was useless. A mousy brunette descended the stairs and walked past.

"Get a room," she muttered.

"Almost there!" Laura laughed.

The brunette rolled her eyes at us. Laura flipped her the bird. I laughed into the nape of her neck. She gave me one more kiss and took my hand.

"Come on," she said, pulling me up the stairs.

We came out into the third-floor hallway. It was lit by harsh halogen lamps. She gave me a quick glance over her shoulder as she moved from one pool of light to another. Every step was foreplay. I was hypnotized by the sway of her hips and the bouncing curls of her hair.

We passed door after door. Mounted on the wall next to each one was a small whiteboard. Some of the whiteboards had messages written on them. Most were short, telling the occupant how awesome they were. Others had funny quotes. I glimpsed one as I passed that read, "May the God of hope fill you with all joy and peace as you trust in Him, so that you may overflow with hope by the power of the Holy Spirit. ~ Romans 15:13". Under which, someone had written, "God don't give a shit."

We arrived at the door marked #317. She took out a key, slid it into the lock, twisted, and pushed it open.

Upon first glance, it was the model of your typical college dorm. There was that invisible line that ran down the center of the room, dividing it in half. The left half had a total "emo" motif, with posters for The Misfits and My Chemical Romance on the walls. The other side was more standard and subdued, except for the large poster of Jesus on the wall next to the bed. He was ascending to Heaven from the cross, surrounded by angels. It sucked all the attention from the room, so much so that I forgot about my erection.

"Um … okay … Which side is yours?"

"Guess."

I pointed to the "emo" side. "This one?"

"Nope."

"Seriously?" I asked, fixated on the Jesus poster.

"Yeah. I know it's a little much, but it's only in case my mom makes a surprise visit."

"Does that happen often?"

"She insists on keeping tabs on me."

Hooking up was still in the cards, but I felt that we had taken a detour and I was intrigued.

"So, you're saying that poster is only for your mother's benefit?"

"Yeah."

"You're not a believer?"

"Nope."

Her tone. Her eyes. Her slight frown. There was a lot in that "nope".

"Interesting. Well, let's see what else I can find out about you," I said, scanning the shelves and desk.

She dropped onto the bed. "Do your worst."

"Hmmmmm …" I said, tapping my finger to my chin as I moved to the photos on the desk. I focused on a silver-framed photo of her in a cheerleading outfit.

"Cheerleader?"

"Brilliant, Sherlock."

I moved to another photo of her with an older woman who had beady eyes and thin brown hair. "Mother?"

"Yep."

"Where's your dad?" I regretted the question as soon as it escaped my lips, but she was unfazed.

"Died when I was three."

"Oh … sorry."

She shrugged. "Never really knew him."

I went to the row of scrapbooks on the shelf. There were five of them, each with a different pattern. I slid the first one off the shelf and opened it. On the first page was the same beady-eyed woman from the photo on the desk. She was holding a baby in her arms and smiling, while a man in his forties stood behind them.

"Ah, there's Dad."

I started flipping through the pages. I watched her grow up through the photos. There were a few of her as a baby, her face smeared with birthday cake.

"Wow. You really liked cake."

She lay back on the bed. "All right. Enough."

"Hold on, hold on."

I flipped a couple more pages. There were photos of her learning to ride a bike, and more than a few of her at church. I came to a photo of Laura dressed as an angel, standing in front of a Christmas tree. If I had to guess, I would have said she was about five. I held the book open to her. "Now that is adorable."

She reached for the scrapbook.

"No, no, no, no," I said, pulling it away.

She watched me with a delicious smile.

I snapped the scrapbook closed and returned it to its spot. I continued down the shelf to an ornate wooden box. The letters 'L.A.' in intricate script were burned into the lid. I reached to open it.

"Please, don't," she said.

I couldn't tell if she was being sincere or playful. Being the jerk that I was, I went ahead and lifted the lid.

A delicate ballerina in a green dress on a spindle rose and began to slowly spin over a glittering glass-beaded surface. There was a mirror mounted to the underside of the lid that was surrounded by a mosaic of blue glass. The mirror and blue glass caught the light that bounced from the beads and scattered soft spots of light over the ballerina. The notes of a haunting waltz filled the room. It was something out of a dream. I was hypnotized by the tiny figure with arms outstretched, slowly twisting to the melody.

"I told you not to open it."

"It's beautiful," I said.

"My dad gave it to me. Mom said it was the only thing that could get me to sleep as a baby."

I couldn't take my eyes off the ballerina. The slow rotation, and the way the figure caught the light, gave the illusion that she was actually moving to the tune.

"Hey," Laura said, snapping me out of it.

I turned.

She was lying back on the bed with a seductive smile. "I'm right here."

Everything came back into focus.

I closed the box and moved to the bed. She laughed, and we

were right back to where we were on the stairs—breathlessly kissing, our tongues darting over one another. Our hands wouldn't stop. She pulled her shirt over her head, revealing an emerald bra.

I shook my head. "Okay, I have to ask—do you coordinate your bra with your hair? Because that is too perfect."

"Shut up," she said and bit my lower lip.

More kissing. More fumbling. My shirt flew above my shoulders and landed on the floor. It was a race to see who could unbutton the other's jeans first. I won by virtue of the fact that I had a belt and she didn't. I flicked the tab of her zipper down in an exaggerated fashion, which created a cartoonish sound effect. She laughed and pulled my belt through the loops of my jeans in her own ridiculous gesture. We slowed. The kissing became more passionate. More purposeful.

My phone buzzed.

I pulled back a fraction.

"Let it go," she whispered, trying to catch up in the "zipper race".

It buzzed, again.

I sighed and lowered my head to avoid another kiss. "I can't. It's my work phone."

She took my face in her hands. "You can't be serious."

"I'm sorry," I said, and pulled away.

She let out an exasperated sigh.

I took the phone from my pocket and checked my messages.

Need to pay a visit to Dara. Account past due.

"Fuck," I whispered.

It was code from Reggie. Our messages were always coded. There was no Dara, but I knew what the message meant.

"I'm really sorry, but I have to go. It's urgent," I said.

I stood up and found my shirt and belt. After hastily putting myself back together, I went for the door.

"Are you sure?" she asked.

I turned back to look at her.

Her sparkling eyes. Her hair draping over the pillow. Her

smooth pale skin. She was one of—no. She was the sexiest thing I had ever seen.

I went over to kiss her.

"I'm really sorry," I said.

We kissed, and she playfully bit my lip again.

"One day, you're going to have to tell me what it is you do," she said.

"I told you. I do IT consulting. They call at all hours of the day and night."

Her face clouded. "No. What you *really* do."

I kissed her one last time. "Gotta go."

I finished latching my belt, and went for the door. Before stepping through, I glanced back. She was still lying on the bed in her bra and unfastened jeans.

She waved her fingers as if to say, "toodle-oo".

"Dammit," I whispered, and left.

*

The hour-long drive to Lyndon, home of Lyndon University, was excruciating. All I could think about was the image of Laura, lying on that bed.

I was finally able to put it out of my mind as I arrived at the squat, brick house a few blocks from the small campus. I got out, walked up onto the porch, and knocked on the door.

It took way too long, but the door was finally answered by Mattie Donovan.

Mattie appeared to have aged ten years from when we used to hang out just last year. He was still a perpetual slacker, and I told him that he needed to get his act together if he wanted to keep doing business. He was still a good guy, just sloppy.

His eyes were bloodshot, and the smell of weed emanated from the open door.

"Hey, Mattie," I said.

"… shit," he replied.

"Good to see you, too."

I stepped past him into the living room, and things were already wrong.

Two guys I had never seen before were sitting on the couch, completely baked, and staring at the television. The coffee table in front of them was littered with spent cigarettes, bags of chips, a bong, and a glass vial next to a pipe. The only sources of illumination in the room were the television and some Christmas lights strung around the borders of the ceiling. Bedsheets covered the windows.

Mattie closed the door behind me.

"Can I get you anything?" he asked. "We've got weed, but if you want something harder, I think we have some—"

"No."

"You want a soda or something?"

"Mattie, you know why I'm here."

"Um … no, man. I don't, uh, I don't know."

"You're behind on your payment."

He scratched the back of his neck, trying hard to feign confusion. This wasn't like Mattie. He could be a fuck-up from time to time, but he had never lied to me.

"Really? You sure about that? I thought I paid."

"Come on, Mattie."

"No, yeah. I paid Reggie. Like, last week, I paid him."

"Mattie, Reggie sent me."

I noticed that the two guys on the couch, while still high, were intensely watching our conversation.

"Oh … Really?" Mattie asked, stalling for time.

"Who are your friends?" I asked with a nod towards the couch.

"They're just friends, you know? From out of town."

The guy with blotchy skin and the bad haircut, sitting on the far end of the couch, flicked his eyes towards the darkened hallway off of the kitchen that led to the bedrooms.

"Is that some of your inventory?" I asked, pointing to the table. "Because if it is, and you're behind on payments, I sure hope your friends have paid for it. Also, if you're keeping your stuff here with the money, you know how bad that is." I was going for bravado, but I worried that I had overplayed it.

Mattie nervously snorted. "Yeah, yeah. Of course, they paid for it."

"Great. Then you can give me the cash, I'll get out of here, and you can continue to entertain your guests from out of town."

No one moved.

Mattie started chuckling. "Yeah, sure." He gestured with his thumb. "It's in the bedroom. I'll go get it."

I nodded, keeping his "friends" in my line of sight.

Mattie disappeared into the darkened doorway of one of the rooms in the hall, but didn't turn on the light. I used his departure to shift my weight and get myself closer to the door.

"This is all wrong," I kept telling myself.

I glanced at the two guys on the couch, who had put down their joints and were staring at me. They locked eyes with one another and right then, I knew what was coming, but there was no time to react.

A guy burst from the darkened room where Mattie had disappeared. He was tall and lean. His tank top revealed a latticework of tattoos that covered his chest and ran down his arm, all the way to the gun in his hand—the gun that was pointed at my face. Mattie followed close behind with a wild, terrified expression. The two guys on the couch jumped up, trying to fight off their high and act alert. The guy holding the gun wasn't high on weed. He was on something else, like coke or meth. His face twitched and his hand shook.

I remained as still as I could, trying to pretend that I was the calmest person in the room. I had only dealt with college kids. This was the first time a gun had been put in my face. Things had gone way above my pay scale.

"All right, listen up," the tattooed guy barked in a frenzied tone. "You tell Reggie that this place is ours. If he wants to do business here, he has to do business with us. You got that?"

I took a moment to try to steady my voice. "Yeah. I'll tell him that. You can lower that gun now."

He shoved the gun closer to my face. "You tell him that! You got that? He has to do business with us from now on!"

I was still trying to exude a calmness that I did not possess. "I got it. I got it … but I don't know who you are, so …"

It was an honest statement, but he did not take it as such.

"You getting smart with me, asshole?" He pressed the gun to my forehead. "I could kill you, right now."

"Then who would give the message to Reggie?" I asked.

"Maybe I should kill you right now to send a message that we mean business."

"You don't want to do that."

"Why not?"

"Because then, you'd have to talk to Reggie yourself, and I don't think he would sit down for a polite chat. I'll give him the message, okay?"

I let it sink in, but was desperate to get out of there.

He considered, and lessened the pressure on the gun.

"Yeah," the tattooed guy said. "Yeah, you do that. You tell him."

"I will."

I glanced over his shoulder at Mattie.

"Mattie, tell me you're not a part of this."

Mattie looked down at the floor.

"Don't talk to him," the tattooed guy growled. "You talk to me."

"Fine. I'll deliver your message. Don't tell me your names. It's better that way." I glanced at the two guys by the couch and back at the ringleader. "And can I give you some advice?"

He blinked. "Advice?"

58

"Yes."

He looked at me like I was crazy. "Sure. Yeah. You can give us some advice."

"As soon as I leave, get underground, fast."

"Why's that?"

"Reggie's not a guy who takes a long time to come up with a plan."

The two guys next to the couch exchanged glances. The ringleader kept his eyes on me, but I could see it. Doubt and fear started to creep out from behind those frenzied eyes.

"Fine. Thanks for the advice," he sneered. "Now, give us all the money you've got."

"I don't have any."

They stopped.

"Bullshit," the tattooed guy said.

"I don't carry any."

"You're Reggie's bagman. You don't have any money?" the guy with blotchy skin and bad haircut asked.

"No. I only do one pickup at a time."

"Why?"

I glanced around. "In case something like this happens."

The ringleader's shock melted into amusement. "You were right, Mattie. This guy's smart. All right, bagman. You go right now, and tell Reggie. Got it?"

"Okay," I said, slowly turning towards the door. I couldn't help stopping and looking back at Mattie.

"This was really stupid, Mattie," I said, and left.

*

Reggie leaned against his car and calmly smoked a cigarette while I told him everything that had happened in Lyndon. Since there was no money to count, the headlights were off. The silent trees stood on either side of the road. Occasionally, a wind would cause them to lean in, as though they wanted to hear. I gave him everything, down to the last detail.

When I was finished, he took a slow drag on his cigarette. I had seen Reggie blow his top before and it wasn't pretty, but this was when he was at his most terrifying—when he was contemplative.

"You didn't get their names?" he asked through a plume of smoke, expelled from the shadow of his face.

"No

"And Mattie is in on it?"

I quickly looked down at the road, hoping he hadn't seen my face. Of course, Mattie was in on it, but if I said it, I'd be signing his death warrant.

"… I don't know," I answered, hoping my inadvertent pause hadn't given it away, but when I looked up at Reggie, it obviously had.

Reggie looked at me and shook his head. "You should really carry a piece."

"Why? So I could have shot my way out of there? I'd end up dead."

He shrugged. "Still …"

"I pick up payments. That's it. And from now on, it's only at fraternity houses. No more private addresses. That's to protect me and to protect you."

He thought it over. "Okay."

"Okay," I repeated.

He took one last drag, and flicked the butt of the cigarette onto the gravel. He went around to the driver side of the Challenger and opened the door. "You have a good night."

He got in, closed the door, and turned the key. The Challenger roared to life. He hit the gas, and the back tires spewed the gravel in every direction.

I watched the car peel away and disappear as the road twisted into the trees.

A wave of nausea hit me and I knelt on the roadside. Once

it passed, I took out my phone and tried to call Mattie, warning him that Reggie knew, but I didn't receive an answer. I tried texting him, but after a few minutes, I heard nothing in return.

I couldn't believe the staggering difference of where my night had begun, to where it had ended. I thought about calling Laura to see if she was still up, but I wouldn't be able to convincingly lie to her.

I had to get out. I still had about twenty thousand dollars to go on my student debt but I would get that elsewhere.

I had bought myself a little time by demanding that I would only do fraternity house pickups but after that night, I knew it was over. I would start planning my exit in the morning, but at that moment, all *I wanted was a—*

"—*beer?*"

I blink at the guy waiting in line on the other side of the counter. He's wearing Coke-bottle glasses, a scarf, and sporting a full beard.

"What?"

"Do you guys sell beer?" he asks, again. "Like a cider or anything that's gluten-free?"

"No. This is a coffee shop."

"I know, but some coffee places sell beer now. Like, even some Starbucks are doing it, now. I thought that maybe—"

"All we got is what's on the board. If you want beer, there are bars all over the place, outside. Go there."

I'm still at Groundworks, churning out drinks on autopilot. The anxiety of my little daydream has carried over, and my tone is incredibly rude.

He's offended, as he should be. "Okay, then. Sure … Great service you got here."

He slithers past the rest of the line and heads out the door. More than a few people who have overheard our exchange watch him leave.

At the register, Sandy nods to Sheila. "Can you take over for a few minutes?"

"Sure," Sheila says.

Sandy forces a smile at me. "Talk to you in the back for a sec?"

I follow her through the swinging doors and into the office. She closes the door behind us.

"What the hell is going on with you?"

"Is that any way to talk to your boss?" I ask, lamely trying to defuse the situation.

"I'm serious, Jacob."

"I know. I'm sorry. A pipe burst in the cottage. I had to cancel some reservations. I'm going to take a hit, and it's messing with my mind."

"What about the franchise? As long as we keep this up, the cottage is going to be small potatoes, right?"

"Yeah."

"Okay. Well, let's not get any bad Yelp reviews before that happens."

"You're right. I'm just out of it, I guess."

"No kidding." She takes a breath and relaxes. "Look, you weren't supposed to be here, today, so why don't you take off?"

"No. I can close. I've been leaning on you too much lately."

"It's fine. Me, Tom, and Shelia can take it from here for the night. It's obvious that you're distracted. Go clear your head."

I surrender way too easily. "You're right. I'm really sorry, but, please call me if you need help."

"Get out of here."

"Thank you, Sandy."

"You can thank me by making me a junior partner in the franchise."

"Done."

"Jacob, I was kidding."

"I wasn't."

She shakes her head. "You're really out of it. Fly, be free, and I promise that I won't hold you to that junior partner thing when you come to your senses."

I go back out into the restaurant and collect Murphy, who is basking in the attention of two young girls. I snap on his leash, and lead him to the door, trying not to make eye contact with any of the guests who may have seen my little outburst.

*

The night air feels fantastic. Sandy was right. I needed to get out of there, but I wasn't joking about giving her a junior partnership. She deserves it. I may have built this ship, but she has been an equal captain.

The decorations on Main Street are beginning to overwhelm the windows of the shops. People are setting up the booths on the green. In three days, this place will look like a movie set. The street is bustling with people. Some of them are locals; a lot of them are tourists. I glance around to see if I can find the guy I snapped at, but I doubt I'll be able to find him in this crowd. He was right, though—a beer sounds really good right about now.

I walk up the street to the Iron & Ivy, The Hollows' upscale gastropub. Since I've got Murphy with me, I grab a small table on the patio. The place is trying to look like a Colonial-era public house, and it's largely succeeding. The patio is filled with long tables and benches made of "distressed" wood. Lanterns hang overhead. An attractive server comes to my table and asks if I'd like something to drink. I scan down the draft selection and choose an imperial stout.

"Anything to eat?"

"No, thank you."

She scribbles in her book and snaps it closed. "I'll be right back."

She walks away, and returns a few minutes later with a goblet of pitch-black liquid, capped by a layer of creamy foam, and a small dish of water for Murphy.

I raise the glass to my lips and take a sip. It's smooth at first, and then the bitterness hits—perfection.

"How goes it, Mr Reese?" a man behind me asks. He steps around the table and sits in the opposite chair. He's in his forties, with salt-and-pepper hair. He leans over and pats Murphy's head. "What's up, Murph?"

"Excellent, Andrew," I reply.

Andrew Paulini is the owner of the Iron & Ivy. He loves his bar and with good reason. It's popular and profitable.

"You gonna tell me your costume for the contest?" he asks.

"Not a chance."

He smiles. "Good."

Andrew is part of our group of business owners who take the annual costume contest way too seriously. He's the guy I dethroned when I went on my yearly winning streak. It's a friendly rivalry.

"What about the parade?" I ask, taking another sip of stout. "What's your float gonna be?"

His eyes light up. "Honestly, I'm more excited about the parade than the costume contest."

"Your float is that good?"

"Yep. You doing a float this year? I know the planning committee keeps asking you."

"Nah. Too much work."

Murphy sits up to receive an ear scratch. Andrew obliges.

"How's the coffee business?"

"Good."

"I heard through the grapevine that you might be branching out. Possibly starting a franchise?"

"That grapevine is pretty loud."

He laughs, and nods at my glass. "What are you drinking?"

"Imperial stout."

"I'll tell your server that the next one is on me."

"You don't have to do that."

64

"Don't worry. I'll buy you another one after I sweep the costume contest, and first prize for the float."

"Bold words, and thank you."

My phone buzzes.

"Speak of the devil," I mumble, reading the screen.

"Did I hear you say that you're dressing up as the Devil? Didn't you already do that last year?"

"No. It's the franchise thing. I'm sorry. I have to take this."

He put up his hands. "By all means." He stands up and pats me on the shoulder as he passes. "Good luck."

"Mr Tiller," I say, answering the phone. "How are things at Alliance Capital?"

"Great, and I think I have some news that will be great for you, too."

"Really?"

"I spoke to Helen Trifauni. You remember? She's our regional director."

"I do."

"I showed her the financials and the photos. She loves the place. She's eager to check it out. She's even cutting her vacation short a little early to come see it. She wants to meet you Friday. Is that okay?"

"This Friday? In two days?"

"Is that a problem?" he asks.

"Well, Halloween is on Sunday, so that's cutting it pretty close. The town is going to be a little crazy."

"She's anxious to check it out, and I don't want to inconvenience her."

"No. It's fine. That works for us."

"Perfect. So, here's what'll happen: she's going to come in while you guys are open, and just watch you work. She likes to get her own feel for the place. She'll be there for a while, peeking over your shoulders, and she'll want to see the night's receipts. It'll be awkward, but that's her method."

"Understood."

"After that, she'll want to sit down with you for a little while. She'll give her opinions about what you need to do. Don't put too much stock in them. She likes to flex her 'creative authority', if you know what I mean. She does it all the time, and she tends to forget her ideas almost immediately."

"Okay," I chuckle.

"One thing I will say is don't bring the dog. In fact, remove all traces of the dog from the shop. That will be a sticking point for her. She's big on cleanliness and sanitation. Make the place shine. If she knows that the dog is there on a regular basis, it's all she'll be able to think about."

"That'll be easy enough. Consider the dog gone."

"Great. I think that does it. Any questions for me?"

"Nope. Thanks for the update."

"We'll be in touch," he says, and quickly adds, "Happy Halloween!"

*

Two hours later, I'm lying in bed with the glow of the three glasses of stout beginning to wane, while talking to Sandy on the phone.

"We're a go."

"This is exciting," she says. "Aren't you excited?"

"Yeah."

"You don't sound excited."

"There's a lot on my plate."

"Well, get excited."

"How was the rest of the night?"

"Good. I emailed you the reports."

"I'll look at them in the morning."

"Cool. Now, get some sleep, and get your head in the game."

"I will. Good night."

"Good night."

I hang up the phone, put it on the nightstand, slide under the covers, and close my eyes.

In forty-eight hours, I have one of the most important meetings of my life and I have to focus.

There's a familiar sigh.

I open my eyes, and turn my head to see Murphy. He's doing that pleading thing where he's resting his head on the mattress, looking right at me.

"Yeah, yeah, Murphy. Whatever. Up-up."

Immediately, he leaps onto the bed and drops down by my side. I've gone from a king-sized bed, all to myself, to a space the size of a twin bed. I scratch behind his ears, and I hear him pant contentedly in the darkness.

I need the distraction of the meeting. I want to focus on the franchise, and not Laura. I don't want to think about what's happening or what might happen next. Whoever is doing this knows my secret. They're toying with me. It can't be Laura. I know it can't. I watched her d— It can't be Laura. But then, who? No one else knows about her. I was the only one to see what happened, and I haven't told a soul.

I roll over on *my side and face—*

—her.

The notes of the music box found us under the sheets.

Her roommate was away again, and we had just made love in her dorm room. Our successful attempt to have sex on her twin bed was almost comical. Now, our naked bodies were pressed together. As a joke, I had gotten up, and started the music box. Then, I returned to her in bed, and pulled the covers up over our heads. We lay there, under the sheet, basking in the afterglow.

"There are words to the song, you know," she said, after a long pause.

"Really?"

"Mmm-hmm. My mother said that my father used to sing them

to me to get me to fall asleep." She waited for the song to cycle through to the beginning, and began to sing to the haunting waltz.

> "Just close your eyes,
> And you and I,
> Will brave the dark, and go dancing.
> Now, time to sleep,
> And safe I will keep,
> Your dreams, as we are all dancing.

> Come with me and soon you'll be
> Dancing on clouds in a star-filled sky.
> Walk with me and you will see
> A magical place we can stay for all time."

The music cascaded before slowing to a crawl for the last verse.

> "There's nothing to fear,
> You're already here,
> With us, and we are all dancing."

The last notes faded away into the corners of the room.

"Your father sang that to you to get you to fall asleep?" I asked.

"Yep."

"That is creepy."

She laughed. "What? It's an old Irish folk song called 'The Dreamer's Waltz.'"

"It's creepy, and if I may say?"

She raised her head and looked at me.

"I'm glad you're a political science major, because I don't think you'll ever get a job as a singer."

She tried to playfully slap me, but we were pressed so close, she couldn't properly execute it.

I held her tightly so she couldn't try again.

After we laughed, I continued to hold her. We relaxed into one another and listened to the music box as it cycled through the song again. As the music came to an end, I could feel her tense, like she was getting ready for the music to stop.

When it finally reached its end, she looked up at me and smiled. "So, are you going to tell me your secret?"

"What secret?" I asked. "Laura, we are naked on a very small bed. There's nothing I can hide from you right now."

"You know what I mean."

"No, I don't."

"Where do you really go when you go out at night?"

So that's what was on her mind. It was on my mind, too. That night at Mattie's had rattled me, and I was trying hard to keep it from her. I also still hadn't heard from Mattie, despite numerous attempts to warn him.

"I told you. It's work."

"Yeah, but it's not consulting."

"It is."

"Jacob, I know it's only been a couple of months, but are you going to keep lying to me?" The question was firm but honest. She was giving me an opportunity.

I decided to try to meet her halfway.

"It's something that's coming to an end. I promise."

"Is that the best I'm going to get?"

"It's all I've got, for now."

Neither of us spoke for a few moments. I was desperate to break the tension, and just threw out a shot in the dark.

"What about you?" I asked.

"What about me?"

"What secrets are you hiding?"

I was only joking, but I saw her change. A guard went up. I had hit on something.

"Hey. It's okay," I said. "You can tell me."

69

"If you're not going to tell me yours, I'm sure as hell not going to tell you mine."

I propped myself up on my elbow to look at her. "So, you do have a secret."

She didn't respond, but she clearly did.

"Tell me," I said.

In the dimness under the sheet, I could see her grow thoughtful and reserved. "We're not there yet."

"We just had sex and are lying naked in bed together, and you're going to tell me 'we're not there yet'?"

She looked at me, all hint of humor gone. "Where do you go, again?"

I didn't answer.

"Yeah," she said. "We're not there, yet."

Our bodies were still pressed together in the darkness under the sheet, but our minds were a thousand miles apart.

Finally, she flipped the sheet off of us. Released from our bubble, the cool air crawled over our skins.

"You should go. Since I'm never going to get that job as a singer, I need to study." She meant it as a joke but there was an edge to it.

"Are you pissed at me?" I asked.

"... No."

We continued to lie there, waiting for the other to speak.

"Listen," she said, "it's only been a while. When you're ready, you can tell me yours and I'll tell you mine." She turned to look at me. "Until then, I just want to have fun, okay?"

"Okay."

I got up, and put on my clothes.

We kissed good night, and I headed back to my apartment.

My mind was in a fog. I couldn't keep it up. I had to get out of my situation with Reggie if I was going to keep Laura. I climbed into my bed and spent hours staring at the ceiling. If I could end things with Reggie, maybe I could tell her that my secret was over and not a big deal. That got me thinking about what it was she was keeping from me. I gave up and rolled over to *try to get some—*

—sleep, but the pain in my side suddenly flares.

I roll the opposite way and bump into Murphy, who groans in protest.

"Shut up, Murphy."

The only response is that of his tail thumping against the mattress at the sound of his name.

Chapter 4

I've been on pins and needles all morning, trying to focus on Helen Trifauni's visit tomorrow, but I'm constantly glancing over my shoulder for anything out of the ordinary. I field calls from Be Our Guest, begging to know if the cottage is back up, and if I can honor some of the existing reservations I've already cancelled. I tell them no.

I call Sandy at the shop. She reassures me that everything is ready to go, but she sounds nervous.

"Do you need me to come in?" I ask.

"Not if you're going to be in the same state as you were yesterday."

"All right, but call me if you need anything."

"Will do."

She's right. I'll be distracted at the shop, but I can't sit at home. So, Murphy and I head to The Sanctuary. I spend the better part of two hours throwing his red tennis ball into the trees for him to race after it. He's so tuckered out by the end, I almost have to carry him back to the house. Thankfully, he makes it back on his own steam. Once inside, he lamely tries to get to his bed in the study, but only makes it halfway through the study door before he lies down and starts snoring.

I try to get some work done at my computer, but my gaze constantly drifts out the window to the forest.

It's been years since I looked to see if there have been any updates about Laura. I used to do it constantly, but after so much time had passed with no changes to the investigation, I walled up that part of my life and moved on. Now, with everything that's happening, I want to know if there's anything new about her disappearance. A quick search proves that no, there's no new information. It gives me a little comfort and I'm able to get some work done.

When hunger comes on around five o'clock, I wake up Murphy, and we head into town. I hit up the Iron & Ivy one more time, and watch the final preparations for the Halloween festivities.

I order the Bacon-Bleu burger, medium rare, with a side of fries, and a seasonal pumpkin ale to wash it down. I "accidentally" drop more fries onto the ground for Murphy than I should. I try to focus on the meeting but every time I do, I think of Laura and—

My phone buzzes. The caller ID flashes "SANDY". I quickly take a swig of beer to wash down the bit of French fry in my mouth before answering.

"Hey, Sandy. What's up?"

"You need to come in, right now," Sandy says, straining to keep her voice calm.

"Why? What's going on? What happened?"

"She's here!"

The sound of the register chimes in the background.

"Here's your change," she says away from the phone with forced cheerfulness.

"Who's there?"

"The lady from the company. The one who's checking us out."

I sit up in my chair. "She's not supposed to be here until tomorrow."

"Um, yeah!"

"Okay. It's fine. Everything's fine. I'll be there as soon as I can but I have to take Murphy home, first."

"Just get here."

The line goes dead.

*

I leave half of my burger but down the rest of my beer. I don't waste time asking for the bill. I just leave way more cash on the table than the bill could possibly be. I take Murphy to the truck and head out.

I glance towards the shop as we drive past. Through the store window, I can see that the line is long. No wonder Sandy is losing her mind.

Ten minutes later, I pull into my driveway.

I take Murphy inside. I tell him to "stay", but when I turn to go back out, he tries to follow.

"Nope. You stay."

He slowly sits on the floor in the hallway, clearly confused.

"Sorry, buddy. I'll be back."

After locking the door behind me, I run to the truck. As I jump in, I quietly curse, because that taillight still isn't fixed, and this would be the worst time in the world to get pulled over.

*

My luck holds out and I'm able to floor it back to the shop without being spotted by a cop.

Walking through the door, the first thing I see is Sandy's face. She's trying to hold the place together. I walk up to the register, where Sandy is making change, while Tom and Sheila frantically try to keep up with the drink orders. This was poor scheduling on my part. It's a Friday, two days before Halloween. Of course, we're going to be packed. I should have been here the whole time.

"Where is she?" I ask, under my breath.

"Corner booth."

I start to turn around.

"Don't look!"

"Sandy, I have to look."

"Well, just don't be obvious."

"Sandy, it's fine. Everything is going to be fine."

I raise my head to look over the line of customers.

There she is, sitting in the same booth where Mr Tiller sat a few days ago. She's a small woman with sharp features, thick glasses, and a nest of gray hair atop her head. She's holding a pen in her bony fingers, and there's an open spiral notebook on the table in front of her. She's looking right at us with a perfectly blank expression.

I smile at her.

She clicks the pen, tilts her head down, and begins furiously writing.

"Shit …" I whisper.

"I thought she wasn't supposed to be here until tomorrow."

"That's what I was told."

"So, what is she doing here? Is she going to be here until we close?"

"Sandy, you've got to calm down, okay? I'll go find out. Did you talk to her, already?"

She squirms. "Yeah."

"What happened?"

"Nothing …"

"Sandy?"

"She just came in and sat down. It was so weird that I asked her if she wanted to order anything. She said no, and I said I'm sorry, but we don't allow loitering. I swear, Jacob, I thought she was just some crazy lady. I mean, look at her … Oh my God. I've screwed this whole thing up, haven't I?"

I've never seen her so wound up.

"You didn't do anything wrong. I'm going to go over and talk to her, okay?"

"Tell her that I'm sorry. If I had known—"

"Sandy, it's fine. Keep the place going. You're amazing. Smile. I'll take care of it."

"Okay."

"Big smiles on everyone, okay?" I add, nodding to Tom and Sheila.

Sandy tries to smile, but she's so rattled, it looks like she's baring her teeth.

I have to leave it at that. I move around the line and make my way to the corner booth.

As I approach, she stops writing. Her eyes follow me from behind those dark, tinted glasses. Every other part of her body remains still.

"Mrs Trifauni?"

"Yes?" Her voice is clipped and surprisingly low for someone so small. I have to assume it's from years of smoking.

"I'm the owner, Jacob Reese. It's nice to meet you."

"Nice to meet you," she says, and extends her hand.

Her spindly fingers are ice cold. After we shake, she gives me her card, which I tuck into my pocket.

"Can I get you anything? Coffee or a latte?"

"I'm fine. Thank you."

"May I join you?"

"Of course."

I slide into the seat across from her.

"I hear that you've already met my associate, Sandy."

"Yes."

"You'll have to forgive her."

"What for?"

"For mistaking you for someone who was loitering."

"Her response was perfectly natural. She should prevent loiterers."

I twist backwards towards the counter. Sandy is trying to pretend like she isn't watching us. I give her a big thumbs-up. She's mortified.

I turn back to Mrs Trifauni. "I am a little confused, though."

"Oh?"

"Mr Tiller said you were coming tomorrow."

"Yes, but when I scout a potential franchise, I want to see them at their most 'normal', not when they are on heightened alert because I'm there. I got here around seven this morning and decided—"

"Wait. You've been here since this morning?"

"Yes," she replies, as though nothing could be more normal. "I wanted to get a feel for the town, how your shop fits in, and how it might fit in with other towns."

"And what do you think?"

I catch the faintest trace of a smile on her lips. "It's charming."

I have the distinct impression that this is as close as she gets to gushing. She's completely under The Hollows' spell.

"I also wanted to see your opening procedures and what the early business was like," she continues. "So, I watched from across the street."

I'm stunned. "I want to make sure I understand this, Mrs Trifauni. You've been scoping us out since seven this morning?"

"I need to know everything about this place," she says, continuously clicking her pen like it's an uncontrollable tick. "I want to see every customer's experience from the moment they walk in the door to the moment they leave. It's the only way to know if Groundworks is worthy of Alliance Capital's money. What I want from you and your staff is to go about your work as if I am not here."

"We can definitely do that, but before I get back to work, are there any other questions I can answer for you?"

She clicks the pen and uses it to point near the register. "Is that a dog bed over there?"

Shit. I was going to get Murphy's bed out of here tomorrow morning before she arrived.

"Yes," I answer, frantically trying to come up with an explanation.

"Do you normally have a dog in here? So much so that it has its own bed?"

It's obvious she doesn't like it, and I'm reminded of Mr Tiller's warning.

"We have a lot of locals come in with their dogs and sometimes, if the line is really long, we let them crash while their owners wait." It's not my best lie, but I try to work in a positive business spin by mentioning that we regularly have long lines.

"Well, if we move forward, lapses in health standards like that will have to go."

"Of course. Absolutely."

Her eyes scan me from behind those glasses, and then drift down to the notebook. She rapidly clicks the pen, and begins scribbling some notes. Although the pages in the notebook are unruled, her writing forms perfect rows across the blank pages.

"Anything else I can answer for you?" I ask.

"No. I believe I have everything I need."

"If you think of anything else, don't hesitate to ask."

"I won't."

I smile. "I'm quite certain of that."

My little joke works, and I can see that trace of a smile return.

I hop out of the booth and go to the register. I collect Murphy's bed, take it through the back to the parking lot, and toss it into the truck. Once back inside, there's a short break in the line, and I gather everyone for a quick pep talk.

"Okay, guys, listen up. She's fine. She's a little strange, but she wants to see the place in action. So, big smiles. You guys are getting triple overtime, tonight, and I'll pay you in cash at the end of the shift. Cool?"

They all eagerly nod.

"Everyone just keep doing what you're doing. It's gonna be great."

*

This is the longest six hours, ever.

The shop is slammed. Outside the window, The Hollows is in full Halloween splendor, and everyone who comes through the door is giddy with anticipation. I, on the other hand, feel like a bomb is about to go off. Occasionally, I glance over at the booth and she's not moving. I swear, she might be dead. I want to go and hold a mirror under her nose to see if she's still breathing. Instead, I keep going. Sometimes, I'll hear the sharp click of her pen over the din of the customers, reassuring me that yes, she is still among the living.

My cheeks start to hurt from smiling, and I know I'm not the only one. The crew is feeling it, too. Sandy has recovered. Out of all of us, she's holding it together the best. When it slows down, I tell her to take a fifteen-minute break.

"I'm gonna go run around the parking lot and scream for a few minutes," she says, blowing by me.

"Knock yourself out."

"Junior partner!" I hear her faintly yell as she opens the back door.

It's drawing closer to closing. We're like marathon runners with the finish line in sight. I've been enjoying this. The shop is alive with laughter and conversation. My crew is knocking it out of the park, and I haven't thought about Laura or the events of the past few days for hours.

Eight-thirty hits and I tell Sandy to put out the "closed" sign. The place is still packed. A few more people straggle in and jump in line until finally, I send Tom outside to instruct anyone else who tries to come in that we are done for the night.

I check Mrs Trifauni. She's no longer paying attention to the shop. She's staring out the window at Main Street. I'm not sure if that's a good or bad sign, but at this point, if she's not impressed, there's nothing we can do about it.

The last order is served, and we start breaking everything down. The crew and I are beat. Sheila begins sweeping the floor. Tom wipes down the cappuccino machine. I'm covering all the food items in cellophane and storing them in the fridge. Sandy is taking care of the register.

An hour later, the last guests are leaving, with the exception of Mrs Trifauni. I thank the last couple as they leave, and lock the door behind them with a flourish.

We're done.

"Mrs Trifauni?" I politely call from the door.

She looks in my direction.

"I'm going to walk my crew out. I'll be with you in just a moment."

She nods.

I lead Sandy, Tom, and Sheila through the swinging doors to the food prep station in the back.

"Wait for me in the parking lot," I tell them.

They leave, and I head into the office. I go to the safe, pull out a thousand dollars in hundred-dollar bills, and go through the back door.

The night air is bracing. Stars dot the sky and the moon has an icy-blue glow.

I join Tom, Shelia, and Sandy under the lone light. I take five hundred dollars from the stack of money I'm carrying, and divide it between Tom and Sheila. "You guys were amazing today. Go have some fun."

"Thanks, boss," Shelia says.

"Thank you," Tom adds.

They walk away down the alley as if they're afraid I may realize I've made a mistake.

I turn to Sandy.

"Well," she says, "there goes a good chunk of the day's profi—"

"And *you*," I say, stomping on her last line. I hand her the remaining five one hundred-dollar bills. "Thank you."

"Jacob, you don't have to do this. That's almost a fifth of the day's profits."

"If my guess is right, we just made a lot more than that."

She looks at the cash like it might bite her.

"Sandy, take the money."

She gingerly grasps it and puts it in her pocket. "Thank you," she says.

"Thank you."

We have a moment that feels a little more than employer and employee.

"I should get back in there," I finally say, and turn to the door.

"Knock 'em dead!"

"Don't say that. She's old."

Sandy's laugh carries through the cold air as I open the door and go back inside. I find Mrs Trifauni in the booth, right where I left her, staring out at Main Street.

"Care if I join you again?"

She turns and smiles—an honest-to-God smile. "Have a seat."

I believed before, but now I know—we did it. All the tension rushes out of me as I sit down for the first time in hours. I also realize how tired I am. My feet are killing me.

"So, what do you think?" I ask.

"I think it goes without saying that I'm extremely impressed. You've got quite a little product here."

"Thank you. I've also got a very good team."

She nods appreciatively, and flips open her notebook. "I do have some ideas that I want to discuss with you," she says with a few clicks of her pen.

"Fire away," I reply, remembering Mr Tiller's warning about her desire to flex her "creative muscles".

She clicks her pen one last time and consults her notes. "What I have in mind is a chain of Groundworks boutique coffee shops. Now, one of the best assets for Groundworks is, of course, The Hollows, and that one can't travel. What Alliance Capital would do is find towns like The Hollows and set up shops. It would be a part of the brand. Towns could wear the fact that they have a Groundworks Coffee like a badge of honor."

"Great."

She flips a page. "Getting down to brass tacks, I love what you've done with the décor. Was that your call?"

"Yep."

"It's fantastic, but I worry that it may be cost-prohibitive to replicate in other locations. This location would be the flagship, and would stay as is, but other locations would be more basic."

"Sure."

She flips another page. "Also, your team is good, but you need more. Other locations will have a bigger staff. We'll flesh out a more detailed structure later."

"Okay."

Click.

I stop. It sounded like she just clicked her pen, but I didn't see her click it. I must be really tired, because it sounded like there was an echo through the shop. She makes no indication that she heard anything. I glance around but shake it off.

"Another aspect we'll have to address is the menu. I like the options that you have, but there are too many. We'll have a team of experts who will work with what you have and come up with some new recipes that will streamline the menu and cut down on inventory."

"Okay …" I answer, my voice wavering.

She looks up. "Don't worry. This is all standard stuff.

Groundworks will still have a unique menu. We're only going to make it more efficient." She goes back to her notebook.

I'm not worried about the menu. It's the furthest fucking thing from my mind.

What caused my voice to waver is the big fat cockroach that's climbing up the wall behind her. It lazily wanders closer and closer to the back of her head.

She's still talking, something about advertising, but I can't hear her.

The cockroach begins moving in more spastic dashes, getting closer to her hair. From behind her seat, another cockroach emerges.

She's looking down in her notebook, giving notes, but it's like she's on mute.

I've got to get her out of here. I have to keep her from looking back. I have to bring this to a close before she sees them.

"Look," I say, trying to keep my voice on an even keel. "It's been a long day. Would you like to head over to the local bar, and continue the conversation over a glass of wine or something?"

"That's all right. I'm almost done," she says, not looking up. "I want to talk about management structure for each location ..."

A third roach appears in the corner, near the window. I'm trying not to breathe. It dashes onto the glass, getting closer and closer to her peripheral vision. It scuttles down towards the table.

No. No. No. No. No.

It halts just above the table's surface. It's perfectly still except for its antennae, which swing back and forth from its glistening head.

I'm so fixated on the cockroach that it takes a second to register that she's stopped talking. I look away from the roach and across the table. She's staring straight at me. No, not right at me. She's staring just past me, over my shoulder.

Something breezes across the back of my neck.

I turn.

The back of my seat is covered in big, thick cockroaches.

I spring from the booth.

Roaches scurry and scuttle across the floor.

They're everywhere.

Chapter 5

It's one o'clock in the morning.

I'm sitting under the lone light post in the parking lot behind the coffee shop.

Helen Trifauni is long gone. At the sight of hundreds of roaches crawling across the floor, she immediately headed for the exit. I pleaded with her, but what was I supposed to say? She left without a word.

I ran to the office, grabbed a binder from a shelf, and found the number for Envo Exterminators. These aren't the guys who come to your house to take care of some ants. These are professionals who work in the food service industry. Most health boards give you a grace period of forty-eight hours to solve any violations they find during an inspection. You have to stay closed for those forty-eight hours, but if you can correct the problem, you can open back up, and keep your health grade. If not, you have to live with the health grade they give you, and as everyone knows, when you go out to eat, the difference between an "A" or a "B" on the door makes all the difference in the world.

This is so much worse than a health violation.

I would have rather have it happened during an inspection. Instead, I just watched millions of dollars walk out the door.

After I called Envo, I called Mrs Trifauni to explain that this had never happened before. She didn't answer. I left messages, begging her to look at the years of pristine health inspections the shop had received. She didn't respond.

I sat back in the chair in the office in stunned defeat. A cockroach ran across the keyboard. I swore, stood up, and decided to wait outside in the parking lot for Envo to arrive.

I've been sitting on the pavement with my back against the light post, my arms wrapped around my knees to guard against the cold. I'm still trying to process the fact that the dream of the franchise is over. Not only that, if this gets out in town, I may have lost everything.

The thing that finally drives it home is a text from Sandy.

Okay. I can't wait until tomorrow for you to tell me. You have to tell me now. How did it go?!!!

I don't have the heart to answer.

The white van finally swings into the parking lot. There are no markings. These guys don't advertise on the side of their van with cheesy graphics of bugs being zapped. They're discreet professionals, and very expensive.

The van parks, and a crew of four men in white coveralls hop out. I catch a glimpse of the interior of the van through the open sliding door. It's loaded with sprayers and bottles of chemicals. The driver, a big guy with a full beard, moustache, and hair pulled into a ponytail, walks up with a clipboard.

"Are you Jacob Reese?" he asks, consulting his clipboard.

"Yeah," I reply, getting to my feet.

"I'm Kyle McGuire with Envo Exterminators and this is my team—Paul, Chuck, and Donnie."

They nod in acknowledgment and I nod back, even though I'm not concerned with learning their names.

"Dispatch said you have a little bit of a roach problem?"

"Yeah," I say, rubbing my eyes. Fatigue is crashing down on me. "Sorry, it's been a long day."

"I understand, Mr Reese. If I was a restaurant owner, I wouldn't be happy to see us, either, but we'll take care of it. Just lead the way."

I take them inside. I try to explain what happened and how freakish it all is. I'm sure they've heard it before and have yet to believe it.

The lights are on, so most of the roaches have gone for cover, but occasionally, one will sprint across the floor and disappear under a counter or behind the bag we use to collect the dirty cleaning rags. The men all have flashlights. As we proceed to the restaurant, they shine their lights into any darkened crevice they find, and small black shapes scatter. The team takes their time as we pass the shelves where we keep our large bins of coffee beans. I show them the refrigerators where we store our cream, milk, and other perishables.

I'm slightly comforted when I hear one of the crew, I think it's Chuck, mumble something to the effect of, "This all looks good."

We head out into the darkened restaurant. I've pulled all the blinds so no one can see inside. I flip the lights on.

"Oh, there they go," Kyle says, as small shapes dart this way and that.

I notice him squint, like he's confused.

"What is it?" I ask.

He shakes his head. "Nothing."

I lead them over to the corner booth.

"This is where it started. They came out of nowhere. It's never happened before."

Kyle gives me a sympathetic look. "Mr Reese, we're not the health board. You can be straight with us. You can tell us if you've seen roaches in here before. It's actually better if you do. It'll help us do our job."

"I'm dead serious. We've had 'A's on every inspection, and I have never seen a single ant in this place."

"Just because you haven't seen them doesn't mean you've never had them in here before."

"I'm telling you, Mr McGuire—"

"Kyle."

"Kyle. We've never had them."

"Scout's honor?" he says, attempting a joke that I'm not in the mood for.

"No," I reply. "And it's been a very long day, and I just lost an unbelievable amount of money, so I'm not really—"

"Okay, okay, okay. I understand. I'm sorry to hear it. Listen, we've got everything we need. Go home and get some sleep. We'll take it from here. I've got your number, and if I have any questions, I'll give you a call."

I'm so tired, all I can do is nod, turn around, and leave.

*

It's past two in the morning when I finally arrive home. I can't remember ever feeling so miserable—well, once but it's been years.

"Murphy?" I call out, walking through the door.

He doesn't answer.

I've left him alone for almost twelve hours. I'm a little concerned as to what I might find.

Sure enough, in the kitchen, I find a tight coil of dog shit in the corner and a puddle of urine. I go to the study, and he's lying on his bed, facing the wall. He turns to look at me with the most guilty, apologetic eyes.

"Not your fault, buddy."

*

Murphy waits in the entrance to the kitchen, his head hanging in shame, as I clean up his mishap. I don't know how to tell him I'm not mad. Twelve hours without a toilet, I'd find a corner, too.

Once I'm done, the kitchen aroma is a cocktail of disinfectant and feces. I take the garbage bag out to the bin in the driveway. Murphy follows, carrying his red tennis ball as a sort of peace offering.

Instead of going back inside, I sit down on the porch. Murphy sits in front of me, head lowered, tennis ball in mouth. I scratch behind his ears.

"It's okay, Murphy."

He drops the ball and it pathetically bounces on the ground.

I pick it up and toss it onto the lawn. He chases it down by the porch light, and brings it back. We repeat the process a few times, and I start to think about this evening.

The franchise is over. There's no salvaging that. These past few days are a nightmare. It can't be a coincidence, can it? But how? How can the events of the past few days have any connection to what happened in the store?

My phone pings with a text. It's Sandy.

Okay, you're not answering. I'm worried. I'm not sleeping tonight. Call me as soon as you get this.

I put the phone back in my pocket.

I don't know what to say. I don't want to tell her but *I don't want to lie*—

"—*but you've been lying*. You've been lying this whole time," Laura said.

We were sitting on a bench in the quad outside her dorm. Some guys were throwing a football on the grass.

Laura and I had hit a wall. We were closed off to one another, at least I was, and it had a lot to do with the news article I had read a few days earlier about a shootout in Lyndon, near the campus, that left five people dead. Among the casualties was Mattie. Reggie had made his move and had been successful, despite my repeated warnings through text messages and phone calls over the last few days to Mattie leading up to the shootout, which had gone unanswered.

I was shaken. Mattie and I weren't necessarily friends but I didn't want him to die and I tried to save him. I was getting out—completely out. I didn't care about the rest of my student debt. I'd find the money somewhere else. I didn't have the mental capacity to deal with relationship stuff. I didn't want to lose Laura but I couldn't tell her what happened. I needed more time. Instead of being honest, I was being defensive.

"What about you?" I said, lamely trying to shift the blame. "You've got something you're not telling me."

"I don't know if I can trust you."

"You can trust me, okay?"

"No, I can't, and I need to tell you if we're going to keep going with this," she said, glancing around the quad, avoiding eye contact.

I had seen this before. The worry. The fear of opening up. She wanted to tell me that she loved me. I had been in my head, but I had noticed that she seemed more nervous as of late. She wanted to open up.

"Do you want me to say it first?" I asked.

She whipped her head around to look at me. "What?"

"I'll say it first," I offered, reassuringly.

She waited.

"I love you, too," I said. It wasn't the truth, but it wasn't a total lie. I did care for her. It just wasn't love and I wanted to buy some time.

Her mouth hung open and her blue eyes shone, but not with happiness or relief.

"What?"

I awkwardly took her hand. "I love you, too."

She continued to stare.

"That's what you were afraid to tell me, right?" I asked. "Fine. I'll be the first to say it—I love you."

She looked hurt. No. Worse. She looked a little horrified.

I thought I was being cavalier. I was expecting a laugh, a sigh of relief, or a kiss—anything but that stunned expression.

"You thought I wanted to tell you—?" Her throat caught before she could finish her question. She stared down at the sidewalk, her eyes welling up with tears.

I leaned forward. "Hey—"

"I have to go." She quickly stood and began walking away.

"Laura?"

She didn't stop. From behind, I watched her wipe her eyes, and then jam her hands into the pockets of her coat.

"Laura?"

She never looked back, and I didn't go after her.

"Heads up!" one of the guys called out, and the football skipped across the sidewalk near my feet.

Thump, thump—

—thump.

Murphy's tennis ball bounces on the ground in front of me.

He looks at me expectantly, waiting for another throw, but I'm spent.

"That's enough for tonight, Murphy."

I take the ball, stand up, and head back inside.

I go upstairs, shower, brush my teeth, and crawl under the cool covers. I leave my phone on the nightstand in case the guys from Envo call.

Murphy doesn't even "ask". He simply hops up onto the bed and lies down. I don't argue.

All I want to do is sleep, but for the next few hours, I stare at the ceiling.

*

I must have fallen asleep at some point because the sun is reaching through the curtains. I don't feel like I've slept. Everything hurts. My eyes are dry and irritated. I roll over and check my phone. There are three more messages from Sandy, which I'm not going to answer. There are none from Envo.

I curse and throw off the sheets. I head downstairs for the only thing that is going to get me through the day—coffee. I sit at the table and drink two cups, black.

I have to answer Sandy's messages, or she's going to go to the shop. Reluctantly, I take out my phone and type.

Sorry I didn't get back to you. It's been a long night. I can't go into it right now, but we're going to be closed for a few days. Everything is fine. Everyone will get paid and I'll let you know what's going on when I get a little more info.

I put the phone down and wait. I know it's coming. Sure enough, she calls. Callously, I reject the call. There's a pause, and she calls again.

"Dammit, Sandy," I groan and reject it, again.

The screen lights up with a voicemail.

I ignore it. I have to. It's not fair to Sandy, but I'm so fried that there is nothing I can do. I can't explain to her what happened, because I don't even know. Once I get a call from Envo, I'll get back to her.

I realize that I have no idea what to do with my day.

I look over at Murphy, who has just finished inhaling his breakfast. "Come on, Murph. Time for a walk."

*

Murphy pads along the path ahead of me, nose pressed to the ground, enjoying the freedom of being off-leash. At least someone's enjoying the walk.

I thought the serenity of the woods would give me a chance to clear my head. Instead, it amplifies my thoughts. The events of last night and the last few days have to be connected. Someone's messing with me. Laura's messing with me.

"She's dead," I say aloud.

Murphy stops and looks back at me, wondering if I have given a command, and he hadn't been paying attention. I keep walking, and he goes back to exploring.

I look up at the trees. The sun's light slashes through the skeletal branches as I continue walking. Distant birds chirp. The cold wind hisses past my ears. We're nearing The Sanctuary. It's just over the ridge

"Laura's dead," I quietly repeat under my breath.

I know this because I watched her die. I watched it happen. I was there. I'm the only one who knows what happened. Then, how? It can't be her ... but people have seen her.

How is that possible?

"It's not," I say, louder.

Murphy stops, but not because I spoke. His tail is up. His head is cocked. I stop, too, scanning the trees for what has him so alert.

"Murphy?"

He twitches, like a sprinter anticipating the starter's gun.

"What is it, Mur—?"

He takes off like a shot. There's no playful bark, like when he pursues the ducks or chases after his ball. I've never seen him move so fast. He sprints down the path and up the ridge.

"Murphy!"

He doesn't break stride as he disappears over the ridge. There's one sharp bark that echoes off the trees and silences the birds.

"Murphy!" I call out.

The only sound is the wind.

"Murphy, here! Come on!"

No response.

I start taking quick strides, and then break into a run.

"Murphy!"

I crest the ridge and look off to the right, down the path to the entrance of The Sanctuary. I wait. There's a horrible silence. I'm about to run down the path, when Murphy suddenly emerges from the pines. He races up the ridge, and darts past me. It's so quick and startling, that I barely catch a glimpse of the stick in his mouth. He swings in a playful arc off the path, and begins another approach. He has what some people call "the zooms".

I lean over and put my hands on my knees to catch my breath, unable to contain a small laugh from skipping out between my inhalations. I've been so keyed up, his sprinting is comical.

Murphy continues to weave in and out of the tree trunks, kicking up dead leaves in his wake. I can see now that it isn't one stick in his mouth. He's got a little bundle.

"Bring it here, Murph!"

Murphy races towards me. I reach out as he nears and he zags to the left, just out of reach. I get a better look at the bundle of sticks in his mouth and my heart stops.

"Murphy, come here!" I command.

My tone catches him. He trots over to me, still wanting to play, but noticing the change in my demeanor. I lean down and take hold of the bundle.

"Drop it."

Murphy obeys.

I hold it up.

It's not a bundle of sticks.

It's a stick doll.

I stare down the path to the opening of The Sanctuary. The birds are still silent. Murphy waits by my side for me to throw it. Instead, I take out his leash, and clip the lead to his collar.

I advance slowly, trying not to make a sound. I'm holding my breath, listening for any sign. As I approach the opening to The Sanctuary, there's no movement from the trees.

I stop and wait, staring into the darkened glen.

"Hello?"

There's no response.

I step inside.

The breeze is muted by the dense pine needles overhead. The serenity that I cherished is now unnerving. The path to the clearing looks like it's a mile long, but I can see it in the distance.

There's something there, lying on the ground.

I slowly make my way down the path.

I'm thirty yards away when I hear it.

"No …" I whisper.

It can't be. It's not possible, but my mind automatically adds the words as the notes reach my ear …

Just close your eyes,
And you and I,
Will brave the dark and go dancing …

I quicken my pace.

The clearing grows larger. I see it, sitting in the middle of the clearing.

The music box.

Laura's music box.

The tiny ballerina that mesmerized me all those years ago slowly turns as the melody fills the clearing. I approach it like it's a snake about to strike. I crouch down and my stomach drops. Impaled on the arms of the ballerina is a dead cockroach. I carefully reach out, and close the lid. The music stops. Engraved on the top of the lid in intricate script are the letters "L.A.".

There's no mistake.

This is Laura's music box.

My mouth is dry and my heart is pounding. I raise my head to look around and nearly cry out. I stumble backwards onto the ground and frantically crawl away until my back collides with the trunk of a tree.

Hanging in the trees are dozens and dozens of stick dolls.

Chapter 6

It takes more than two hours to cut them all down.

I went back to the house and brought two large garbage bags to haul them away, but the first thing I put in a bag is the music box. I then use the stick dolls to bury it. I don't know what's coming, but I don't want any evidence that I might have to explain later. Murphy's bored, and lies down in the clearing to chew on his tennis ball. Most of the stick dolls were within reach from the ground, but there are a few I have to climb a couple of branches to reach. Twice, I think I'm done, only to glance up and see another one slowly twisting overhead. I cut the last one down and scan the trees one more time, verifying that yes, that's the last of them.

I carry the bags back to the cottage. I'm about to empty the first bag into the fire pit when my phone rings.

"Hello?"

"Mr Reese?"

"Yes?"

"It's Kyle McGuire with Envo Exterminators. Got some updates for you."

"Okay."

"We're almost done, but there's something I need to show you."

"What is it?"

"Something I've never encountered before, and you won't believe me unless you see it for yourself."

*

I store the bags of stick dolls in the cottage. I'll take care of them later.

Murphy and I hop into the truck, and head towards town.

We drive down Main Street and past the shop. The blinds are still drawn. There are a few people reading the sign on the front door, informing them we're closed and apologizing for the inconvenience. At the next intersection, I take a left, turn into the alley, and then take another left into the lot behind the shop. I park next to the big, white, unmarked Envo van. The back door to the shop is open, and one of the crew, I think it's Chuck, walks out, heading for the van.

"Hey, Mr Reese. Kyle's inside."

"Thanks." I open the truck door for Murphy, and he jumps down to the pavement. "Is it safe for the dog?"

"Yep."

I take Murphy inside and find Kyle standing in the restaurant, holding a clipboard. The air has an acrid smell but no one is wearing a mask. He turns at the sound of the swinging door and Murphy's panting as we enter.

"Afternoon, Mr Reese."

"Hi."

"We're finishing up here. Just doing a few last sweeps. You'll want to do another one tonight, in case any of them stagger out of their hiding places to die. Also, you'll need to stay closed for at least three more days."

There goes the Halloween business. My biggest hope now is that I can keep the real reason for staying closed under wraps from the town.

"What is it you wanted to show me?"

"Yeah." He puts the clipboard down on a table. "From the start, this whole thing seemed off. Like you said, you've had all 'A's on your inspections and you said you never saw a roach in this place."

"I haven't."

"And I believe you."

"Good," was all I could think to say.

"I mean, the place is clean—immaculate, really. So, that didn't add up. Now, as part of our routine, we look for concentration points. That's where we think the roaches might be coming from—the drains, the food storage areas, under the fridges, stuff like that. It's going to be near their food source, which means it's almost always in the kitchen. We checked everywhere, and there is nothing. It was like they all were in the dining room, and not in the back where the food is. It's one of the damnedest things I ever saw. Then, I remembered you saying that you were sitting in that booth over there when you first saw them. So, we popped off the cushions of the seat, and we found something."

He leads me over to the corner booth. By this time, the entire crew has gathered around and follows us.

The interior of the booth comes into view. Sitting on the table is a squat, cardboard box. There's a small square that's been cut into the side, near the bottom, and there's a plastic valve fitted into the hole to close it off. Mounted to the box, next to the valve, is another piece of plastic, which is connected to what looks like a small nickel battery.

"What the hell is that?" I ask.

"Took me a while to figure it out, myself," Kyle says, leaning in closer to the valve, "but this is kind of like a trapdoor. This here," he says, pointing to the bit of plastic above the battery, "is a receiver. You can get them at any electronics store. Once it gets a signal, it opens the door," he says, flipping the valve, which creates an opening to the box. The clicking sound it makes is the clicking sound I had mistaken for the clicking of Helen Trifauni's pen. "That allows whatever's inside to get out, and what we found inside is what's really crazy." He lifts the flaps on the top of the box, and reaches in. He lifts out a smaller, white cardboard box. One end has been cut away. Inside, I can barely make out what looks like egg packaging. As Kyle lifts it out and sets it on top of the larger cardboard box, a few dead roaches fall out onto the table.

I glance back and forth in confusion from the box to Kyle.

"I … I don't understand."

He turns the white box over to show me a red stamp that reads, "LIVE DELIVERY". There is a postage label that has been obscured by thick, black lines of marker.

"People order live cockroaches online for a number of reasons," Kyle says. "Most times, it's to feed a pet lizard or snake. Some schools order them for science classes. Point is, anyone can get them. This right here," he says, indicating the two boxes, "is a sort of 'cockroach bomb'. They let the cockroaches loose in the bigger box and then opened the valve with a phone to let them out in your restaurant."

"Wait," I say, shaking my head. "You're saying that someone put them here, under the seat in this booth?"

"Not just this booth. We found one of these under the seat of every booth in here," he says with a sweep of his hand around the dining room. "We destroyed the other ones, but I wanted to keep this one, because I didn't think you'd believe me without proof."

I believe him. I believe every word, but can't tell him why, because *he* won't believe *me*.

"Do you have any cameras in this place?" he asks.

"No. I don't even have an alarm."

He blinks. "Really?"

"Yeah. I mean, it's The Hollows. I didn't think I would ever …"

I feel stupid, but it's true. Crime is non-existent in this town. All I had was a simple lock and no cameras. What would anyone steal? Come to think of it, how did they get inside?

He shrugs. "Well, we've taken care of it. You may find a dead roach now and again for a few days, but other than that, you're good to go."

"That's it?" I ask.

"That's it." He takes a look around the shop. "I don't know how else to say it, Mr Reese, but it looks like, and please excuse my French, but it looks like someone is fucking with you."

"No shit."

*

I go home and sit in the living room chair by the window. I stare out and watch the cottage and the woods for hours. I don't answer my phone. I only get up to feed Murphy and take him outside to do his business. Once he's done, we go back inside and I resume my post.

Chapter 7

No … no … please …

The handle turns with a groan that echoes through the basement. Silence.

I slowly reach down to pull the door open. The instant before my fingers touch the handle, the door explodes outwards. I'm blown backwards and sent careening across the grimy floor. Shrapnel from the steel door flies past me.

My body slides to a stop. My ears are ringing as the dust settles around me. I can't move. Every bone in my body is broken, but I somehow manage to pull myself to my feet. I cough and splutter, attempting to catch my breath.

There's a wet, ragged whisper behind me.

"Jacob …"

I bolt upright in bed.

Sunday. Halloween morning.

I don't remember coming upstairs to my room last night. Murphy's here, too, taking up two-thirds of the bed.

I throw off the sheets, head to the bathroom, and take a shower. I reach for the shampoo bottle and miss, knocking it off the side of the tub. I quickly reach to catch it, and the pain in my side flares.

I look down at the matching scars—two small, round patches that look like someone plastered and painted over to match my skin. Standing there under the stinging water, I lose track of time. I think about what happened, what's happening, about Laura, and I feel so helpless that I'm hit with an impulse—it's Sunday, and I'm going to go to church.

I can't remember the last time I went to church. It was something my parents were never really big on. I asked my father about it one time. I must have been ten or eleven years old.

"Dad, is God real?"

"Some people think he is. Some people think he isn't," he replied without looking up from the computer at his desk in his office.

"Do *you* think God is real?"

Dad shrugged.

That was the extent of my theological studies. At ten or eleven, there were more pressing issues, like Little League Baseball or Nintendo, but this morning, I feel compelled to go.

I finish up in the shower, shave, and put on what I guess I would call my "Sunday Best". Fastening the last button on my shirt, I stare in the mirror at my reflection. The clothes are sharp, but they can't hide the fact that I look like a wreck. I've aged five years in a few days. I massage the heavy bags under my eyes in the hopes of getting the blood going, but if it has an effect, I can't tell.

Murphy watches from the bathroom doorway, confused by this new procedure.

"Yeah," I sigh. "I'm not sure I get it either, Murphy."

*

Standing in front of the open doors to the Old Stone Church, the only thought in my head is that this is a huge mistake. It's a beautiful autumn morning, people are pouring in around me, and I'm hit with that same feeling I had at my parents' funeral—I'm a fraud—but I start walking, as if I'm being pulled by a tractor beam through those doors.

Once inside, I can't turn and leave without having to go against the flow of people, like a fish fighting upstream. I move off to the side and watch the people file in and find their seats in the pews. Their polite conversations echo in the rafters overhead.

It's the standard church layout. There are two columns of pews, divided by the aisle leading to the altar, which is bathed in light from the stained-glass windows surrounding the apse. A large crucifix with Jesus on the cross hangs above the altar. The original church had been built in the 1600s, but it burnt down shortly after the witches' trial. Only the tombstones and the Hanging Tree out front were spared. This new church had been completed in 1810, over the site of the original structure. While other parts of the church had been updated through the years with modern touches like drywall, the chapel hasn't changed since 1810. It looks even older. Standing in the room, you might have thought you were in a medieval village church somewhere in the English countryside.

More people pour in, and the pews are starting to fill. I wonder if there will be a bigger congregation than normal because it's Halloween. I accidentally lock eyes with a few people as they enter. They are Groundworks regulars who are mildly surprised at my presence. I say a quick hello to a handful of them, but move further away from the doors, keeping to the wall at the back of the chapel.

It doesn't help. People still continue to recognize me. I'm sticking out like a sore thumb, especially since I'm standing up. I go and sit down in the furthest spot from the doors in the last pew.

There's almost no angle of recline. I have to sit perfectly straight. I try to find some way to have a little slouch in my posture, but the pew in front of me is too close. It's like I'm sitting in an airplane and not first class. I can't believe God would want us to be this uncomfortable while singing his praises.

More people file in. There are handshakes and "good mornings". Every now and then, a laugh rises above the conversation. I catch occasional snippets of people talking about tonight's celebration. Thankfully, my pew is empty and no one comes to speak to me. I keep my head down and pretend to be looking at my phone to deter any contact.

This is ridiculous.

What was I hoping to get out of this? Why did I think this would help?

The congregation grows quiet.

I should go. I'm going. I'm going to get up and—

Too late.

Reverend Williams emerges from a side door in the apse and steps to the podium. He's tall and thin, with a shock of white hair and glasses that give him a scholarly look. I know him enough to say "hello", but not much else.

"Good morning," he says.

There is a collective cheerful murmur of "good morning" in response.

"Happy Halloween," he adds.

It gets a few warm laughs.

"We have just a few things to go over about tonight's festivities before we begin. First of all, I hope to see you all there. You have put so much of your time and effort into tonight, and I think that's really what makes The Hollows so special. Our social director, Mrs Ronson—" he nods to someone in the front pew "—will be running a face-painting booth on the green, and Mr Dempsey has graciously offered to manage the Dunk Tank. So, don't miss a chance to throw a softball, and possibly dunk him in some water. I know I'm looking forward to that, and have been practicing all week."

Mr Dempsey rises from his seat, turns, and waves to everyone.

"There are also some raffle tickets still available," Reverend Williams continues. "We have some great prizes from our local businesses, and all proceeds go to the high school marching band, which will also perform tonight. Speaking of which, as a reminder, there is no parking on or around Main Street. If you're attending, you'll be directed to park at the high school and walk to the celebration." He consults the papers on the podium in front of him and smiles. "Well, that's it for the formalities, and now, on to business. Please take your hymnbooks and we'll begin with …"

I mumble my way through the songs, feeling more foolish than ever. I'm being disrespectful to everyone here. I'm an imposter.

The hymns end, and everyone has a seat.

Reverend Williams takes to the podium, again, with a short stack of papers in his hands. He gathers his thoughts, and begins to speak.

"You know, the other day, it occurred to me what this day must have meant to the generations before us. As most of you know, November first was 'All Hallow's Day' or 'All Saints Day', and the night before was 'All Hallows Eve', which became 'Halloween'. That was a night when spirits, and ghouls, and goblins would roam the Earth. The popular perception today is that everyone was terrified on All Hallows Eve, but that's simply not true. They viewed Halloween the same way we do. It was a night to cut loose a little bit. On Halloween, they weren't really scared of werewolves or witches or vampires. They got to *be* them. For one night, they got to *be* the monsters. It was the one night when you weren't scared, because by pretending to be the monster, you take away what is scary about them, which is the unknown. And let's face it—it's fun. Becoming our fears, pretending to be these monsters, and in a way, mocking them, takes away their power over us. It takes away our own fears. It helps us understand why we fear them, and that's a good thing. Anyone who says that we shouldn't celebrate Halloween because it's a pagan holiday, well, they've just told you what they're dressing up as—a stick in the mud."

He's good. I even chuckle at that one.

"But I thought we'd have some fun. We're going to look at these classic Halloween monsters, because I think they have something to teach us. So today, I'm going to present to you my stab at a doctoral thesis. Mike?"

He motions off to the side, and a young man wheels in a digital projector on a cart. He then brings in a projector screen, and sets it up behind the podium.

"Mike is my grad assistant for the morning," Reverend Williams says as Mike sets up.

Mike pulls down the screen and positions the projector. He also brings out a laptop, and sets it on the podium. Mike hits a button on the projector and the screen fills with the image of the home screen from the laptop. It's a strange juxtaposition to see these modern items in a stone chapel that is stuck in the past.

"Thank you, Mike," Reverend Williams says, and pats him on the back. Mike nods and walks off to the side in the apse. "Round of applause for Mike, everyone." There is good-natured clapping, and Mike waves. "He helped me put all this together, so you can blame him."

Standing behind the podium, Reverend Williams' hands go to the laptop. On the screen, the pointer glides over to the PowerPoint icon and clicks. The home screen disappears and is replaced by a title card with a photoshopped image of the Reverend wearing a large graduation cap. The text under the image reads, "Reverend Alexander P Williams, PHD, Esq., LLC., TBD, ASAP presents ..."

"Now, as many of you may have guessed, this is not an entirely serious dissertation, but it's kinda fun, and I believe we can learn something from our favorite monsters." He takes a thoughtful breath. "You have to ask yourselves—what are those classic Halloween monsters? Monsters like Dracula, witches, mummies, werewolves, Frankenstein's monster? More importantly, what *were* they? The answer is people. They were, and sometimes still are, people. They are humans who have been corrupted. The truly scary part about these monsters is that we can become them. All of them are cursed people, people who have given in to the worst sins, and that got me thinking—what if these monsters are the personification of sin?"

He pauses for dramatic effect. Then, he comically mimes his head exploding, drawing laughter from the pews, and I'll admit it, I am totally hooked. "And so, ladies and gentlemen of the jury, I give you my doctoral thesis." He taps a few keys on the keyboard and the screen advances to the next slide.

Seven Deadly Sins & Seven Halloween Monsters:
A Comparative Study

Underneath the title are photos of the various classic monsters—a vampire, a witch, a werewolf, Frankenstein's monster, a mummy, a ghost, and a zombie.

"The Seven Deadly Sins are pride, sloth, lust, greed, wrath, envy, and gluttony. What I'm going to try to show you is that each of these monsters represents one of those sins, and again, I must reiterate, this thesis will be published absolutely nowhere, but if you would like to offer me a grant, I'm okay with that. So, let's start with the one our own town has a little history with." He taps the button and the slide show advances to a picture of a stereotypical witch with green skin, warty nose, and a pointy hat.

"Now, which sin do you think a witch represents?"

"Lust!" someone calls out.

Reverend Williams turns to the picture, studies it, and turns back to the person who said it, who I can't see.

"Really, Bob? You look at that, and think 'lust'?"

That one gets a laugh. From behind, I see someone shrug their shoulders.

"I know, I know," Reverend Williams laughs. "There are more modern-day representations of witches that might make you think that, but I'm going with the old school. I drew a different connection. I think that a witch represents envy. A witch is someone who has made a pact with the devil because she wants something. She is so envious of something that she's willing to sell her soul to Satan to obtain it. Then, what does she do? She feeds off other people's envy. People bargain with the witch to get things they want because they are envious. They want to be beautiful, or they want riches. They only want these things because they are envious of those around them, and they will give up their soul to get them. And when we think of envy, what color do we think of?"

"Green," the congregation murmurs, making the connection to the witch's skin in the photo.

"So, you kind of see how this works. Next up, we have Dracula." Reverend Williams taps a key, and the screen fills with the image of Dracula. Like the witch, it's the classic version, with the cape, slicked hair, and pointed fangs. "Anyone want to take a guess?" He tilts his head towards the pews. "Bob?"

"Lust?" Bob answers, tentatively.

"Lust! There you go, and I know this one for a fact. Our modern image of Dracula is straight out of the Victorian views of morality. Here is a monster that corrupts with an intimate physical act. It is almost literally a kiss that goes too far. It's a metaphor for …" He looks around like he's unsure if he should say it, and then dramatically whispers, "intercourse." Everyone chuckles at his feigned embarrassment. "Dracula is seductive. He's mysterious. He is the perfect personification of temptation that will lead you to ruin." He pauses and looks at the congregation. "Ain't gonna lie, this one was the easiest argument to make. Some of these other ones might be a bit of a stretch."

He taps the key, and the slide show advances to a picture of a werewolf. It has pointed ears, red burning eyes, a snarling snout, and a muscular chest barely contained in a tattered shirt. His sinewy arms end in black claws. His whole body is covered with gray hair. His head is thrown back in a howl.

"The werewolf," Reverend Williams says. "Any guesses?"

"Wrath!" a woman chimes.

The Reverend puts one finger on his nose and points at her. "Bingo! Kelly Woodward, right out of the gate! Well done."

There are grumblings of "of course" from the pews.

"Want to do the rest of the sermon?" Reverend Williams asks.

"Nope," she replies.

Reverend Williams laughs and goes back to the slide. "Yes. The werewolf is wrath. The werewolf is special because out of all the monsters, it is the one most like a human, because it is a human. It only becomes a werewolf during the full moon. When it is the werewolf, it is blind with power. It's savage. It preys on the weak. As a werewolf, it will destroy the ones it loves as a human. It brings destruction to itself and all those around it. He may not be aware of what he is doing, but the werewolf is wrath. It is in his nature."

The Reverend's analogy hits me like a ton of bricks. My eyes fall to the back of the pew in front of me. I squirm in my seat. I'm thinking about my costume for tonight. For weeks, it's been sitting in a closet. The words tumble through my mind. *It brings destruction to itself and all those around it. It is in his nature.*

"Moving on," the Reverend says.

I'm barely listening.

The distance to the front of the chapel has suddenly expanded into miles.

"Frankenstein," Reverend Williams says. "This one is different because we're not going to talk about the monster. We're going to talk about his creator, Doctor Victor Frankenstein."

It brings destruction to itself and all those around it.

I can't get those words out of my head.

"Now, I mentioned Dr Frankenstein's monster before, but I want to focus on Dr Frankenstein, himself. Dr Frankenstein created his monster by giving it life, and we know that there is only one being who bestows life, and that is the Lord. So, who can tell me what sin Dr Frankenstein personifies?"

"Pride?"

110

"Yes! Pride. Well done, Mr Hampton."

It brings destruction to itself, and all those around it.

"Mary Shelley's original title for *Frankenstein* was *Modern Prometheus* and Prometheus stole fire from the gods and gave it to humans. Dr Frankenstein is pride, and if he had been real, God wouldn't have sent a lightning bolt to reanimate that dead body. God *would have said*—"

—We need to talk.

I leaned back in the chair on the back porch of my apartment, read the text message again, and shook my head. I hadn't seen Laura since our argument on the quad, and that was over a month ago. Since then, I hadn't tried to talk to her, either. I had way too much on my mind, and just assumed our relationship was over.

I was trying to figure out how exactly I was going to get out of the whole business with Reggie. He had agreed to my conditions and I stuck to fraternity house pickups and other public places where I could be relatively sure that no one would pull a gun on me, but I was done with the whole thing. I still owed a lot on my debt, but I didn't care. Maybe after it was over, I would try to salvage the relationship with Laura, if we even had one. I assumed that she wanted to talk about it. I wasn't going to answer it. I couldn't answer it, that night. I was waiting on another message.

I got up and went back inside. As I was reaching to lock the back door, another message came through, this time on my "business phone".

552 FYXPIV V 3 4B

This was the message I was waiting for.

I had gotten word to Reggie that I wanted to talk, and he had just given me the time and meeting place. I had decided that this was going to be the night I told Reggie I was out.

I went to the kitchen and got out a scratch pad from the junk drawer. I wrote the original message, and then scribbled underneath.

It was a simple shift code. When I first started working for Reggie, he had no problem texting me the addresses of places he wanted me to go, or the names of people he wanted me to do business with. I told him it might be wise to try hiding that information just a teeny bit, in case the cops ever wanted to match us to people and places. Reggie thought I was being overly cautious, but I told him that there was no such thing as overly cautious when it came to stuff like this. He laughed and finally agreed.

Shift codes are easy. You take each letter or number and shift it a certain number of places to decode it. The key is to make it a different number of places for each message. For instance, in the text I had just received, the last number was the "key". The 4B meant I needed to move each character back four places. The 5s became 1s. The 2 was an 8, because you included 0 as a digit. F became B, Y became U, and so on. I decoded the message on the scratch pad. It read "118 Butler R." I had the address—118 Butler Road. The 3 became a 9, which meant nine o'clock. Our meeting was set. I checked the directions online. It was a bit of a drive, and I would need to leave in the next ten minutes if I wanted to make it. My regular phone rang. It was Laura. I silenced it, set the phone on the kitchen table, and went about my preparations to leave.

Since the whole affair at Lyndon, I had started taking way more precautions in case the cops ever came to question me and I had to try to prove I was home, instead of somewhere I shouldn't have been. It wasn't foolproof, but it would provide enough doubt to whomever was asking. The first thing I did was leave my personal phone at my apartment. I had heard that the police could use cell phone towers to track the location of your phone by finding out which towers had been used to relay messages to your phone. Next, I turned on my television and cable box. I clicked through the pay-per-view options, and found a movie that had just been released that I had already seen. I selected the 'rent' option, and a window popped up on the screen. "Would you like to start this movie now?" I hit 'yes', and the opening credits began to play. I went to the fridge, took out six bottles from a twelve pack I hadn't touched for just such an occasion, popped the tops, and poured them down the sink. All of this may sound like overkill, but as I explained to Reggie, there's no such thing as overkill when you're covering your ass.

I did a last look, headed out to the car, and drove off into the night.

I cranked up the stereo to heighten my adrenaline and resolve. "This is it," I kept repeating in an attempt to psych myself up. I didn't know what Reggie would say. What could he say? I just kept repeating "this is it" over and over.

I was feeling good until I noticed that I was closing in on the address, but I was still in the middle of the woods. I flicked on my high beams, which only revealed more trees and empty road. I worried that I had passed my destination in the dark, but I finally spotted a light up ahead, through the trees. I turned off the road and into a gravel parking lot. The light was a single lamp centered in the parking lot of a massive, rusted warehouse. The walls were littered with graffiti. There wasn't a single window intact that I could see, but I could only see the bottom floor. The rest of the building reached up into the darkened sky. On the right side of the building was a large set of bay doors that had been wrenched open a couple of feet.

I got out and scanned the parking lot. Reggie's Challenger was parked by the side of the building, nearly hidden in the shadows. There were three other lampposts around the parking lot, but the bulbs of two had been busted out, and the light on the third had been ripped off. It stood there like a decapitated body.

I walked over to Reggie's car, hoping he would be waiting there, and I wouldn't have to go inside, but it was empty. I made my way over to the bay doors, the gravel crunching under my feet, and stood at the opening.

"Reggie?" I called out.

My voice echoed from inside, but there was no response.

I cautiously stepped through the opening. In a moment of absurdity, I worried about the tetanus I might get if I scratched myself on the door. Once inside, I stopped to allow my eyes to adjust. The light from the parking lot filtered through the opening, and the broken windows overhead.

After a few seconds, the warehouse came into focus.

In front of me was a vast, open space, with piles of rotting wood pallets stacked up to eye level, littering the floor. There was other debris about the floor—newspapers, discarded food containers, garbage, and a few shopping carts—I had no idea how they came to be there. To the left was a darkened hallway. There was also half of a stairway leading to an office that overlooked the entire floor. The top half of the stairs had collapsed and twisted into a replica of a broken spine.

I took a few more steps inside. "Reggie?"

My echo ricocheted around the warehouse, but there was still no answer.

My blood ran cold. I had built up my own resolve so much that I had been blind to the danger I had so casually just walked into. I pivoted to leave, my heels grinding into the grit on the floor.

A silhouette was standing in the opening of the bay doors, blocking my exit.

"'Sup, Jake?"

"Goddammit, Reggie!" I gasped, pulling in gulps of air. "What the hell are you trying to do, give me a heart attack? Why didn't you answer when I was calling for you?"

He ignored the question, and glanced over his shoulder towards the opening.

"I wish you would have parked your car next to mine," he said in that lazy drawl that carried so much menace.

"You want me to move my car? I can move my car."

"Nah. This won't take long." His hand emerged from his coat pocket. The faint light glinted off the barrel of the massive gun in his hand as he pointed it at me. He flicked the barrel towards the darkened hallway. "Start walking."

"Reggie, what th—?"

"Walk."

"Listen, Reggie, I don't—"

He extended the gun in my direction. "Last time … walk."

I put my hands up. "Okay. Okay."

I started walking towards the hallway.

"You don't gotta hold your hands up. I know you don't carry, but right about now, don't you wish you did?" He chuckled.

I stayed quiet.

As we navigated through the warehouse to the hallway, my mind raced. I could try to run, but where? Also, I had my back to him. I couldn't tell when would be the best chance to make a break for it. I was so mentally paralyzed that I continued walking into the hall. My eyes had already grown accustomed to the low light, and I could see that there were three offices on each side. All of them were missing doors.

"To your right," Reggie said as we approached the second door.

I turned, and entered.

It was a medium-sized office with a handful of decrepit desks. In one corner was a scattering of syringes and a spent condom.

"Stop," he said, once I had reached the center of the room.

I obliged.

"Turn around, slowly."

I did.

His figure filled the doorway. The gun was still trained on me.

"Have a seat," he said, nodding to a decimated office chair.

"I'd rather stand."

"I'm not asking you."

"Look at that thing. It's not going to hold me."

Even in the darkness, I could see the anger flash in his eyes. He advanced closer.

"Sit the fuck down."

"If you're going to shoot me, what the fuck do you care?" I snapped.

It was a calculated risk. I had regained some of my wits, and survival mode was kicking in. If he was going to shoot me, he would have done it already. That meant that he wanted something from me, which meant I still had time. If I was going to try anything, I had to stay on my feet.

Reggie extended the gun towards my face. The end of the barrel was so close, I couldn't focus on it. I thought about making a grab for it, but Reggie was tense. One move from me, all he had to do was flex his finger, and it would be over.

We had a brief standoff, and the anger in his eyes waned.

"Yeah, whatever. You're right. Stand if you want."

"Thanks."

We both took a breath.

He grinned, and relaxed the gun back to his side, but kept it pointed at me.

"You hear about Lyndon?" he asked.

"Yeah. I saw it on the news."

"That shit went sideways, man. When we left, I thought we had them all wiped out."

"You did. The news said that everyone was dead."

He shook his head. "Nah, man. Turns out one was still breathing. Cops got him. He died later at the hospital. It was your boy, Mattie."

Right away, I knew what he was thinking, but I had to keep him talking.

"So, what? He's dead. Problem solved."

"Ain't that simple, man. See, it went sideways because they were ready for us. Like someone told them we was coming. And now, I'm worried that before he died, your boy might have talked.

116

He could tell the cops about you, and that could lead to me. You see my problem here?"

"Reggie, he didn't know shit and now, he's dead. He was probably in a coma when the cops found him. He couldn't say a thing."

"Maybe. Maybe … but put yourself in my position. I can't really afford to take that chance, can I? I mean, you said it—no such thing as being too careful when you're covering your ass."

"What? You're going to kill me, just to be sure? You're only going to make it worse for yourself. Someone will come along and find my body out here, and that will definitely lead the cops back to you."

"No one's gonna find you. I've been stashing out here for years. No one knows about this place until I tell them to meet me here. And they never leave."

'Stashing' was slang for the hiding of dead bodies. I was screwed and knew it, but he still needed something from me, and I was holding out for any chance to act.

"So, why haven't you killed me?" I asked.

"I need to know—did you tell anyone about what happened in Lyndon? Tell me the truth, and I'll make this painless. If I think you're lying …" He shrugged.

"Of course, I did," I said, seizing on the opportunity to buy more time.

He cocked his head, and steadied the gun.

"You don't think I covered my own ass? I've got it all ready to go," I said. "I set it up the day after I found out about Lyndon. I have a contact, and if I don't check in every forty-eight hours, they go to the police. And guess what? Tomorrow morning is forty-eight hours."

He stared at me with his mouth open. I caught a glimpse of the gold tooth in his upper incisor. For a second, I thought I had him. Then, he laughed.

"Nah, man. Nah. You smart, but you ain't that smart." He

shook his head in admiration. "You seriously just come up with that shit on the spot?"

I tried to exude confidence, like I was daring him to call my bluff, but I couldn't hold it. I was terrified and he could sense it.

"I'm impressed," he said, but then extended the gun, aiming it right at my face, and cocked the hammer, "but too bad."

"Jacob?" a woman's voice called out from somewhere back in the warehouse.

Reggie blinked, and instinctively glanced back towards the door.

Now.

I was just as confused as Reggie, but for the past few minutes, I had been a coiled spring, waiting to burst.

In a flash of movement, I wound up, and threw my whole body into a punch that was leveled at Reggie's jaw. My fist slammed into the side of his chin. I could feel a bone in my hand give way.

The force of the impact caused Reggie to spin and stagger sideways. My follow-through momentum carried me towards the door. I briefly tangled with Reggie's legs, and tumbled into the hallway. I scrambled to my feet as the gun roared behind me. The drywall next to my head chipped in a small burst of dust as the bullet buried itself in the wall. I found my footing and broke left, back towards the warehouse.

"Get back here, muthafucker!" Reggie screamed.

I reached the end of the hall just as Reggie emerged from the office. I was about to go right, towards the bay doors, when Reggie fired. The bullet tore into the stack of pallets in my path. I changed direction and went to the left as Reggie's boots began to thunder down the hall towards me.

I wove through the stacks of pallets, trying to circle back towards the bay doors, while using the stacks for cover.

I could hear Reggie giving chase.

I turned a corner, and was about to make a mad dash for the doors when I froze.

Laura.

She was there, staring at me with a breathless expression of shock and surprise.

There was a sound behind me.

I turned.

Reggie emerged from behind the stack of pallets I had just rounded. He raised the gun.

I began to dive to my left, in between a stack of pallets and a rusty garbage drum.

The gun kicked in Reggie's hand. The muzzle flash illuminated his livid face. The sound ripped through the warehouse.

There was an incredible pain in my side, just above my hip. I slammed into the concrete floor, and rolled onto my back. I bumped into the debris that was sitting next to the garbage drum. Some pieces of brittle wood, short metal pipes, and rotting garbage fell around my head. My hands instantly flew to the pain in my side. I looked down and could see trickles of blood running through my fingers. I was so stunned, I didn't make a sound.

The echo of the gunshot faded into silence.

Then, there was a soft choking sound.

"What the fuck?" Reggie whispered. I couldn't see him because I was wedged between the pallets and the garbage can.

I could hear the shuffling of Reggie's feet. A moment later, he slowly walked past the opening, seemingly forgetting about me.

The soft choking sounds continued.

I looked around and saw a short section of pipe lying on the ground next to my head. As quietly as I could, I pulled my hand away from my hip, and gripped the end of one of the pipes. I bit my lip to keep from crying out.

"… shit …" Reggie whispered.

I heard him turn, and there was the sound of his approaching boots. I put my head back down, and held my breath.

I kept my eyes open a fraction of an inch, and watched as Reggie returned to the opening. He looked down at me, and stepped closer. The gun was still in his hand. He crouched, and reached with his other hand to explore my wound.

I opened my eyes.

The top of his head offered a perfect target.

With everything I had, I lifted the short pipe from the ground and swung.

It connected with Reggie's skull with a sickening, hollow crack. Reggie never made a sound. He was dead before his body collapsed on top of me. I pushed him off, and grabbed the gun from his hand. I wasn't going to take any chances.

I sat up, groaning at the sharp ache in my side. I lifted my shirt. There was a clean entrance and exit wound, just barely inside my hip, above my pelvis. Any further out, it would have simply torn away the flesh. Any further in, and I would have been in a lot of trouble. I was bleeding, but I was okay. That's when the realization finally hit me.

Laura.

I crawled out of the opening.

She was lying on her side with her back to me. She was the source of the soft choking sounds, and I could see her body lightly rise and fall with each labored breath.

"Laura?"

I crawled to her, and gently turned her onto her back. Her eyes were open, but I couldn't tell if she could see. Her hands clutched at her upper abdomen, and were covered in blood. Her breath was slow and shallow.

Panic seized me.

"Oh God … Oh God … Laura …? Laura, can you hear me?"

She made no sign that she could.

I dropped the gun to the floor and put my hands on the wound, trying to stop the bleeding. I frantically searched for anything I could use. The only thing available was some old filthy newspapers. Instead, I put my finger into the hole in my shirt left by the bullet and pulled. The bottom of my shirt came away in a crude strip. I was barely aware of the pain in my side as I wadded it up and tried to stuff it over the wound. Instantly, it began to soak up the blood seeping from her abdomen.

"Laura?!"

Her eyes were open but still unfocused. She made no sign that she could hear me.

The strip of shirt was already soaked in her blood. I wasn't going to be able to save her. She needed medical attention, now.

I reached into my pocket and pulled out my burner phone. I was about to dial 9-1-1, but saw the gun on the ground, which made me stop. I stared at the gun, then the phone, then Laura. I turned around. Reggie's feet were sticking out of the opening behind me. Laura was bleeding out in front of me, and I had the gun that shot her. My prints were all over it. It had also probably been used at the shooting in Lyndon. What would the police think? They would only have my word, unless Laura lived. I unlocked the phone with my thumb, but stopped when the dial screen appeared. I'd have to tell them everything. I could be tied to the killings at Lyndon. I'd go to jail, and there was the possibility I'd never get out. I'd known Reggie was going to do something. I was pretty sure what it was going to be, and I didn't go to the authorities after it happened ... but, dammit, Laura was dying right in front of me!

I pressed my hands to my head and screamed. I paced back and forth, racked with indecision.

I had to think. I had to come up with something, goddammit. I quickly formulated options, but immediately found flaws in each one. Maybe I could call the police and leave before they got there, but even if I did, they would ask Laura who—

I realized that the choking sounds had stopped, and looked over.

Laura's chest still rose ever so slightly, but it was almost imperceptible.

That was when I knew.

It was too late.

If I had called right away, she may have had a chance, but I'd panicked, and waited too long. She was beyond hope.

I went and knelt beside her.

"Laura?"

Her eyes were open but still. Her face was serene.

I sat on the floor in shock, unable to process that I had watched someone die, right in front of me. I didn't know how she found me, but I was the reason she was there, and I had taken too long to save her. She may not have made it, but my indecision had cost her that chance.

I couldn't move, but I couldn't look away as Laura took her last breaths. I placed my hands on the side of her face. I didn't know how to comfort her, if I could comfort her. Tears began streaming from my eyes. I was scared, and in pain.

I don't know how long I sat there. It couldn't have been more than a few minutes, but I was snapped out of it by a lonely car passing the warehouse, outside. I got up, and looked out. The car was long gone, but Laura's car was sitting next to mine. It was still running with the driver's side door wide open.

Something snapped inside me and a reflex took over. It was some animal instinct of self-preservation, the instinct to save yourself at all costs. It seemed to speak in a cold voice from somewhere in my brain; a voice unfettered by morals, only interested in survival. Laura was dead and there was nothing I could do about it. If I was caught here, with two dead bodies, I was just as good as dead, too. I was going into shock and the instinct took over; the instinct that kept me from going to the police after the shooting at Lyndon and the instinct that crafted the plan of covering my tracks whenever I went to meet with Reggie.

I only vaguely remember going over to Reggie's body and taking the car keys from his pocket. I ran out into the parking lot, to the side of the building, started his car, and drove it around to the back of the warehouse. I parked it there and ran back to the lot. I got in Laura's car, and drove it around back, as well. I parked them side by side. I made one more trip to the lot and pulled my car into the shadows, hiding any evidence that someone was at the warehouse. I went to their cars and did my best to cover them in leaves and dead branches. I wasn't going to be able to completely camouflage them, but I wanted them hidden from the casual observer. There was nothing but woods behind the warehouse and Reggie had assured me that no one ever came there, but I wasn't taking any chances.

I went back inside the warehouse, and started what I knew would be a gruesome search.

I found a stairwell in the corner of the building that went down to the basement. Using the light from my burner phone as a flashlight, I descended the stairs. The darkness was nearly total, and the phone's light only gave me about three feet of visibility. I reached the bottom of the stairwell, and stepped out into a corridor. The sides were lined with more storage rooms. I slowly moved down the hall. The walls were grimy, and there was the constant sound of dripping water from somewhere in the darkness. There were two other sets of hallways that branched off, but I continued on my path. I knew I was heading in the right direction from the stench that was steadily building in my nostrils.

The hallway finally ended in a heavy steel door with a padlock. On a hunch, I pulled out Reggie's keys, which were still in my pocket. I tried two or three keys before one slid home. I twisted it and the lock sprang open. I took a large inhalation of breath, held it, and pulled open the door. The smell was unbelievable. The attempt to hold my breath didn't work. I turned to the side, leaned against the wall, and vomited. I waited for the wave of nausea to pass and for my senses to adjust to the smell, but after a few minutes, I couldn't wait any longer. I pushed my sleeve over my hand, and held it to my mouth. I took a step through the door. Once inside, I held up the phone to illuminate the room, saw what was in it, and promptly vomited, again.

I had found where Reggie had been "stashing".

*

An hour later, it was over.

I stepped out of the storage room and quickly closed the heavy steel door. I had lost count of the number of times I'd vomited. At that point, I was only dry heaving. I reached down, and quickly snapped the padlock closed. I had made sure to leave the keys in the room, behind the locked door. I stood there in the dimness. It was only then that the instinct left me and I felt myself come to my senses. I stared at the padlock on the door, comprehending the full horror of what I had done. I turned and walked as fast as I could through the darkness of the basement.

*

Once I got home, I took off my clothes, and stuffed them into a garbage bag. I bandaged my wounds in the bathroom with the supplies in the cabinet under the sink. It hurt like hell, and I had lost a good deal of blood, but the wounds were superficial. I would live. I went back into the living room and stopped when my eyes rested on the scratchpad where I had deciphered the message from Reggie. I had left it on the counter, but now it was on the kitchen table. Someone had moved it. Someone had been there.

Laura.

That's how she knew where to find me. It was the only way she could have known, but how did she get in?

I knew the answer the instant the question floated through my mind.

I went to the sliding back door and pulled. It opened without resistance.

I had been distracted by Reggie's coded text message, and forgot to lock it. Laura had been here, opened the back door, and saw the deciphered message.

I quickly grabbed my phone from the end table by the couch. I checked the screen.

Six new texts. Three missed calls. All from Laura.

I have to talk to you.
Please, it's really, really important.
Please, answer your phone.
Whatever you are doing, stop it right now and call me!
Jacob, please! Call me. I need to talk to you.
Where are you?! Please! Call me!

Although she called three times, she hadn't left any messages.

I deleted all the messages, dropped down to the couch with my head in my hands, and waited for the sun to come up.

*

For the next few days, I didn't leave my apartment. I spent them cleaning my wounds, and torturing myself with all the things I should have done to save Laura. I tried to remain as immobile as possible to help myself heal, but it meant that all I could do was lie there with my guilty thoughts. I should have called for an ambulance, no matter what might happen to me, but I didn't. Even as I lay there healing, I knew the right thing to do was to call the police, but I couldn't bring myself to do it. I told myself that I would wait until my wounds healed completely so I could think straight, and then come up with a way to explain it without incriminating myself.

Part of me wished that someone would miraculously find their cars, which would lead to a search of the area, which I was sure would somehow lead to me, and bring it all to an end, but if Reggie said that no one went out there, then I felt sure they would never be found.

Instead, I had begun the process of compartmentalization. I had done something horrible, and subconsciously, I was walling it up in my mind. Victims of trauma do it, but so do people with a guilty conscience.

*

A week later, I was lying on the couch, watching the news, when a report came on.

"And our top story tonight, county police are asking for the public's assistance in the search for a Wilton University student who has gone missing." A picture of Laura appeared over the reporter's shoulder. I sat up on the couch, wincing from the pain in my side. "Laura Aisling is a senior at Wilton University and was reported missing four days ago. Authorities are also searching for her car." The reporter checked her notes, and gave a description of Laura's car and license plate number. "Anyone with any information on her whereabouts is urged to call the number at the bottom of the screen ..."

From that moment, the horror inside me turned into a ball of guilt that began to grow ...

Over the course of the next week, I only left the couch to buy food, medicine, clean my wounds, and to go to the bathroom. The news stayed on the television twenty-four-seven. I made sure to catch every local broadcast, and flipped between the major cable news networks at regular intervals. It never reached the national networks, but local news stations would have updates from time to time, always pleading for anyone who knew anything to come forward.

Search parties were organized and canvassed the area around the university. I was the only one who knew that Laura was dozens of miles away in a place they would never search for her. Some of Laura's friends who I had never met were part of the search parties, and gave brief sound clips to the news teams, talking about what a good person Laura was. Their interviews were interspersed with helicopter images of lines of people, combing the woods.

"Officials state that despite the time that has passed," a local reporter was saying, "hopes are high that Laura Aisling will be found. Her mother, Gretchen Aisling, has issued this statement."

The image cut to a woman standing in front of a forest. A row of cameramen pointed cameras at her while reporters shoved microphones in her face. She was short, but had a fierce expression that was highlighted by her wry hair, and sharp, beady eyes.

"I ask everyone to pray to our Lord and Savior, Jesus Christ, for Laura's safe return. If you're watching, Laura, know that God is protecting you, and I can't wait for you to come back to me, my angel. Your room is waiting, and God will bring you home."

The video cut back to the field reporter, who was wearing his "gravely concerned" face. "And we, too, hope for Laura Aisling's safe return. Anyone who may have any information is urged to call the anonymous tip line that the police have established. The number is there at the bottom of your screen."

They cut back to the studio.

"We all hope for her return," the anchor with an unbelievable amount of foundation on his face said. "When we come back, Channel 7's own Daniel Chance has a look at the weather. Stay with us. We'll be right back."

I turned off the television. I had a decision to make, right then and there.

They were going to find me. They were going to ask me questions. It was unavoidable. All they had to do was check her cell phone records, which I assumed they had already done. If I waited to say anything, they would want to know what took me so long. I could claim I hadn't heard anything, but with each passing day, that excuse became less and less plausible.

127

I took out my phone, took a deep breath, and dialed. I was going to tell them. I was going to tell them everything, but as soon as I began dialing, the instinct was back …

*

"Mr Jacob Reese?" the man at the front door asked.

"That's me."

"I'm Detective Laurie with the Addison County Police Department," he said, flashing a badge. "May I come in?"

"Yes, please."

I opened the door and stepped aside to allow him to pass.

He stopped in the kitchen and looked around.

"Thanks for coming out to talk to me," I said. "I would have come to the station, but I'm not feeling too hot."

He smiled. "You don't look so hot, but thanks for getting in touch with us."

"I've been laid up for a week with a stomach bug, so I've been cut off from the world. I saw the news this afternoon, and I couldn't believe it."

"We're talking to everyone, trying to find out what happened. You mind if I ask you some questions?"

"No. Please," I said, motioning to the kitchen table. "I'd offer to get you something to eat or drink, but all I've got at the moment are Sprite, saltines, and some soup."

"No, thanks. I'm good," he said, settling into a chair.

I poured myself a glass of water and joined him at the table.

He took out a small, spiral notepad, removed the pen that was tucked into the binding, and flipped the notepad open.

"So, as you heard, Laura Aisling has gone missing. We just want to talk to anyone who can give us an idea of where she might be."

"Sure."

"First of all, how did you know Laura?"

"Well, like I told the person on the tip line, she was a friend. We met at a frat party a few months ago. We, um, we actually dated for a while."

He stopped writing and raised an eyebrow. "Really?"

"Yeah. I didn't know how much detail to go into on the tip line. I figured it would be better to speak to someone in person."

He considered it, and nodded.

"When did you last see her?"

"It's been like a month and a half. We sort of drifted apart. We weren't that serious, at least I didn't think so, but about a week ago, she texted me a couple of times. She seemed upset." I squirmed, playing up my unease. "I figured she wanted to talk about our relationship, but like I said, I thought we were done. I didn't respond. In fact, the last time we saw each other was at her school. We had an argument."

"An argument? About what?"

"It was nothing really—just stupid relationship stuff. We had been seeing less of each other. It was one of those, you know, 'what-exactly-are-we?' conversations."

"And?"

"We called it off. That was the last time I saw her. Do you think it has anything to do with her disappearance?"

He didn't look up from his notepad as he wrote. "Don't know. We're simply talking to everyone right now. You said that she sent you some text messages a week ago where she sounded upset?"

"Yeah."

"Do you still have those messages?"

"No, I deleted them."

"Why?"

"I thought she wanted to talk about us, and to me, we were through. I didn't want to encourage her. I'm sorry. I shouldn't have deleted them."

He waved his hand. "It's okay. We can get them through the phone company."

"She also called that night, but didn't leave any messages," I added.

"Do you know what she wanted to talk about?"

"No."

That was an honest answer, but whatever it was, it was important enough for her to come find me at the warehouse.

"Why didn't you respond?"

"Honestly, that night, I rented a movie, got really drunk, and passed out on my couch. I woke up at like, four in the morning, saw the texts, and deleted them."

"She send you any more messages?"

"No."

I could feel the weight of his stare as he peeked over his notebook at me. "And you have no idea what she wanted to talk about?"

I helplessly shrugged without overdoing it. "I hadn't spoken to her in a month and a half."

"When you two fought?" he asked, a little too pointedly.

"I don't even know if you could call it a fight. I took it as a breakup, and it wasn't all that dramatic—like we had both decided that we had had our fun, but it was over."

He digested what I said.

"Is there anyone who can vouch for your whereabouts the night of these texts?" he asked, lightly waving the phone in his hand.

I shook my head. "No. Just got drunk alone and rented a movie."

"What movie?"

I told him.

"Any good?"

"Honestly, I don't remember much about it. I ended up passing out at some point."

"Where did you rent it from?"

"On pay-per-view."

He made a note on his pad. I assumed it was to check my cable records.

What am I doing? I thought. This wasn't me, but I couldn't stop myself. I worried what might happen if I told him what really happened. Would Reggie's guys come after me? Would I be held responsible for Laura's death? I sure as hell was responsible for Reggie's death. It seemed the panic and guilt in my head was detached from the tone and actions of my mouth, which had no problem lying to this detective.

"Did you have your cell phone on you?" he asked.

"Yeah. Why?" I asked.

"No reason," he replied.

I knew the reason. They could check cell tower records to see if I was telling the truth, assuming that my phone and I were in the same place. Laura and Reggie's phones were off, making them untraceable. The instinct had seen to that.

He wrote one more note in his pad and glanced at me. "Is there anything else you can think of?"

"No. Not at the moment."

He took out his wallet, extracted a card, and handed it to me. "Well, if you think of anything, give me a call," he said.

I took it. "Thanks, and if there's anything else I can do, let me know."

"Thanks. We're still looking, but with every day that passes, the odds go down. We're still trying to establish when exactly she went missing, but it looks like your texts may be the last time anyone heard from her."

"I … I don't know what to say. I mean, I'm sorry I didn't answer those texts. I have no idea what she was worried about."

He shrugged. "No way to know, now." He closed his notepad, and leaned back in his chair. "You have any theories about where she could be?"

"Me?"

"Sure. You knew her."

The question threw me a little. I wasn't sure if my confusion

131

was a good thing or a bad thing. "I'm still trying to process it. I mean, I only heard about this a few hours ago."

"If you had to take a guess—anything you know of that would cause her to disappear or maybe run away?"

The second he said "run away", the instinct clicked.

"The only thing I can think of, and it's only because you asked, is her mother. She said that her mother was very controlling, and that they did not get along—and, please," I quickly added, "I'm not saying I think her mother did something to her, but if you think she may have run away, she may have done it to get away from her. I don't know. She might pop up somewhere far away from here."

The slight change in his expression told me that the same exact thought had crossed his mind.

A wave of guilt made me sick to my stomach, but I continued.

"Have you met her?" I asked.

"Oh yeah," was all he would say before standing from his chair. "Well, thank you for contacting us, Mr Reese, and for answering my questions."

"Of course," I said, following him to the door.

"If you think of something to add, give me a call."

"I will," I said, opening the door.

He stepped onto the porch and turned to me. "Also, let us know if you plan on going anywhere, okay? We may want to ask you some more questions."

"Sure."

"Again, thank you for your time." He extended his hand. I grasped it. "Feel better. Load yourself up on those saltines and Sprite. It's what my mom did for me when I was sick, and I swear, it would cure cancer."

I managed a chuckle. "Thanks. I will."

"Have a good night."

"Good night, Detective."

He walked away.

I closed the door. The instinct left and the ball of guilt grew heavier in my stomach. I barely made it to the bathroom before I began vomiting uncontrollably.

That night, I had my first nightmare about the door in the basement of the warehouse.

*

Weeks passed.

My wounds healed, but from time to time, I would feel a sharp pain if I turned too quickly, or sometimes, for no reason at all. I tried to convince myself that it was just a phantom pain, but it would not go away.

The search for Laura continued, but there were no new leads. I constantly watched the news for any updates. Over time, the coverage grew further and further apart. There was no new information to keep the public's interest. Detective Laurie called a few more times, but only to ask me if I had anything new to add. I told him that I didn't.

Ironically, the more and more it looked like they weren't going to find Laura, the worse the guilt consumed me. The instinct wasn't there to banish it. It was simply a constant crushing guilt.

I felt like a prisoner. I couldn't move on while the investigation was still open out of fears it would raise a red flag to Detective Laurie, but it was torture. I was waiting for my door to be kicked in at any minute and to be dragged off to jail. The nightmares continued.

I tried to wall up my guilt—to distance myself. I began to treat the whole thing as if it had been some other person who had allowed Laura to die on that floor. In those moments where I did permit myself to recognize what I had done, and what I was doing by covering it up, the guilt was all-consuming. I would throw myself out of bed in the middle of the night with the intention of calling the police to confess. I would begin to dial

Detective Laurie's number but stop. I would sit there staring at the phone until I returned to bed, only to be haunted by nightmares of that door.

My savings dried up. I pleaded with my bank to give me some more time on the remainder of my student loan. They agreed but only after raising my interest rate over a longer period of time.

I had to get a job.

I didn't have much in the way of a résumé, so I got one of the only jobs I could—a barista at a coffee shop. The work sucked, but I was one of the better employees. I was trying to keep myself squeaky clean and worked as many hours as I could. I became a manager, which was a meager upgrade in pay. I would bristle as I watched the place take in money, hand over fist, and dole out pennies to the employees.

I was miserable and saw nothing but misery in my future. There was nothing I could do until I was rid of this guilt.

Then, one night, after a full year had passed, I was watching the news. They had just wrapped up a story about the Middle East, when the camera went to one of the anchors, and the photo of Laura appeared over his shoulder.

"And a final update on the case of the missing Wilton University student, Laura Aisling."

I sat up on the couch, wincing at the pain in my side.

"With no new developments for months, Addison County officials have decided to close the case. The tip line will be discontinued, but the police still urge anyone with information to call the sheriff's office. We reached out to the Addison County Police Department for any further comment, but they declined. We did, however, contact Laura Aisling's mother, and she had this to say …"

The image cut to the same woman I had seen before, standing in front of the woods. This time, she was standing on the front steps of a home. It was clear that Laura's disappearance had taken a toll on her. Her wrinkles were deeper. Her hair had thinned, and her eyes had sunken in their sockets.

"I'm not going to give up," she said, defiantly. "I know the Lord will bring my angel back to me, and I have everything ready for her return. We'll be a family again."

It cut back to the anchor.

"Again, if you have any information on the whereabouts of Laura Aisling, you can call the Addison County Sheriff's Department at the number below. That'll do it for us tonight here at Channel 7. Thank you for joining us. Stick around for an all-new episode of—"

I turned off the television.

I went to the kitchen and pulled a beer from the fridge. I sat at the table, staring at the chair Detective Laurie had occupied. I should have been relieved. I had made it, but I felt worse than ever. I knew it would never truly be over. It would always be there in the shadows. The nightmares would continue, as would the guilt and the fear … unless I decided to end it.

For the next few days, I walked around in a fog, trying to formulate a plan. I was going to confess. I tried to research what I would be looking at as far as jail went. It caused me to hesitate, but I steeled myself to the fact that it was the only way to move on with my life.

Then, I got a call from my father, telling me about my mother's failing health. I was so stunned, that I sat there, speechless, with the phone to my ear.

Everything happened so fast with their passing, I put my plans on hold until after the funeral.

Then came the reading of the will.

I sat in their lawyer's office, as he read the declaration that I was to receive everything.

"To our son, Jacob," the lawyer read, "we know that things have not always gone smoothly between us, but we could not be prouder of the change you have made in your life. You have

135

proven yourself responsible and know that we love you. We hereby leave the entirety of our estate and all financial holdings to you, Jacob …"

The lawyer's voice trailed off.

They left me everything.

In an instant, the guilt and the instinct returned but seemed to speak with one voice. This was a chance, the only chance, I'd ever have to make something good of my life. If I confessed, Laura would still be gone, and what would it do to her mother to find her daughter's decomposing body in a room full of dead addicts and dealers? Wouldn't she be better with the fantasy that her daughter was somewhere happily living her life? And if I confessed, where would the life savings of my parents go? I could pay off my student loans and start a new life, a life that I could do some good with.

Before, I only thought the guilt would go away by serving my time, but now, I saw a way to pay my penance by taking this opportunity and making myself a better person. That was the only way something good could come of this. Yes, I had done something horrible and I would still live with it every day. Nothing would change that, but I could try to be the person I always should have been.

As I made my decision, I faintly heard the lawyer talking from behind his desk.

"Jacob? Are you okay?" he asked. "*Jacob—*

—Jacob?"

I look up to see Reverend Williams standing next to the pew, staring at me. I glance around. The church is empty.

"Oh my God," I say. "I am so sorry. I promise you, I wasn't asleep."

He smiles. "No. I know. Your eyes were open, but you were really somewhere else."

"Yeah … Also, I'm sorry for saying 'Oh my God' just then."

136

He shrugs. "I've heard worse. Mind if I sit?"

"Uh, okay."

I scoot over and he sits next to me. He fidgets with his knees in the cramped space.

"Ugh. I spend so much time up there, I forget what it's like out here." He gives up and slouches. "I guess this is a good reminder to keep the sermons short."

"It was a good sermon."

"Thanks. Where did I lose you?"

"Somewhere around werewolves."

"Ah."

"No, it really was good. It got me thinking. That's all."

"Well, mission accomplished, I guess."

We stare at the figure of Jesus on the cross, hovering above the altar.

"Everything all right, Jacob?"

"Sure. Fine," I answer without a hint of conviction.

"I saw that Groundworks is closed."

"Burst pipe."

"Mmmm … but that's not what brought you here today, is it?"

"No. I just felt like it had been a while since I went to church. It was time."

"A 'while'?"

"Yeah."

"Jacob, when was the last time you went to church?"

"I don't remember."

"I see …"

We sit silently, for a moment.

"Why don't you tell me what's on your mind, Jacob?"

"Nothing."

He sighs. "Jacob, I've been at this long enough and I can tell you, there are three types of churchgoers—those who go every week, those who go on the holidays, and those who go when

137

something is tearing them up inside. I've never seen you here at Christmas or Easter, so I'm guessing you're in the last category."

"I'm just trying to figure some stuff out."

"Want to talk about it?"

"I don't know if I can."

"You can try."

"I wouldn't know where to start. I—"

I almost start to talk. I want to tell him. I can feel it bubbling up inside me. I want to get it out. I understand confession. I understand the urge, but I tamp it down. I can still get through this. I'm not going to tell him, but a question suddenly seizes me.

"Reverend?"

"Yeah?"

"Do you think God punishes us for our sins?"

"That bad, huh?"

"… I don't know, yet."

"As someone who has been doing this job for, oh, twenty-five years or so, do you want to know what I think?"

I nod.

"I think more often than not, God lets us punish ourselves for our sins."

My head drops in contemplation.

"Jacob, you can tell me. No matter what it is, I can try to help you."

"Thanks, Reverend, but I don't think you and I are there, yet."

"You know, in this place, it's never just you and I," he says with a tilt of his head to the crucifix over the altar.

"I don't think God and I are there, yet, either," I reply.

Chapter 8

Halloween has been my favorite night of the year for the past six years running.

The first year I decided to dress up and join the fun, I went as the Headless Horseman. I bought my costume at one of those stores that pops up mid-September, and then disappears two days after Halloween. It was cheap and flimsy. The cloak was vinyl, as were the overlays for my shoes that were supposed to make them look like boots. The "coat" that came with the costume was made of felt and durable for one night only. The buckles that were supposed to look like brass were made out of cheap plastic. There was also a plastic sword that even a child would have been embarrassed to have.

The worst by far, was the black cardboard apparatus that was supposed to create the illusion that I was headless. It was simply a box that went over my head, with small squares cut into it for my eyes. The holes were covered by black, mesh fabric. Driving to the festivities, I thought that the costume was perfectly fine—albeit a little cheesy—but I had paid $100 for it, so it had to be good, right? Once I arrived in town and saw the costumes of the other Main Street business owners, I came *this* close to getting back in my truck and driving home.

Sally and Emmett Irving, who own the flower shop two doors down from Groundworks, went as Frankenstein and Bride of Frankenstein. It wasn't an entirely original idea for a couple, but they had gone all out. She had the wig with the high hair and white stripe running through it. She also had the pale make-up with the puckered lips, and wore a white dress that draped from her body. She looked like she had stepped right off of the screen. Emmett was unreal. He had traveled all the way to Boston that morning to have his make-up done by a special effects company. Everything from his square forehead to the bolts in his neck were amazing. Even up close, it was fantastic.

Maggie Vaughn, owner of the Elmwood Hotel, was dressed as a witch, but it wasn't some generic witch, like the one Reverend Williams had displayed in his sermon with a pointy hat and black smock. Nope. She had a stringy wig, hunched back, and wore rotted-looking clothes. She wore sallow-toned make-up, and had applied warts everywhere on her face. The final touch was yellow contact lenses. I didn't even realize who she was until she broke character. I had been speaking to her for ten minutes, wondering, "Who the hell is this crazy woman?" when she stood up straight and said, "For Christ's sake, Jacob. It's me, Maggie."

There were vampires, zombies, a Freddy Krueger, and every single time I saw a new costume, it put mine to shame.

The final blow was the arrival of Andrew Paulini, the owner and operator of the Iron & Ivy gastropub.

A small knot of us Main Street business owners were gathered on the sidewalk, admiring the costumes and waiting for the parade. Behind me, I suddenly heard the sound of boots, accompanied by the jingle of spurs.

Doug Leontes, a banker at Citizen's Bank who was dressed as a pirate, looked over my shoulder and gasped, "Oh, wow …"

We all turned and … just … damn.

He was the Headless Horseman, and I mean he was *the* Headless Horseman. His heavy, leather boots thudded on the

140

sidewalk, and the spurred heels clicked against the concrete. An actual sword and sheath hung from his hip. He wore black gauntlet gloves, and in his left hand, he held a real jack-o'-lantern. Inside was a flickering LED light that perfectly mimicked the light of a fire. The real brass buckles on his doublet coat glittered in the light of the gas lamps. His black cloak billowed as he walked. The collar of the cloak was turned up, and this is where his costume was genius. Over his head, he wore a black stocking, but he, or someone with some artistic skill, had painted the stocking to match the red lining of the turned-up collar, with a black hole painted at the base. From any slight distance, in that light, the effect was flawless. It looked like the man had no head.

He won the costume contest that year. He also won it the year after that, when he went as the Terminator, with amazing latex pieces that made it look like there were rips in his skin with machinery underneath.

After that night, I vowed that I was never going to half-ass my Halloween costume again. I went as V from *V for Vendetta* one year, and a demon the year after that. The demon was frustrating, because I had to order the kit and apply the latex pieces myself. It required hours of watching tutorial videos on YouTube, but it paid off. I won my first title that year, breaking Andrew Paulini's reign. Since then, we've had a little bit of a good-natured rivalry.

After church this morning, I'm thinking of not going, but I know I have to. If I don't, and the shop is closed, people are going to know something is wrong. If I want to keep my standing in town, I need to go, but I don't know how long I can keep this façade going.

I arrive home from church, and let Murphy outside to do his business. I throw his tennis ball a couple of times, and then head back inside. I go to the hall closet and take out the box that has been sitting on the shelf for over a month. I ordered it from a special effects company in Los Angeles that does make-up for a lot of television shows and movies. The kit cost almost $300, due to the pieces being specially made, and came with a how-to manual that was over ten pages long. There was even a personal note included from one of the make-up artists who had assembled the kit.

> *Dear Mr Reese,*
>
> *Don't know who you are, but I admire your balls in trying this one on your own. The how-to manual isn't going to cut it. I'm not supposed to tell you this, but a rival company makes a similar kit, and instead of a manual, they have an online video. I suggest you use that. The link is at the bottom of the page. When you're done, send us a pic of the finished product, and we'll post it on the wall in our shop.*
>
> *Happy Haunting!*

I had been looking forward to this night since 12:01 a.m. of November 1st of last year. Normally, this is my Christmas, New Year's, and Super Bowl Sunday, all rolled into one, but I've just watched potentially millions of dollars go up in smoke in addition to the fact that I have no idea who's doing this. However, if I'm going to keep the shop open, I need to keep a presence in The Hollows. It's the only thing I can do.

I check my phone. It's three o'clock. Time to start suiting up.

I take the box into the bathroom, along with my iPad. Murphy attempts to follow, but I close the door. He waits outside, sniffing near the bottom of the door. A few moments later, I hear him give up and go to his bed.

I unpack the box on the counter, and double-check the inventory. I lay out all the pieces of plastic and latex, along with the brushes, make-up, a full wig, and a bag of braided crepe hair. I pull up the browser on my iPad and type in the link for the tutorial video listed in the letter.

The video starts with a guy sitting at a make-up counter—the kind you see in the movies, with the mirrors, bordered in light bulbs. Lined up on the counter are items almost identical to what's in front of me.

"Hi, I'm Jesse Whitaker, and today, we're going to show you how to apply your werewolf prosthetics and make-up."

In a moment of serendipity, "Little Red Riding Hood" by Sam the Sham and the Pharaohs begins playing on the online radio station.

I look in the bathroom mirror, take a breath, and say, "Let's do it."

*

It takes over two and a half hours to apply the make-up. At first, it's hard to take my mind off the cockroaches and the shop, but eventually I'm able to focus on the video. My mind is desperate to think of anything else and latches on to the instructions. I follow them to the letter, pausing and rewinding to make sure I'm doing it correctly. I scrub my face, apply the base coat, and move to the finer details, like heightening and sharpening my cheeks and jawbone. Then come the pieces of foam latex. I apply the spirit gum to anchor them to my skin. I know from experience that it's going to hurt like hell to rip them off later. I blend the edges of the pieces to my skin with liquid latex. Then, I use the base coat make-up to blend the colors.

The effect is flawless. Gradually, my image in the mirror goes from a confusing image of some guy with white bits of plastic and latex all over his face, to something vaguely wolf-like, to full-on werewolf. Next comes the snout. I fasten the nose and upper lip piece over my own nose, so that it looks like I'm permanently snarling. I put on the wig over my slicked-down hair, and fasten it with hairpins. I use more liquid latex to blend the edge of the wig with my forehead. I pull strands of hair from the braided crepe hair to create a hairline all around my jaw, leading to my neck. Now, for the latex ear pieces that turn my dull, human ears into pointy canine ears. Surprisingly, these are the hardest part of the whole affair.

The sun is going down outside the window when I finally complete the last two steps.

I take the false teeth, and pop them out of their packaging. These aren't some cheap knock-off teeth you get from a Rite Aid or Walgreens an hour before you want to be at the party. These are the latest in false canine tooth technology that go over your teeth. The tops are firm, but the bases are water soluble and your saliva will cause them to shrink and mold to your teeth. The result is natural-looking fangs.

The last step is the red and yellow contacts.

I've never worn contacts, so it takes a moment for me to ready myself and put them in. Instantly, there's the instinctual horror of touching your own eyeball. I'm filled with an urge to rip them out. I brace myself against the counter, and wait for my tear ducts to calm down. I worry that it might smear my make-up but it holds. Finally, my eyes adjust.

I slowly look up into the mirror.

"… wow …" I breathe.

The costume contest is over.

"Eat shit, Andrew Paulini." I chuckle. I remember the werewolf from Reverend Williams' sermon and growl, "I am Wrath."

I wash my hands, and open the bathroom door. Murphy's there, waiting for me.

As soon as he sees my face, he bolts.

"Oh, Murphy! I'm sorry, buddy! It's me!"

He runs out of the room, and I hear him haul ass down the stairs. Of course, I feel bad, but it's kinda funny. I go to the bed, and put on the ripped jeans and flannel shirt I've trashed, just for the occasion. I also pull on the elbow-length gloves, which are designed to look like werewolf hands with claws and hair.

I go downstairs and find Murphy cowering in his usual hiding spot behind the couch.

"You okay, buddy?"

Between the voice he knows so well, and my appearance, he's really confused. It's not like this is something new. He wasn't too high on the demon costume, either. I tried taking him to the festival last year, but he was so freaked out by the costumes, I had to leave a little early. I don't want to put him through that again.

"I'll be back later, Murphy."

I put some treats in his bowl, which still isn't enough to get him out from behind the couch. I grab some bags of candy from the pantry, and head out the door.

The ragged flannel shirt isn't very effective against the dropping temperature, but werewolves don't wear coats.

I hop into the truck and glance at the cottage in the rearview mirror. I haven't thought about Laura or the shop in hours ... and I don't want to.

*

The drive into town on Halloween is the closest thing The Hollows has to a traffic jam. Once I reach town, the local police and volunteers direct everyone to the high school, where it's a half a mile walk to Main Street.

Even before I park the truck, I'm getting thumbs-up from other drivers, and wide-eyed stares from kids who press their noses against the car windows for a better look. I wave to them, and their faces light up.

After parking at the high school, I get out of the truck, carrying the bags of candy I'll hand out at the shop after the parade. Even though we're closed, it's still tradition. The walk towards downtown brings more compliments. Everyone is going in the same direction, towards Main Street. Marissa McCormack, an English teacher at the high school who is dressed like a cowgirl, breaks away from her husband and kids, and crosses the street to walk beside me.

"That is unbelievable." She smiles, peering closely at my face.

"Thank you."

"My kids wouldn't come over because they were too freaked out. Who is that under there?"

"It's Jacob Reese."

She rolls her eyes. "Of course, it is. For God's sake, are you and Andrew ever going to let someone else win this thing?"

"Nope."

She lightly punches me in the arm. "You look great. Have fun."

"You, too."

She hurries off to rejoin her family.

There's a thickening of the crowd, one last turn, and Main Street bursts into view in all its Halloween glory. Kids and parents are swarming the green, playing the games and enjoying the food stands. Most of the lights in the shops are off, leaving the gas lamps to illuminate the festivities. There are jack-o'-lanterns everywhere. In one corner of the green, there's a concentration of them, waiting to be judged for a contest. The smell of kettle corn and caramel apples hangs over everything. Everyone is in costume, children and adults, alike.

For this one night, The Hollows is a fairy tale.

My stroll down Main Street adds to my ego as people stop and ask for photos. Parents point me out to their kids, who wave apprehensively until I wave back, letting them know that I'm not a Big Bad Wolf. I'm a Big *Good* Wolf.

The Old Stone Church is a scene-stealer by virtue of the fact that it carries no decorations or lights, as if to say, "I'm the real deal." The soft glow of the gas lamps causes the shadows of the graveyard to crawl across the ground, with the Hanging Tree looming over the headstones.

I spot the collection of business owners on the green. They're easy to identify because it's a grouping of the best costumes around. Maggie Vaughn is dressed as Cleopatra—simple, elegant, and she looks good. She's standing next to Marcus Stanton, owner of the hardware store, who's dressed as Dracula. He's not as impressive. It's the stereotypical Dracula, so even if he went all-out, which he has, it's not entirely original. Sally and Emmett Irving have done another "couple's costume"—The Mad Hatter and Alice from *Alice in Wonderland*. If I have any competition this year, they're it. Thomas Martinez, who owns The Hollows Diner, is dressed as some sort of steampunk guy. There's one other person who's part of the group. They've got their back to me, so I don't know who it is, but they've got green hair.

Maggie glances at me, and her eyes light up as I approach.

"Oh my God! That is amazing!" she cries.

The man with green hair turns to look. It's Andrew Paulini, dressed as the Joker from *The Dark Knight*. Lame. I think I've already seen a dozen Jokers on my walk to downtown.

"Since Andrew is right here," Maggie continues, "that can only be Jacob!"

I bow. I can't help the feeling of satisfaction as Andrew rolls his eyes. The trophy for Best Costume will be on display at Groundworks for at least another year. The others all chime in with their approval.

"Great costumes, everybody," I say. "Except you, Andrew. Why didn't you dress up this year?"

"Oh, ha ha ha," he says with a sneer. He points to the darkened, blind-drawn windows of Groundworks. "What's up with the shop?"

"Burst pipe," I reply.

"Burst pipe?" Maggie asks. "Didn't you have a burst pipe in your cottage?"

Shit.

"Yeah," I say. "What are the odds?"

"I saw a van parked in the back of your place, yesterday," Andrew continues. "Didn't look like plumbers. They looked more like exterminators. Got a little vermin problem?"

For a brief second, I think that Andrew may have been behind the cockroaches, but quickly realize that's a stupid conclusion. How could he have Laura's music box? No. He's just trying to get my goat.

"We'll be back up by Wednesday."

I try to sound confident, but I see a flash of doubt in Maggie's eyes, like she's suddenly worried about rat droppings in the free coffee I give her.

The mention of the shop also causes me to do an involuntary quick scan of the crowd for anyone with red hair, but there's no one.

We exchange a few more pleasantries and talk about the costumes, decorations, and the parade. Every year, this town gets better. We wish each other good luck in the costume contest, the winner of which will be announced after the parade.

As we slowly scatter, I tap Andrew on the shoulder. "Hey, I can't wait to see the Iron & Ivy's float in the parade."

He smiles. "You won't be disappointed."

I stroll around the green, checking out the kids carving pumpkins next to the display of elaborate jack-o'-lanterns that have been entered into the carving contest, while other kids decorate caramel apples. The dipped apples look like bronzed orbs perched on the end of sticks. The compliments I receive for my costume are constant, and every few moments, someone stops me and asks for a photo. I'm loving it so much, I start passing out the candy I've brought for the trick-or-treating. I'm not supposed to officially start until after the parade, but I don't care. I run out of candy and decide that when the trick-or-treating starts, I'll run into the shop, grab all the cookies we've got, and hand those out. We moved the cookies to one of the coolers and they're individually wrapped, so they'll be free of any pesticide. Sandy will flip because it will mess with the inventory.

At eight o'clock, some of the volunteers who are running the festivities, begin clearing Main Street, and string twine between the gas lamps. There's a slow exodus from the green, and everyone begins lining up to watch the parade. I take up a spot outside the window of Groundworks. That way, when the parade is over, I can go inside and grab the cookies. The sidewalks become crowded. The smaller kids are sitting on the curb to get a good view. Main Street is a gallery of families, kids, and adults, all enjoying the spirit of the occasion. There are even smatterings of high school kids, who would normally be too cool for such things, but they are just as enthusiastic as the youngest kids.

The walkie-talkies mounted to the hips of the volunteers begin to chatter. A hush falls over the crowd, and everyone turns their heads towards the shadows at the south end of Main Street. Through the walkie-talkies, there's a call of "go". The volunteer closest to me raises her walkie-talkie and replies, "Go." It passes down the street to other volunteers.

Everything falls under an expectant silence.

From the shadows at the south end of Main Street, there are three sharp chirps from a whistle. It's followed by the tapping of a snare drum to establish a cadence. Then a bass drum picks it up and continues the beat. It grows louder, and out of the shadows, into the soft glow of the gas lamps, appears a drum major, accompanied by a color guard, carrying a banner that reads, "The Hollows High School Devils Marching Band". The marching band begins to play "Werewolves of London". I shake my head and smile. More than a few people turn to me and point or give me a thumbs-up. It's a fluke, but I bask in it.

It's a high school band, so the horns are a little soft, and the note precision is far from perfect, but it only makes the hometown prouder. The marching band comes into view, sporting their red and black colors. The crowd erupts in cheers. The kids sitting on the curb strain their necks to watch as the band approaches. The music grows louder, and gives way to "The Monster Mash". That gets a big round of applause. Next is the theme to "Beetlejuice", followed by "People are Strange" by The Doors. It's odd to hear these songs played by a marching band, but in the present setting, it absolutely works. Parents are snapping photos. You can tell when it's their kid walking by, because the light from the camera on their phone becomes a strobe.

The marching band is followed by Mayor Ballard and her husband, riding in a convertible. She's got a sash over her shoulder, identifying her as the Mayor, as if there was some chance that we wouldn't know. Next up are the Homecoming King and Queen. They, too, are sitting in the back of a convertible, and waving. He's the star of the football team, which, admittedly, has won one game and lost five, but hey, Hollows Pride! I don't know anything about the Homecoming Queen, except her name because of the festival program that was dropped off at the shop two weeks ago.

After that come the floats built by the various high school clubs and teams, each being pulled by a pickup truck. First is the homecoming committee's float, which is a giant jack-o'-lantern, constructed out of wood and papier-mâché. Its crude construction gives it a sense of charm. The football team is next. Just like every year, it's kind of half-assed. It's mostly players in rubber devil masks, dancing around a "fire" that's made of strips of red and orange tissue paper attached to a fan. There's a Devil mascot dancing on a raised platform.

There's a float for the show choir, and one for the science team, which is a mock-up of a Doctor Frankenstein's lab. There's a student dressed as Frankenstein's monster lying on a table. Other students in bloodstained lab coats run around on the float, mixing different-colored concoctions that occasionally lead to a burst of smoke. They must have spent a fortune on dry ice, because the mist drapes off the base of the float down to the asphalt like a curtain. There's also one of those machines that makes sparks between two wires. For the life of me, I can't remember what it's called.

The student playing Frankenstein's monster raises his hand,

and the main mad scientist shouts, "It's alive! It's alive!" The monster sits up, waves at the crowd, and throws out candy, which is quickly scooped up by the kids. After the lame effort by the football team, the science team's effort is much appreciated.

Next are the floats from the Main Street businesses. They ask me to do one every year, but with my limited staff, it would be too much work. I'd rather just win the costume contest and enjoy the parade.

The float for the Elmwood Hotel is next to roll down the street. It's a replica of the pumpkin patch from *It's the Great Pumpkin, Charlie Brown!* Pumpkins litter the float. There are two high school kids dressed as Linus and Sally, waiting among the pumpkins. The kid dressed as Linus holds a sign that reads "Welcome, Great Pumpkin!" in one hand, and a blanket in the other as he sucks his thumb. Sally is playfully annoyed. Every few moments, a girl dressed in all white sweat pants and shirt, with a black-painted nose rises from the vines, and Linus screams, "There he is! There he is!" It's really cute.

There's a collective gasp from down Main Street, and the float for the Iron & Ivy comes into view.

"You have got to be kidding me …" I whisper under my breath.

The float depicts the hanging of the three witches in the Old Stone Church cemetery. There's a mock-up of the Old Stone Church and the Hanging Tree. The witches are played by three of Andrew's staff, one of whom I recognize as my server from a few nights ago, and they are dressed as sexy witches. Around each of their necks is a noose that is draped over a branch of the Hanging Tree and leads to the hangman, who stands off to the side. He's played by one of the Iron & Ivy's barbacks. They are surrounded by short vertical planks of wood that have been painted to look like the slate headstones of the cemetery.

The "witches" plead with the hangman and the crowd in sultry voices and suggestive puns. "I'll be good. I prooooomise," one says while leaning forward to bare her cleavage. "I don't want to be hung," another witch says, and turns to the hangman. "But I bet you're hung," she says with a wink. The hangman pretends to be embarrassed.

I'm going to win the costume contest, but Andrew Paulini has just won the night. I take in the reactions around me. The more aged citizens of The Hollows look a little stunned. The kids don't seem to get it. Everyone else *loves* it. As the float moves down the street, it steadily gains applause and cheers. I scan the crowd, and easily spot Andrew across the street, thanks to his bright green hair. He's holding a cup of cider, and receiving pats on the back. We lock eyes, and I humbly bow my head. He smiles and toasts his cup in my direction.

I scan the other side of the street in an attempt to note every smile, every laugh, every wide-eyed stare from every kid, every pers—

Laura Aisling.

She's right there, across the street, staring at me with those unearthly blue eyes. The scar is there, just above her brow. She looks older, as if she didn't die on the floor of that warehouse. Her red hair flows out from under the hood of her red cloak. There's a picnic basket in her hands.

Little Red Riding Hood.

Her expression is neutral, but as we stare at one another, the corners of her mouth curl into a devious, sinister smile—a smile made all the more unnerving due to the fact that she's not blinking.

I can't move. I can't breathe. The shock is so great, my eyes begin to water under my contact lenses.

She bows her head, turns, and steps behind the row of spectators who are focused on the parade. She's tall enough that I can see her hood, moving down the sidewalk, behind the gallery of monsters. It all feels like it's happening in slow motion, in a dream, with the sound of the parade and crowds far away.

I mirror her movement from my side of the street, desperately trying to keep her in view. I rudely bump into people, who voice their displeasure, but I take no notice.

This can't be real. It can't be, but every time she disappears behind someone and I think that the hallucination is over, she reappears.

We come even with the Old Stone Church. She turns, and goes up the stairs into the cemetery, her cloak flowing behind her.

I shoot forward through the crowd. I'm dimly aware of the people around me.

"Hey! What's your problem?" someone asks.

I duck under the twine and dart into the street.

"Sir! Excuse me, sir!" a volunteer patrolling the street protests, but I keep going. I race in front of a float. The pickup truck pulling the float hits the brakes. Even though it's only going a few miles an hour, the people on the float lurch forward, and drop to their knees. I continue running, trying to keep the red cloak in view as Laura enters the shadows of the graveyard, and moves off in the direction of the Hanging Tree.

I reach the other side of the street. The people who have been watching me approach lean out of the way as I duck under their section of twine and hop onto the curb. I can't see her anymore. The graveyard is too dark. I jostle my way through the crowd to the steps to the church. I take them in one leap and race into the rows of headstones.

I whip my head left and right, searching for any signs of her. I trip over one of the shorter headstones, bashing my toe, and smacking my knee on another as I stumble. The pain is excruciating, but I'm right back up. I go further into the shadows and graves. There's no sign of her.

I arrive at the Hanging Tree.

She could be anywhere. She could be hiding behind one of these graves. She could have doubled back, and be long gone.

I spin in place, searching the shadows.

I stop.

There, at the base of the Hanging Tree.

The picnic basket.

I approach slowly and crouch beside it. I gently slide my hand under the handle and lift. By the weight, I can tell there's something in it. I glance around, but she's gone. I slowly open the lid. It's too dark to see inside. Shaking, I reach into the basket and feel around. There's something round and fuzzy. I carefully pull it out.

It's a chewed, worn, red tennis ball.

Murphy's tennis ball.

*

The roads are empty as I keep my foot on the accelerator. Everyone is at the Halloween celebration.

Checking my rearview mirror, I see the reflection of the were-wolf staring back at me. I begin ripping the pieces of latex from my face. My phone starts lighting up with phone calls and texts, asking where I am, and informing me that I've won the costume contest. The picnic basket and tennis ball sit on the passenger seat next to me. I try to stop myself from constantly glancing at it. I keep praying that it will simply disappear—that this is all a bad dream.

I glance again, and it's still there. I focus on it for too long, and suddenly hear the gravel under the wheels of the truck. I look up. I'm drifting off the road. I yank on the wheel to correct myself, but it's too late, and the truck plows into a mailbox. It flips up into the windshield, sending a small cobweb of cracks in the corner where it strikes, before flipping over the top of the truck. The truck fishtails, and for one agonizing second, I think I'm heading for the ditch. I grip the wheel and try to hold it steady. The tires scream across the pavement, and the truck corrects itself. Adrenaline courses through me. I can taste the bitterness in my mouth. My heart has been pounding since I saw Laura in the crowd. I scream in frustration and punch the steering wheel.

One last turn onto Normandy Lane, and it's a straight half-mile shot home. I keep my foot on the gas, topping eighty miles an hour as the house comes into view. I crest the last small hill, and the truck's tires briefly rise off the road before crashing down again.

The lights in the house are still on from when I left them on for Murphy. I whip the truck into the driveway, and past the pond, spraying gravel behind me. I bring the truck to a sliding stop in front of the porch.

The front door of the house is open.

I leap out of the truck and hurtle up the steps. Tears are starting to fall from my eyes.

"Murphy!" I yell as I enter the front hall. "Murphy! Here, boy!"

There's no answer. No familiar sound of paws across the floor. I check behind the couch.

"Murphy!"

I know the horrible truth, but I can't accept it. He's not here.

I run to the study.

"Murph—?"

Murphy's bed has been dragged to the middle of the room. Sitting in the bed is a cheap cell phone and a Polaroid. I walk over and pick them up.

Murphy stares at me from the photo. There is a hand, reaching in from out of frame, holding his collar. He looks scared. His head is down, but his eyes are looking at the camera, like he doesn't understand. Every human who has ever come in contact with him has shown him nothing but love.

There's a message written in the margin below the picture.

You can save him, but you can't save yourself. You left me in that room to rot. Before you sleep, you have to know everything you took from me.

I turn on the phone. There are no contact numbers or any extra features. It's a burner phone, just like the one I carried around those years when I worked for Reggie. I assume that this is how she, whoever she is, will communicate with me.

I walk back to the front hall in a daze, staring at the phone, and stop at the door.

I tuck the phone and Polaroid into my pocket, and crouch down to inspect the lock.

It hasn't been forced.

I look out into the night, past the light that spills from the open door, to the tree line.

How? How did she get in without—?

My eyes drift to the cottage.

I begin walking. I use the back of my hand to wipe away the tears of frustration and anger. I can't believe I've been this stupid. I can't believe I didn't realize the danger I was in from the moment I found the guestbook that morning. Now, she has Murphy.

I twist the key in the lock, and nearly kick open the cottage door. It's freezing in here, due to the fact that no one has used it for days. I snap on the light, which allows me to see my breath, as I move through the living room to the hall. I open the closet door and pull the chain overhead. The single bulb bursts to life. The vacuum cleaner stands at the ready, and the stacks of towels are on the shelf, right where I left them. I go up on my tiptoes and feel around the back of the top shelf. I find the ceramic dish, hidden behind the towels, and bring it down. I know the answer, but I take the lid off, anyway.

The keys are gone.

This is how she did it. This is how she got into the shop. This is how she got into my house tonight.

"Fuck!" I scream, and hurl the dish at the wall. It cracks the drywall and shatters into dozens of sharp, jagged pieces.

*

The raging fire chews through the dozens of stick dolls.

The pile is so high, it overflows the circular fire pit. I can feel the heat from the flames on my cheeks as I keep my eyes on the woods. The light from the flickering flames gives the illusion of movement to the trees. I know the glowing ashes drifting upwards are dangerous if they settle onto the roof of the cottage, but I don't care.

The last thing I pull from the bag that contained the stick dolls is Laura's music box.

I open it. There is still a little tension left in its gears from when I closed it before in the woods. The song begins to play at a slow, tortured pace. The ballerina barely turns.

I toss it on the fire.

I watch as the flames reach around the open lid. The notes continue to chime, but they come further and further apart. The ballerina blackens as the intense flames close in. The notes stop, and the box begins to pop and hiss.

I look out into the woods.

"You're there, aren't you?" I quietly say, then yell, "You're there, aren't you?!"

My voice echoes through the trees. I wait for an answer that I know isn't coming.

"You're not her. You're not Laura!"

The flames continue to eat into the ballerina. I keep my eyes on the dancing shadows of the trees.

"I don't know who you are or what you want, but you need to know this—if you hurt that dog, you had better just kill me … because I will sure as hell kill you."

I stand there at the fire for hours until it has almost completely burnt itself out, never looking away from the trees.

I don't go back to the house. Instead, I go into the bedroom of the cottage.

There's something about being in this room—the room where she's been, whoever she was. The woman I saw tonight was not

Rebecca Lowden. It wasn't Laura, either, no matter how much she looked like her. It can't be, but she did look older, like she was the right age. I glance over to the mirror in the corner of the room. The wasted remains of my make-up are more hideous and grotesque than any professional make-up artist could ever achieve.

I pull myself onto the bed, not giving a damn about getting make-up on the sheets. I don't care about anything in this cottage anymore. No one is going to stay here, ever again.

I lose track of time. I don't know how long I've been lying here, staring at this phone she left me. I don't think I fell asleep but the pitch black outside the window is transitioning to the deepest shade of blue, signaling that the sun is on its way.

I'm trying to formulate a plan. I can't wait for her to call me. I'll go mad, and I don't want to play her game by the rules she's trying to set. I need some sort of counter-play. I can't go to the police. I can't explain this to them, but I want help. I want people to be on the lookout for Murphy. In addition to possibly getting him back, it will lead me to her. I'll tell people he ran away, and was last spotted with a woman who has red hair and a scar. I'll post flyers around town. It's all I can come up with at four in the morning after one of the most insane days of my life, and I want to start fighting back, now.

I need a photo for a flyer.

When I went to the shelter to pick out Murphy, there was a wall full of flyers for missing pets. While they were filling out Murphy's paperwork, I stared at the wall. The photos broke my heart.

"Have you seen any of them?" the woman behind the desk asked.

"No. It's so sad."

"I know. Hopefully, you'll never have to use this advice, but just in case your dog ever goes missing, use the best photo you have of them on the flyers. You want people to remember him."

"Got it."

So, I needed to find the best picture of Murphy I have.

I know that there's a ton of them on my computer at the house, but there's also always a bunch on my phone. I take out my phone and begin thumbing through my gallery.

It's painful to flip through the photos. Each one is a reminder that I may never see him again. I clench my eyes shut and drive the thought from my mind. I can't go down that road.

The next-to-last photo is the one I took on the porch, the afternoon Rebecca Lowden arrived. It's the one where Murphy is lying on his back and the cottage is in the background between his open legs. Murphy's face is upside down. His jowls droop, and his tongue almost touches the floorboards. I laugh and choke up at the same time. It's a great photo. The only thing out of place is the car in the background, which had just pulled up when I took—

I sit up.

I move the photo so that the car is center frame.

I use my fingers to carefully zoom in.

It's blurry, but readable, just to the side of Murphy's right hind leg.

My feelings of helplessness vanish.

A fire ignites in my stomach.

I have a license plate, and I'm done playing defense.

Chapter 9

The sign above the small brick building proudly proclaims:

Royalty Car Rental
Where you're always treated like a King! … or a Queen!

I'm parked in my truck across the street, watching the front door, and sipping my venti coffee.

Normally, I'd do everything in my power to avoid giving a competitor any money, but I haven't slept, I need the caffeine, and their coffee's not bad.

"A large coffee, please," I told the barista.

He smiled at me. "Do you mean "venti"?"

"We're not fucking doing this today," I replied.

Once I fiddled with the picture of the car so that I could clearly read the license plate, I went back to the house, and fired up the computer. If I had been trying to find the owner of a car based on the license plate twenty years ago, I would have had to go to the DMV, fill out a form, and wait six weeks for them to get back to me. Now, I can get the results instantaneously online for the low price of $40. Thank God for the internet.

The car rented by the woman posing as Rebecca Lowden

belonged to the fleet of Royalty Car Rental in Hammersmith—a short, thirty-minute drive from The Hollows.

I went to the Royalty Car Rental's website. Thankfully, it was a smaller operation, and not some big, national car rental chain, which would have made things much more difficult. On their website, they had a "Meet the Team" section with photos. There was a group photo on the page and then individual photos of the associates with their bios. I needed to find the associate who stood out from the rest—the one who wasn't really part of the team. I didn't want the Employee of the Month—quite the opposite. I wanted the one who was possibly the most willing to break the rules if the price was right.

The horse I picked was a rental associate named Derrick Slauson. From his picture on the website, I'd say he's in his mid-twenties. In the group photo, his hair and clothes were much less tidy than his coworkers, and his smile was the definition of "uninvolved". His prematurely aged face also indicated that he was a smoker.

I arrived in Hammersmith well before Royalty Car Rental opened, hit up an ATM next to the Starbucks, and set up shop across the street with my coffee.

I watch the staff arrive and go through the front door. The first person to arrive is Mr Martzen, the manager. Everyone else begins arriving a few minutes later. Nine o'clock rolls around and there's still no sign of Derrick Slauson. I'm worried that he's no longer employed by Royalty Car Rental, and they haven't updated the website.

It gets to the point that I take out my phone and pull up the website to find another target, when a beat-up Saturn turns into the parking lot. Derrick Slauson gets out and hurries through the front door. He's late, reinforcing everything I had hoped about him.

Perfect.

Now, it's a waiting game until lunch.

I move the truck, and park in a spot where I can see not only the front entrance, but the side door, as well. I use the time to return some emails and texts, most of which are about the costume contest. Sandy's written an email. She normally prefers to call or text, so an email is an indication of how worried she is. I briefly write her back to assure her that everything is fine, and that everyone is getting paid while we're closed. I end the email by encouraging her to enjoy her time off, but I know she won't.

There's not much in the way of customers coming and going from Royalty Car Rental. As lunch nears, I put away my phone and keep a constant eye on the doors. Without the busy work of emails and text messages to keep me distracted, thoughts of Murphy creep into my head.

There's no way she would hurt a dog. No way. No matter how crazy she is, and she has to be crazy, right? She's gone to these lengths to mess with me; she has to be crazy. But if I'm so convinced that she's crazy, how can I be certain that she won't hurt Murphy?

I'm saved from any further mental torture by the emergence of Derrick Slauson from the side entrance of the building. He turns and starts walking to the neighboring strip mall, which is home to a deli, a liquor store, a Chinese take-out, and a Chili's.

Thankfully, he's alone.

I hop out of the truck and cross the street. I hastily catch up with him as he reaches for the door handle of the Chinese take-out place.

"Hi, uh, Derrick?" I ask.

He stops and turns to me. He looks around before answering, "Yeah?"

"You work at Royalty Car Rental, right?" I ask, with a thumb over my shoulder towards the building.

"Yeah."

"Great. My name is Matt Becker. Nice to meet you." I hold out my hand. He regards it for a few moments and weakly shakes it.

"Hi …"

"Listen," I say, reaching for my wallet. "I was wondering if you could do me a favor."

"… Okay."

"Let me buy you lunch?" I ask, holding my wallet open just enough so he can see the multiple one hundred-dollar bills inside.

He's interested, but still suspicious. "I don't eat that much."

"Yeah, I know. It's a business thing."

*

Fifteen minutes later, we're sitting at a table in Chili's.

"How long is your lunch break?" I ask.

He sucks on the straw, downing the better part of the blended beverage the Chili's waitress delivered less than five minutes ago. "It's an hour. I've got plenty of time."

"Great," I say, over my glass of water. "So, do you like your job at Royalty?"

He blinks, fighting off the brain-freeze he's brought on himself. "It's a job."

"How long have you been there?"

"About a year. Why?"

"I need a favor."

"What's the favor?"

"A few days ago, someone rented a car from your place. I've got the license plate number. I need you to tell me the name of the person who rented it."

He shakes off the brain-freeze. "You're going to need more than three hundred. I could get fired."

"No one's going to know."

"Why do you want to know who rented the car?"

"That's my business. You can find out, right?"

"Sure. I'm just not sure it's worth three hundred bucks."

"Come on. What are you pulling in over there? You're probably part-time, barely making over minimum wage with no benefits, yeah?"

He shrugs. "That's my business." He takes down the rest of his drink, pleased at his cleverness of using my own words against me.

"Go easy on those, okay? I don't want you getting fired for being drunk on the job."

"Look, man, I don't really need this." He gets up to leave. "So, thanks for the lunch and the mai tais, and you can try your luck with someone else."

"Fine, fine, fine. How much would it take to make you 'need this'?"

He makes a show of thinking it over, and sits back down. "How many hundreds you got in there?"

"You're good, I'll give you that, but I'm not going to tell you."

He mulls the slushy remains of his mai tai. "I'll do it for a grand."

I quickly grab the attention of our server as she passes. "Can I get the check?"

She nods.

"Wait. Hold on," he says. "We're negotiating, all right?"

"Negotiations just ended."

"You could make a counter-offer."

"Here's my counter-offer—I can go into your work, find your boss, his name is Mr Martzen, right?" The fact that I know his boss's name unnerves him. "I go in there, and tell Mr Martzen that I asked for a customer's personal information, and you were willing to give it. Then, you won't have the money, and you'll be out of a job."

"Oh, come on. You don't— I was trying to— We're just talking, okay? We're cool."

The bubbly server returns, drops the check, thanks us, and leaves.

I open the check presenter, eye Derrick, and return the bill to the table. "I guess we don't have to go anywhere, just yet."

He sighs. "Good."

There's a long moment where we size each other up, waiting for the other to reopen the negotiations.

I need to get this going, so I'm the first to cave. "I'll give you five hundred. Final offer. For that, I want a name and an address."

He considers it, and nods. "Deal."

*

I lead him out of the Chili's and to the liquor store next to the Chinese take-out.

"You're a smoker, right?" I ask.

"I quit two months ago."

"Well, today, you're going to relapse." I take two one-hundred-dollar bills out of my wallet, and hand them to him. "The rest you get when it's done, okay?"

He nods.

I hold the door open and we go inside.

We're greeted by the *bing-bong* of the door chimes. I take him over to the counter and point to the various packs of cigarettes in the display.

"Pick your brand."

"Uh, Marlboro Reds."

"One pack of Marlboro Reds," I tell the clerk.

She takes a pack and places it on the counter. I pay for them, and push the pack into his chest.

"How long will it take you to get the records?"

"I don't know. Like, five minutes, maybe."

"Okay, here's what you're going to do," I say, leading him back outside. "Find the records and write them down on a slip of paper. Then, you're going to have a nicotine fit, and need to head outside for a smoke break. Is anyone going to question that?"

He shakes his head.

"Great. Walk outside and bring me the paper. This will all be over, and you'll be five hundred dollars richer."

"Wouldn't it be easier for me just to text you the name and address, or something?"

"No. I don't want any records of this, okay?"

For some reason, that rattles him. He still has the two one hundred-dollar bills in his hand, but he suddenly looks at them like their used tissues.

"What's the problem?" I ask.

"I'm … I'm having second thoughts."

"Derrick, in ten minutes, you'll be five hundred dollars richer, okay?"

He still hesitates.

"I'm kind of in a time crunch, Derrick. I need to know if we're going to have to go the Mr Martzen route—"

"Okay, okay, okay. I'll be out in a minute."

He jams the cash in his pockets, and heads off in the direction of Royalty Car Rental.

I watch him disappear through the door, and I begin pacing behind the strip mall, incessantly checking the time on my phone.

Ten minutes pass. Then twenty. Then thirty.

I finally stop pacing, and stare at the door to Royalty Car Rental.

Something's wrong. He got caught, or he's not going through with it. I don't know what it is, but something's up.

I curse under my breath and start trying to think of other options. There are none. This is it.

Thirty minutes becomes forty. Forty stretches into fifty. An hour.

"Fuck it," I mumble, and start walking.

I reach the entrance of the building. I grip the handle of the door and yank it open.

There's a reception desk with cubicles arranged behind it. Right away, I spot Derrick, sitting at his desk. There's a large, windowed office at the back of the room. Through the window,

I can see Mr Martzen. He's talking on the phone, and he damn well sees me.

A charming girl in a button-down shirt, name tag, and khakis, sitting at the front desk tries to engage me.

"Hello. Welcome to Royalty Car Rental. How can I help you?"

I glance at Derrick. He's trying to pretend that he doesn't see me.

I point to Mr Martzen, through the window.

"I need to talk to that guy, right there," I say, loud enough for the whole office to hear.

Looking directly at me, Martzen speaks into his phone and hangs up. He steps out of his office and starts walking towards the main desk.

"Um, sure. I can have Mr Martzen speak to you," the girl says. "If you'd like to take a seat—"

"It's all right, Kelly," Martzen says, cutting her off, while keeping his eyes on me.

I haven't slept in over two days, so I'm sure my appearance warrants caution.

"Is there something I can help you with?" he asks.

"Boy, is there ever," I say, casting a glance over to Derrick.

Derrick springs from his cubicle, and hustles over to us.

"Mr Becker," he says, trying to sound cheerful. "I'm so sorry, I didn't recognize you when you walked in. I meant to return your call to let you know that yes, I do have that Ford Explorer you were asking me about buying." He turns to Martzen. "I'm sorry, Mr Martzen. This is Mr Becker. He and I have been in contact about purchasing that 2015 Ford Explorer from us." Derrick turns to me. "If you'd like, I'd be more than happy to show it to you right now, Mr Becker."

I look between Slauson and Martzen. "That'd be great."

Martzen is baffled.

"Right this way," Derrick says, motioning to the door.

He leads me out the door and into the parking lot. Neither of us says a word as we head to a corner of the lot and stop next to a Ford Explorer.

"Well?" I ask.

"Just keep staring at the car like you're thinking about buying it," he says, gesturing with his hands towards the Explorer, like he's showing it off.

"What the hell happened?" I hiss. "Do you have the name?"

"Yeah, I got it."

I wait for him to hand it over.

"Derrick—?"

"Why do you want it?"

I turn to him. "What?"

"Keep looking at the car," he says.

I do.

"Why do you want the name and address?" he asks, again.

"I told you, that's not your business."

He bites his lower lip. "It's just that I thought you were looking for a guy."

I don't reply.

"We keep scans of the driver's licenses. I pulled up the records and saw her picture."

"So?"

"She's pretty."

"What does that have to do with anything?"

He hesitates. "You're not some sort of crazy stalker ex-boyfriend, are you?"

"If I was an ex-boyfriend, don't you think I'd know her name?"

It wasn't the answer he's looking for.

"Listen, Derrick. I promise, I just want to talk to her."

"Why?"

"Because she has something of mine. I have to get it back."

He glances over his shoulder towards the building. His frustration builds. He jams his hand into his pocket and pulls out a slip of paper. "Her name is Veronica Sanders."

I quickly take the slip of paper from his hand and stuff it into my pocket.

"What about the address?"

His jaw hardens. "I'm not comfortable giving you that. I'm sure you have ways of finding that out on your own, now that you have her name. Don't ask me why that makes me feel better. You say you just want to talk to her? Why should I believe you?"

"Derrick, trust me—"

"Trust you?" he snorts. "Why should I trust you? Is your name really even Matt Becker?"

My hesitation tells him that it isn't.

"Yeah … So, her name is all you're going to get from me." He produces the pack of cigarettes I just bought for him, takes one out, and stuffs one end in his mouth. He also takes out a lighter, lights the cigarette, and takes a long drag. "I'll keep the two hundred. You can keep the other three, and I never see you, again. Deal?"

I nod. "Deal."

He takes another long drag, drops the cigarette onto the ground, and crushes it under his heel. He turns and starts walking back to the small, brick building.

"Thank you for showing me the car," I call after him.

He turns. "You're welcome, Mr Becker," he answers, while discreetly flipping me off.

Chapter 10

Night has fallen by the time I park the truck in the gravel lot.

"You've got to be kidding me," I say from behind the wheel, staring up at the blinking neon sign that casts a sickly glow over the dashboard.

> *Whispers*
> *Cocktails! All Nude! Private Dances!*

Derrick Slauson's attempt to protect Veronica Sanders had been partially successful. I couldn't find her home address, but I did find her Instagram account.

Earlier this afternoon, she posted, "Come see me tonight! Only one dance! Who's it gonna be?!" It was accompanied by a photo and a tiny url that linked to her place of employment—Whispers Gentlemen's Club, halfway between Burlington and The Hollows. Veronica Sanders is not the woman I saw last night at the parade. She's not the one who has Murphy, but she is the woman who posed as Rebecca Lowden, and I need to know who sent her. I've got a hunch that she doesn't know what's happening, but she's the only lead I've got.

The Polaroid of Murphy is sitting on the passenger seat. I tuck it into my back pocket, get out of the truck, and start walking towards the front entrance. This place is in the middle of nowhere. I get it. It's a place where you're not going to bump into anyone you know who's not there for the same reason you are. I show my ID to the doorman, who waves me through without looking up from his phone.

Once inside, I'm greeted by the aroma of stale beer, which reminds of the countless frat houses I used to visit in the days of Reggie's employment. The lighting is low, and only slightly brighter near the stage. There's a mirrored ball hanging from the ceiling that slowly twists, casting spots of light over everything and everyone. The music is cranked up to a headache-inducing level. I've never been to a strip club before. They're just not my thing. In my opinion, this is what the internet is for.

For being in the middle of nowhere, it's surprisingly busy. There's not a seat available near the stage, where two women in thongs, high heels, and nothing else dance under the red and blue lights. One is working the pole, while the other seductively crawls to a group of guys sitting next to the stage, who are waving dollar bills. There are two bouncers stationed at either side of the stage, making sure the patrons keep their hands to themselves.

Veronica's not up there, so I scan the room to see if she might be behind the bar, or one of the handful of girls serving drinks.

I'm startled by the tap on my shoulder. I turn to see the doorman smiling at me.

"You okay?" he asks, shouting over the music.

"I'm fine."

"First time?"

"Yeah."

"You can sit anywhere you like. One of the girls will be with you in a second."

"Thanks."

"Two-drink minimum."

"Got it."

He goes back to his phone, and steps back outside.

I find my way to a booth in the corner and slide in. I position myself to keep as much of the place in view as possible, but there are nooks and crannies everywhere. The shadows are almost impenetrable. It's a place designed for customers to keep their anonymity.

Next to the stage, there's an opening to a corridor. As I watch, the group of guys next to the stage head over to the bouncer and flash him some money. He leads them into the corridor to an open door that's just in my field of view, and they go inside. A few moments later, a blond girl in fishnets, thong, heels, and pasties over her nipples appears from behind the curtain on the stage, goes down the steps, and heads down the corridor, escorted by the bouncer. He opens the door for her, and she enters. He then stands guard at the door. I'm not entirely up to speed on strip club procedure, but through there has to be the VIP rooms.

"Something to drink?"

I snap out of my observations to see a cocktail waitress next to my table. She has flowing black hair, heavy eye-shadow that makes her eyes pop, and a tight corset, which is struggling to contain her breasts.

"Can I get a Bud Lite?"

"Sure," she says, making a note in her check pad. "You know it's a two-drink minimum, right?"

"Yeah. They told me."

She nods and goes off.

I turn my attention back to the stage, where the two girls continue dancing. The pounding bass shakes the booth, and my ears are ringing, but my eyes are starting to adjust to the surroundings. It's easier to keep track of the movements around the floor, but I still don't see Veronica.

The song wraps up to cheering and catcalls. The two dancers gather the money that litters the stage.

A booming, base-distorted voice comes over the sound system. "All right, everyone! Give it up for Amber and Cherie! They're working hard for you. Show them some love!"

A few more bills fall onto the stage and are quickly scooped up. The girls blow kisses to the surrounding men and disappear behind the curtain.

"Don't forget to take care of your servers! They're working hard for you, too. Stay hydrated! Keep ordering those drinks! And if you want some private entertainment with any of our beautiful dancers, we've got private booths and VIP rooms. Just let Hank over there by the stage know, and he can set that up for you!"

The bouncer by the corridor raises his hand to indicate to everyone that he is Hank.

"All right, let's keep this party going!" the DJ continues. "Next up to the stage is the lovely, talented, smoking-hot Ashley! Give it up for Ashley!"

A tall, lithe girl emerges from behind the curtain as a new song begins to play. She effortlessly drapes her body around the pole and spins. The patrons surrounding the stage cheer and extend their dollar bills.

I stop paying attention to her and go back to scanning the floor. The cocktail server arrives with my beer.

"Bud Lite," she says, placing it on the table.

"How much?" I ask, going for my wallet.

"Eight bucks," she says.

I take out a twenty and hand it to her. "Keep it."

Her face lights up, and she gives me a wink. "Thanks." She tucks it into her corset. "Let me know if you need anything else."

"Will do."

I have no intention of drinking my beer. Between the stress and lack of sleep, if I have a sip of alcohol, I'll be in trouble. I need to stay sharp. I still have plenty of cash at the ready from this morning.

I keep a lookout in case Veronica has slipped on to the floor without my noticing. I check the burner phone, which has no messages, and my personal phone, which only has messages from Sandy.

The song reaches its conclusion. Ashley has her legs wrapped around the pole. She leans back, and does one last rotation with her torso parallel to the floor. She pulls herself back up, and slides all the way down the pole. She playfully crawls across the stage to take the money from her admirers. She allows a few of them who are holding larger bills to tuck them into her G-string.

"Ashley! Ashley! Ashley!" the voice booms over the speakers. "Give it up, guys! Keep those dollars coming! Keep those drinks flowing! Next up to the stage, please welcome the ever-so-delicious, the ever-so-sensual, the ever-so-sexy Veronica!"

A slower, sultrier song begins to play.

I sit up in my seat and lock my eyes onto the stage.

The intro to the song plays, beginning with heightening notes that crash into a guitar melody. She steps out from behind the curtain. The guys roar their approval.

It's her—the woman who passed herself off as Rebecca Lowden, but not the woman I saw yesterday at the celebration in The Hollows. I have a hunch Veronica Sanders doesn't know what she's become a part of.

Like the dancers before her, she's only wearing heels and a thong. Unlike the other dancers, her routine is slow, seductive, and hypnotic. The shoddy red hair dye from the day we met is gone, replaced by her natural brunette. She's undoubtedly beautiful. The crowd agrees, not by applause, but by its muted response. Everyone watching is mesmerized. She's not doing a pole dancing routine. This is performance art. She plays to the guys next to the stage, but not nearly as much as the other dancers. She takes in the whole room. From the moment she begins to move, she has everyone under her spell.

The song builds towards its climax, she slinks up the pole, holds it with one hand while facing the crowd, crosses her legs around the pole behind her, and spins. On the last note, the lights go out. Everyone cheers, but there is the noted absence of catcalls, and whistling. The lights come back up, and she smiles. She playfully picks up the bills that carpet the stage. Arms reach out to eagerly tuck bills into her G-string. She has to have just made hundreds of dollars in a matter of minutes.

I get ready to make a beeline for Hank, but I don't want to approach the stage while she's still there. I don't want her to see me. Not yet.

She scoops up the last bill, winks, and disappears behind the curtain.

I'm out of the booth and heading for the side of the stage before the curtain stops moving. Two other guys have also left their seats and are approaching Hank.

"Oh my, Veronica!" the DJ calls. "Give it up for Veronica one more time! We're gonna take a little break to give you guys a chance to grab another drink. Maybe get yourself a private dance with any of the lovely ladies you've seen here tonight! Don't go anywhere! We still have some of the hottest ladies who want to have some fun with you coming up in just a few minutes, here at Whispers!"

The music resumes, but the volume is mercifully lower. Conversations, however, still require almost shouting.

I reach the side of the stage. The two guys have already beaten me there and are talking to Hank. One of them is a middle-aged businessman. The other looks like he's in his mid-twenties, lanky, and wearing glasses. Both of them have money in their hands.

Hank looks at me as I take my place next to them.

"You here for Veronica?" he asks.

"Yeah."

"All right, gentlemen," he says with all the panache of an auctioneer. "Here's the deal. She only does one VIP dance. It's up to you to decide who it's gonna be. Got it?"

We all nod.

"All right, let's do it. Who's gonna start?"

We glance at each other. The lanky guy chimes in. "Two hundred dollars."

Hank gives him a look of pity. "All right, we're starting with the lowball." Hank turns to the businessman. "You gonna do better?"

"Three hundred," the businessman says with a little more confidence than Lanky.

"Five," I say, almost on top of him.

"There we go. There we go." Hank nods, and turns back to the young guy. "You still in, Poindexter?"

He hangs his head, and goes back to his lonely table.

"Have a good evening," Hank calls after him. "All right, gentlemen. It's heads up poker time. My man here bid five hundred. You willing to do five-fifty?"

The businessman nods.

"Six," I immediately reply.

"My man says six. You got six fifty?"

The businessman hesitates, and then nods.

"Seven," I say.

Even Hank is a little shocked by my brazenness.

"My man here wants it," he says, admiringly. He turns his attention to the businessman. "All right, we're at seven. You still in? You've seen the goods. You know she's worth it."

The businessman thinks. I'm pretty sure he's got the cash on him.

"Seven-fifty," I say.

They both stare at me.

"You have to let the man bid," Hank says.

"Let him bid eight hundred if he wants to."

This is insane, I know, but I'm not going to take the chance of waiting until the end of the night to catch Veronica in the parking lot. I'm sure Hank will probably walk her out, and I'll get nowhere. I have to get this dance. I don't care about the cost.

The businessman looks at me. "Have fun," he says in a tone that suggests I should do something else.

Now that I'm alone with Hank, he gives me his full attention. "You ever been here, before?"

"No."

"Well, I like your style. Gotta admire a man who knows what he wants. Let me see the cash."

I open my wallet so that he can see inside. There's a lot more than the seven-fifty in there.

"Damn, you came to play." He shakes my hand in admiration. My hand is swallowed up inside his vice grip. This guy is a mountain. "Follow me."

He leads me down the darkened corridor. There are curtained booths near the entrance and doors at the back. Some of the curtains are open to reveal empty chairs next to poles that run from the floor to the ceiling. Others are closed and have bouncers stationed outside. Hank leads me to one of the open doors.

"All right, let me explain the rules to you. You're gonna get two songs. You have to remain seated with your hands underneath you. Got it?"

I nod.

"She can touch you. You cannot touch her. I'm going to be right outside this door. You do anything stupid, I'm gonna come in there and fuck you up. Understand?"

"Yeah."

He smiles to let me know that we're cool. "Just something I have to say. You're spending the cash, so I assume you know how this works."

"Yep."

"It's a lot to splash out, but Veronica will be very appreciative."

"Great," I say, eager to get this thing going.

He laughs. "All right, man. I get it. I get it. I'll take the cash and you can enjoy the dance."

I hand him the money.

"Thank you." He takes hold of the door and gestures inside. "Make yourself comfortable, and I'll go get her."

I step through the door.

"Be right back," he says, and closes it.

The room is lit by the purple neon lights overheard. There are smaller, spinning lights mounted next to speakers in the corners. The effect mimics the lighting in the main room. There's a black vinyl bench against the wall, and a solitary pole in the center of the room. I walk around the pole to the bench, and hesitate before sitting. For a moment, I really wish I carried some disinfectant wipes. I shake my head, sit down, and wait … and wait.

It's taking forever. At least, I think it is. Instead of sitting in a strip club VIP room, waiting for a lap dance, I feel like I'm waiting in a doctor's office. I try to listen for the sound of approaching footsteps, but the thumping speakers rule out any advance warning.

I haven't even thought of what I'm going to say. I've been so bent on tracking her down, I haven't formulated what I might—

The knob turns, and the door opens. Music from the main room floods in.

There she is.

She's standing in the doorway, looking off in Hank's direction.

"Thank you, Hank." She smiles, and then steps into the room, closing the door behind her. She's still in high heels, a thong, and nothing else. She beams as she turns to me. "I don't know who you are, mister, but I hope you are ready for one hell of a dance." She finally gets a good look at me. There's the hesitation, then the slow realization that she's seen me before. Then comes the recognition. Now, the fear.

"… shit …" she whispers.

I stand up. "Wait!"

She turns to the door. "Hank!"

I take two steps towards her. "No! Hold on! I just want—!"

The door flies open, and Hank busts in, ready for business. He sees me standing, and his eyes flash.

"What the fuck is going on?" he asks.

"No, this isn't— I only wanted to—"

"Why are you standing up? I told you, you've gotta be seated with your hands under you. What's so hard about that?"

Veronica moves backwards, and Hank steps between us.

"I just wanted to talk to her," I plead.

"We don't do that talking shit, here."

A moment ago, Hank and I were friends. Now, he's ready to kick my ass.

"I need to talk to you!" I shout over Hank's shoulder at Veronica.

"She don't want to talk to you, man."

"You have to tell me who put you up to it!" I yell towards Veronica. "I have to know!"

Her eyes go wide.

Hank steps closer. "We ain't got time for the weirdos and the crazies. You gotta go."

I'm blowing my chance, and if I don't talk to her tonight, I'll never get near her again. Panic sets in.

"Please! Listen to me! Just listen!" I begin to reach for my back pocket.

Veronica lets out a sharp gasp.

"Hey!" Hank charges forward, locks my arm with his massive hand, and grabs my neck with the other. He spins me, and slams me up against the wall. "Don't you fucking move!"

"No! Please, listen to me!"

"Shut the fuck up!" Hank yells.

"She took my dog!" I shout, straining to look at Veronica.

My comment is so out of left field, that Hank blinks. His grip loosens by a fraction. "The fuck did you just say?"

I take the opportunity to pull in a breath, but don't fight his grip. I nod towards Veronica. "She knows what I'm talking about."

Hank glances over his shoulder at Veronica. She's tense, but it's obvious that she does know something, and she's listening.

Hank turns back to me, his face inches from mine. "Keep talking."

"Veronica, that crazy woman took my dog, and I need your help. In my back pocket, there's a photo this woman left for me. I can show it to you so you know I'm not lying. That's what I was reaching for."

Hank glances over his shoulder and waits for instructions from Veronica.

She watches me, and nods.

Hank relaxes his grip. "You go slow. Got it?"

"Yeah. I got it."

He lets go of my arm, but keeps the other hand on my throat.

As instructed, I slowly reach back and take the Polaroid out of my pocket. I bring it around in a wide arc, so Hank can see it coming. He takes it from my hand and studies it. He hands it to Veronica, who brings it close to her face so she can see it in the low light.

Her shoulders drop. "Shit … You can let him go, Hank."

He does so, but stays ready for action in case I make any sudden moves.

Veronica looks at me, not knowing what to say.

"Listen," I say as calmly as possible. "I don't think you knew what was going to happen, but you're the only hope I have of finding her and getting my dog back. Okay?"

She glances at the photo again.

"All I want to do is talk," I repeat.

She looks up and sighs. "Hank, can you please bring me a robe from the dressing room?"

He gives me one last threatening glance. "Sure thing," he says, and leaves.

She hands me the photo. "Let's go somewhere a bit quieter."

*

We're standing under the harsh halogen lamp mounted to the wall over the back door of Whispers. Wrapped in a thick robe against the cold, she lights a cigarette. I'm gingerly massaging the spot on my arm where Hank had me on lockdown.

"You okay?" she asks.

"I'm all right. Aren't you cold?"

She shrugs, takes another drag, and leans against the wall.

"So, what do you want to know?"

"First off, did she give you a name?"

"No."

"Of course not. That would be too easy," I say, more to myself than to her. "Then tell me everything you remember."

She collects her thoughts over another inhalation of smoke. Her cigarette is going quick. She blows the column of smoke into the air as she begins speaking.

"She came in a few months ago. I didn't think anything of it. We get women in here all the time. She was wearing this old baseball hat and her was hair down, like she was trying to hide her face. That's not anything new, either. You should see some of the stuff the guys do. They're so afraid of running into their neighbor or their wife that they dress like they're in a spy novel, you know? Anyway, one night, she sees me on stage and pays Hank a shit ton of money for a dance."

She looks at me, and lets out a little laugh. "Kinda like you. So, I go to the room and she's there, sitting down. I start doing my thing, and she says that she just wants to talk. Again, kind of like you." Veronica takes another drag. "I hate the talkers. I hate the people who either say they want to save you or they want to

181

fuck you. I don't need saving. I'll bet I make twice as much as they do, and in half the time."

After watching her on stage, I believe it.

"Anyway, I tell her that I'm not interested in a personal connection, and she says that it's a business thing. Says she'll give me five thousand dollars for one night's work. I'm thinking that she's got to be talking about sex, right? I tell her no way. I'm not sleeping with her. She says that it has nothing to do with sex, it's not illegal, and I won't have to touch anyone. All I'll have to do is a bit of acting. She gives me a thousand bucks cash, in addition to what she's paid for the dance, and calls it a down payment. She tells me to meet her at this coffee place in Burlington the next day, and she'll give me another grand just to hear her out. After that, she got up and left. I figure, hey, I could use another thousand dollars just to hear her out and then tell her no, whatever it is she wants me to do. So, I meet her the next day and we—"

"What did she look like?" I interject.

Veronica cocks her head. "She was tall. She had red hair, and was wearing that baseball hat again. Gray jacket, I think, and blue jeans."

"Did she have a scar, right here?" I ask, pointing to a spot above my eye.

"Yeah. That's her."

"What color were her eyes?"

"Green."

"Not blue?"

"No."

I always knew that whoever I had seen was not Laura. It couldn't be. This sealed it. Whoever she was, she had gone out of her way, even giving herself a scar and dyeing her hair, but the eyes weren't lying. She had been wearing contacts when I saw her.

"She was cute, but not my type," Veronica continues, tapping

182

the butt of her cigarette. The ashes drift to the ground like snow.

"Then, what?" I ask.

"She lays out this plan. She says that for one night, I'm supposed to pretend to be someone named Rebecca Lowden. She gives me a backstory that I'm supposed to memorize and then, I'm supposed to mess with this guy—the guy being you."

"Yeah. I figured that out. Did she tell you about Be Our Guest?"

She nods. "She said you might ask about it, so she filled me in a little. She said she'd make the profile and book the reservation. She also showed me your page and pictures of the cottage. She was really insistent about that stick thing in the living room. Told me to make sure that you saw me with it, and that I should just kind of fuck with you."

"What about your hair?"

She rolls her eyes. "Oh, yeah. That was the other thing she was really hung up on. Said I needed to dye my hair red. I guess it was a thing with her, because she did it, too."

Whoever this woman is, she's gone way over the top to get the image of Laura in my head.

Veronica crushes the stub of her cigarette against the bricks, extracts another one from the pack in the pocket of her robe, and places it between her lips.

"Keep going," I say. "I'm kind of in a rush."

"I'm trying to remember, okay? Give me a second." She flicks her lighter and kisses the flame to the end of the new cigarette until it begins to glow. She pulls in a breath, savors it, and returns the pack and lighter to her pocket. "The hair thing was last minute, and it made me feel really weird. Also, she told me to leave your place early in the morning, and to keep the front door open. I asked her why, and she said not to worry about it … That felt a little creepy."

"Really? *That* was the point where it felt 'a little creepy'?"

She shrugs. "I thought that maybe she was just playing some

sort of prank on you. I didn't know that she was a complete psycho."

"The rental car—her idea or yours?"

"Mine. I didn't want to use my car because I worried you might use it to find me … Wait. Is that how you found me? The rental car?"

"Yep."

She blows smoke through her nose, and shakes her head. "Fuck … Well, you can tell how good I am at this shit. Whatever. She gave me another grand for listening, and says if I go through with it, I'll get three thousand more, once the job is done."

"You said yes?"

"Well, obviously. The day I left your place, I showed up for work, and there was an envelope waiting for me with three thousand dollars in it. That's the last I heard from her."

"Did you write that message in the guestbook?"

"What message?"

"Did you take the keys from the closet?"

"What keys? What message? What are you talking about?"

"Never mind."

She waits for some further explanation but gives up.

"Anything else?" she asks.

I'm going over her story, trying to find anything that I can use, and coming up empty. "She never gave you any sort of name? Not even just something to call her?"

"No."

"Nothing else? You didn't see what kind of car she drove?"

"No."

"What about her clothes? Anything unusual? Anything stand out?"

She takes a long drag on her cigarette. "Not really. Just the hat. It was old and beat up and had some sort of logo on it."

"What was the logo?"

"I don't know. I'd never seen it before. It was faded, but it looked like some sort of saber-toothed cat or something, with big fangs."

My heart skips in my chest. "Do you remember the colors?"

She blows an exasperated, smoke-filled sigh. "I don't know. It was old and beat up, but I think it was blue. Like, blue and gray."

Gotcha.

"That's all I need."

She stops. "Really? That's it?"

"Yeah. Thank you." I turn towards the door, eager to get going.

"Hey," she says.

I turn around.

"Why does she want to mess with you so bad?"

"I'm still trying to figure that out, but I won't know until I find out who she is."

"But you know something, don't you?"

"… yeah."

"Is it bad?"

"It's not your business."

She shrugs. "Fair point." She looks down, and scrapes the toe of her shoe thoughtfully on the pavement. "She took your dog?"

"Yeah."

She shakes her head. After a moment, she reaches into her robe and pulls out the money I gave Hank. "You can have this back."

I take it from her hand.

"Thank you."

"Don't thank me. It makes me feel like shit. Good luck."

*

I jump into the truck and fire up the engine. I crank the heat on high and warm air starts pumping from the vents.

It's not much, but it's a start.

Veronica Sanders may have no idea what that logo was, but I do. I saw it countless times on my rounds of pickups from various campuses. I had seen that very same logo on lots of hats topping a lot of heads.

That blue-and-gray, saber-toothed cat was Wild E. Cat, the official mascot of the University of New Hampshire, where Laura Aisling had spent her first year and a half of college before transferring to Wilton University.

Chapter 11

My body slides to a stop. My ears are ringing as the dust settles around me. Every bone in my body is broken, but I somehow manage to pull myself to my feet.

There's a wet, ragged whisper behind me.

"Jacob …"

I have to get away from that whisper.

I stumble forward and hit a wall. No. It's not a wall. It's a door—the steel door that was just blown apart a moment ago. It's in front of me. I look around. There's an unearthly dim light that gives off just enough illumination to see. I'm in a room—the room. The smell of rot and decay is overpowering. I reach for the handle of the door, but it's not there. It's on the other side.

There's a scraping sound behind me.

I don't want to look. I know what's there.

There's the scraping sound, again.

Don't turn around. Don't turn around.

I push against the door, but it won't budge.

There's the sound of someone breathing behind me. It's low, ragged, and wet.

I slam my fists into the door.

"Help! Somebody help me, please!"

Footsteps—slow, dragging.

Something touches my shoulder. I can feel the cold, rotting breath on my ear as it whispers, "Jacob ..."

My head flies up from my computer desk. I furiously wipe at my shoulder. I can still feel the pressure of whatever it was, touching me.

I breathlessly look around my study.

Outside, the sun is staring to rise. The computer is still on. I must have fallen asleep.

Last night, after I got home from Whispers, I went straight for the computer. Whoever has Murphy is somehow connected to Laura's time at New Hampshire University. I searched every possible angle on Laura's time there but found nothing. There are no records I could access that would tell me which dorm Laura lived in, or what clubs she may have belonged to. I scoured Facebook, Instagram, and even LinkedIn for any alumni that may have had a connection to her, but there are too many people who graduated from UNH. All I need is one connection—one person who might have known Laura.

I check the burner phone for any communications that might have arrived while I was asleep, but there are none. I go to the kitchen to make coffee. From the window, I look out at the tranquil morning. The pond is absolutely still. The cottage is dark. It's remarkable how much the trees have lost their leaves in the last few days. More and more, they look like dark, bony fingers, reaching up out of the ground behind the cottage.

The Polaroid of Murphy is on the counter. I try not to look at it. Every time I do, I feel like I'm having a heart attack, but I can't help myself. Seeing him alive in that photo keeps me from imagining the alternative.

I need to take a break before resuming my research of New Hampshire University. The last time I checked the clock before falling asleep, it was four a.m. It's now a little after seven. I've only had a short nap, and I'm fried.

I'll work for a little bit on the flier for Murphy. I want to get those up as soon as possible, so that people will start looking for him. I have to pick which picture to use.

I go back to the study, collapse the browser window that holds all the stuff I've found on UNH, and pull up my "photos" folder. They're in no particular order, so I use the preview function to flip through them. There are pictures of him sitting by the fire pit and splashing in the pond. There are photos of him with his red tennis ball, and even one of a road trip we took through Maine. For one of the photos, I recklessly took my eyes off the road for a moment to snap a photo of him with his head out the window as we drove. His jowls were flapping in the wind, sending ropes of spit everywhere. There's even one from the day I brought him home from the shelter. I need to create a backup for these. I need to print them out, and put them in a scrapbo—

A realization cuts through the fatigue, and I sit back.

"… holy shit …"

Laura's scrapbooks—the ones I saw in her dorm room. They must have given them to her mother.

She would still have them, right? She has to. She has to have kept them, and they might have the answer I'm looking for, but how can I see them?

There's no way that I can try to get them without arousing suspicion, but there's no other options. Maybe I'm wrong. Maybe she doesn't have them, but she might. The more I think about it, the more I'm convinced she has to still have them. There's no way the mother I saw in that news footage would destroy them, and it's the only thing I can think of that can give me any clues.

That's it. It's the only place I can think of to find answers.

I begin pacing around the house, trying to think of a way to approach her without alarming her. She doesn't know me.

We never met. How can I ask to see the scrapbooks without her thinking I had something to do with Laura's disappearance, which of course, I did?

The short answer is, I can't. It's too risky. I need another way to find what I—

The burner phone pings from the kitchen.

I race to the kitchen and snatch it off the counter. There's one message, but the number is blocked.

I open it.

Murphy.

He's lying on a concrete floor in a darkened room. He's hanging his head and looking up at the camera as if he's being scolded, but looks okay.

A moment later, a message appears below the photo.

You can save him but you can't save yourself. You have to know what you took from me. Then, you can sleep.

I put the phone down. I take deep breaths, and run my hands through my hair. I tense every muscle in my body, then slam my fist into the counter so hard, the window above the sink rattles. I go back to the phone, and study the photo. I look for anything I can use to identify the location, absolutely anything, but whoever took it has been careful. Nothing about it can help me. I can't even reply, due to the number being blocked. I delete the message. I don't want it there to distract me like the Polaroid.

The message has made the decision for me. I have to call Laura's mother.

I go to the computer, and bring the web browser back up. It's easy to find Gretchen Aisling, mother of Laura Aisling, who lives in the town of Thistleton, Maine. There are so many old news stories that mention her. I use one of those services that seem designed for online stalkers to get her phone number and address.

I go to the kitchen and pick up my phone. I don't know what I'm going to say, and I don't care if she's suspicious. I'll figure something out.

I punch the numbers in, and wait for the familiar purr of a ring at the other end. Instead, three blaring, ear-punishing tones answer back, and a voice declares, "We're sorry. The number you have dialed is disconnected, or is no longer in service."

I hang up.

I still have an address. It's a two-hour drive to Thistleton. I don't want to be away from The Hollows, but I don't have a choice.

I grab the keys for the truck and head for the door.

Out of habit and muscle memory, I call out, "Come on, Murph!"

I stop at the door, realizing what I've done. Rage and frustration course through me again. The physical urge to tear apart everything around me passes, but the desire remains.

*

Thistleton is the definition of a one-light, New England town. It's just off the highway among the hills and forests of Maine. I drive through the intersection containing the light and think that maybe this is only just one end of Thistleton, but no, the GPS lets me know that this is "downtown". I continue on, following the directions on my phone. The buildings, which mainly consist of the odd specialty store or auto mechanic, begin spacing out. Soon, I'm in the gently rolling farm fields. I could only imagine what it was like for Laura to grow up here, and then go to a college like New Hampshire University. It must have been like going to another planet.

I crest a hill and a small valley comes into view. Farmhouses dot the landscape, each isolated by the surrounding fields. The voice on the GPS announces that my destination is ahead on the right. In the distance, there's a rusty mailbox at the end of a dirt drive, leading to a small, two-story house with wooden siding and a black roof.

That's it.

I turn the truck into the driveway and stop. The withered brown grass of the lawn is accentuated by patches of resilient weeds. At first glance, the house appears gray, but upon closer inspection, I can see that it's just dirty. It's not dilapidated, but it hasn't been cared for in some time. There's a beat-up station wagon at the end of the drive, parked in front of a sagging wooden shed. I sit there, waiting for any sign of life from the curtained windows of the house, but there's no movement.

I take my foot off the brake, and the truck begins rolling forward. The house grows bigger as I approach.

"This is stupid," I say out loud. "This is where you get caught."

I almost hit the brakes and throw it in reverse, but I look at the burner phone on the front seat and know that at any minute, I could get a message that says, "You didn't save him," accompanied by a photo I don't want to imagine. I allow the truck to continue forward, keeping my eyes on the house. I park behind the station wagon and get out. There's taller, withered grass around the tires of the station wagon, proof that it hasn't moved in a while.

With no resistance from the forests or mountains, the bitterly cold wind hisses through the tall, dead grass. I shut the door to the truck and wait to see if the sound alerts anyone inside. Nothing. I peek inside the station wagon. The upholstery is torn and rotting. The floor is littered with dirt and leaves.

I slowly walk up the cracked concrete path to the porch. I take one last look at the windows, and press the doorbell. There's no sound. I open the screen door, knock, and wait. After a few moments with no response, I knock again.

"Hello?" I call out.

The only answer is a gust of wind.

"Mrs Aisling?"

I wait, but there's no reply. I take out my phone and try the number again. I want to see if I hear ringing inside, but I get the same message as before.

I turn and scan the scattered houses in the valley, wondering if anyone knows—

The lock on the door clicks open.

I nearly stumble back off the porch as I spin around. I watch as the knob slowly turns and the door opens a few inches.

"Laura? Is that you?" a voice whispers from the darkness within.

I hold my breath. My eyes are fixated on the empty space.

"Laura?" the whisper repeats.

I take a cautious step towards the door.

"Mrs Aisling?"

There's no answer, but I can feel someone staring at me from the void.

"My name is Jacob Reese," I gently say. "I was wondering if I could speak to you."

I wait, trying to peer into the darkness.

The door is pulled open a few more inches, and the face of Gretchen Aisling appears from the shadows. Her beady eyes have sunken further into their sockets since the last time I saw her on television and are surrounded by liver-spotted skin. Her thinning hair is stringy, and her pallid scalp is visible underneath. That fierceness I saw in her all those years ago is gone. She looks confused and afraid.

"Do you know Laura?" she asks through stained teeth.

My first instinct is to correct her and say that I "knew" her, but I catch myself. "Yes. I was wondering if I could speak to you about her."

Her bony hand clutches her housecoat tighter around her fragile frame.

"Did Laura send you?" she eagerly asks, her voice like sandpaper.

"Yes," I reply, giving her the answer I know she wants, but I have no idea what's happening.

She opens the door the rest of the way, and I tentatively step forward through the doorway.

Oh my God, the smell. I almost gag. It's not like in the basement of the warehouse. This is dust, rotting garbage, and human waste. I try to hide my reaction, but it's not easy. I also quickly realize that she is the source of the smell.

I take shallow breaths through my mouth to avoid using my nose, and scan the surroundings. There's a set of stairs to the left, leading up to the second floor, and there's a chair in front of me, facing the door. There's also an old worn couch across from an ancient television. It's the big, bulky kind from when TVs were considered furniture. It looks like it hasn't been used in a while. There's a dining table at the far end of the living room.

However, all of this is secondary. The first thing, the only thing, I see are the crucifixes, figurines, and images of Jesus. They're everywhere—on every shelf, and on every wall. Some of the images are framed and sit on the shelves. I count at least seven on the walls. Some are of the variety you can find at a gas station or flea market. Others are prints of famous works of art. There appears to be no rhyme or reason to their placement—like she tried to fill every space with the Lord. This isn't devoutness. This is dementia. There are also burnt-out candles on the shelves and tables throughout the room. The wax from some has dripped down and collected onto the threadbare carpet. There is a layer of dust on everything. It all comes into focus—her electricity has been disconnected, as well as her phone.

My scan of the room brings me back to her. She's standing before me in her housecoat and slippers. She's trembling from the cold and I can see her lightly fogged breath descend from her nose. She's frail, anxious, and those eyes, staring back from the pits above her cheeks, tell me her mind is broken.

She stares at me with frenzied hope. "Laura sent you?"

I inhale to answer, and the smell hits me, again—a smell of which she seems to have no inkling. I fight the gag building in my throat.

"Yes. Laura sent me. I wanted to talk to you about her."

She looks past me to the door. "Is she here?"

"I'm sorry?"

"Is Laura with you?"

"No."

"When is Laura coming back?"

"I—I don't know."

Her hope turns to disappointment.

"Can I ask you some questions about Laura?"

She mumbles something, and goes to the chair. She eases herself into it, and looks right through me to the door. "I'm waiting for Laura."

I glance at the closed door and back to her. It's unnervingly quiet. There's no hum of a refrigerator or rumble of central heating. There's only the wind blowing against the side of the house.

She sits in the chair, smiling expectantly at the door.

In horror, I realize that this is what she does. She sits in this chair and waits for Laura to come home ... and she does this because of me, because of the hope I left her by not telling anyone what happened to Laura. I know right away that I have to help her, and I know how, but I have to do something, first.

I calmly go over and crouch beside her. "Mrs Aisling, I need to ask you about Laura."

Her smile widens and her eyes stay on the door. "You can ask her when she gets here."

"But I want you to tell me, okay?" I wait to see if she'll look at me, but she doesn't. "Mrs Aisling, do you remember when Laura went to New Hampshire University, then transf—?"

She grimaces.

"No, no, no. That was wrong. She was wrong, but it wasn't her fault. It was the Devil. The Devil was to blame. Not my angel. And God forgave her."

"Mrs Aisling, what did the Devil make Laura do?"

"No. No, we don't talk about it. God has forgiven her. He forgives all. If we confess our sins, He is faithful, and just, and will forgive us our sins and purify us in all righteousness."

"Please, Mrs Aisling. I need to know what happened."

"You can ask Laura when she gets here."

My calm veneer is cracking. The smell is getting to me again. "Mrs Aisling, Laura's not coming back."

She slowly turns her head, and smiles at me through those sunken eyes and rotting teeth. "That's what they said all those years ago … and they were wrong. God gave my Angel back to me. She came right through that door."

The blood freezes in my veins.

"Laura was here?" I choke.

Her eyes glow with happiness. "Yes. Right there."

"What did she want?"

"She wanted her music box."

"And did you give her the music box?"

"Of course. It's her music box. She went upstairs to her room and got it."

I glance over to the foot of the stairs.

"When she came downstairs, she said she would come back to me very soon, but first, someone had to pay for what they had done. She said she was going to make it right. So, now, we wait for her," she says with loving pride.

My eyes haven't left the stairs.

She had been here. Whoever *she* was, she had posed as Laura to fool Mrs Aisling's riddled mind. Immediately, I formulate a plan. I'm not happy about it, but this has to happen.

"Mrs Aisling, Laura did send me."

She turns to me with those sparkling, sunken eyes.

"She wanted me to get something from her room and bring it to her."

The brighter her smile grows, the worse I feel.

"Can I go up to her room, and get it?"

She eagerly nods. She tries to stand but I calmly put my hand on her shoulder to keep her in the chair.

"No, no, no. I don't want you to hurt yourself on the stairs. I'll get it," I say, softly.

Tears of happiness spring from her eyes and flow down her cheeks.

"You wait here, okay?"

She nods again, but she wants nothing more than to join me. I turn and go to the foot of the stairs.

There's a window at the top that throws down a shaft of sunlight. Particles of dust drift in and out of the beam. I begin to climb. The wooden stairs creak under my weight. The foul smell diminishes the further up I go. At the top of the stairs, the hallway goes off to the right. There are three doors—one at the end of the hallway, leading to a bedroom, a smaller door halfway down that I assume is a bathroom, and the closed door immediately on my right. I grasp the knob and push it in.

It's a girl's room—Laura's room.

There are pictures of Laura everywhere, from every stage in her life—as a baby, as a toddler, as a child, and as a young woman. There are some crucifixes, and porcelain figures of Christ, but nothing like downstairs. While the rest of the house is a shrine to Christ, this room is a shrine to Laura, just waiting for her return. The floorboards broadcast my movements as I slowly walk about the room. There are posters on the walls for movies and boy bands, and an army of stuffed animals on the bed. There's a framed photo of her graduation from elementary school. Even as a young, awkward girl with braces, you can see the beauty that she would become. Next to that is a framed photo of her graduation from high school.

I'm suddenly consumed with guilt. I'm standing amongst the remains of a life I helped end. I had never seen this part of her. I had only caught a glimpse of it in her scrapbook, but to see the physical objects of her life, laid out before me, is crippling. Seeing these different phases of her life makes me feel like I let multiple Lauras die, not just one.

The guilt is growing but when I arrive at the bookshelves, a blank space reminds me of my purpose. There's a rectangle in the dust. This is where the music box once sat. This is where she took it. The rest of the shelf is filled with books such as *Alice in Wonderland, The Giving Tree, The Wizard of Oz*, and *Where the Sidewalk Ends*. I go to the next shelf, and stop. Scrapbooks. Here's the one I looked at in her dorm—the one that was filled with her childhood. I find the one that's blue and gray and take it out. All I can think of is the blue and gray hat that Veronica described. I hold it for a moment.

"Please …" I whisper, and flip it open.

Pasted in the first page is a letter, congratulating Laura on her acceptance to New Hampshire University.

I flip another page. It's a group photo of a bunch of girls, standing on the grass in front of a dorm. The caption reads, "Royce Hall, UNH, 2005". I'm tempted to sit on the bed and begin reading, but I want to get out of this house.

I snap the scrapbook closed, carry it out of the room, and walk back down the stairs.

Mrs Aisling is still sitting in her chair. She tries to stand as I approach.

"I want to see Laura," she says. "She promised she'd come back."

I gently ease her back down with one hand, while clutching the scrapbook in the other, trying my best to keep it from her view.

"No. It's okay," I whisper. "Everything is going to be okay."

Reluctantly, she allows me to help her back down.

"Now, you wait here, and Laura will be back before you know it."

She's about to cry, but appreciatively pats my hand.

I get up and walk to the door. I pull it open, but stop when she begins to speak.

"Thank you. Thank you for staying with my Laura. She said it was so dark in that room. Tell her to come back, and that I love her."

My heart sinks into my stomach. "I will."

I step outside, close the door, and walk back to the truck feeling like the disgusting, wretched human being that I know I am.

*

As soon as I'm back on the road, before I even look at the scrapbook, I find the nearest Target store, which is about ten miles away. I walk in and go straight to the electronics section. I purchase a disposable cell phone and load it with the lowest number of minutes I can. The sales clerk doesn't even bat an eye when I pay in cash.

I drive to a bridge spanning the Crookshaw River and park. I get out and go to the guardrail. The water churns thirty feet below me. I've been charging the phone while driving, and it's up to seven percent. That's all I'll need. I dial, and it's answered almost immediately.

"Nine-one-one. What's the nature of your emergency?"

"Hi, can you please send an ambulance to six-one-eight Falstaff Road in Thistleton? There's an old woman living by herself, and she's in bad shape."

"Are you with her now?"

"No, but I was just there. She's got no heating and she … she needs help."

"What was the address again?"

"Six-one-eight Falstaff."

"Can I have your name, sir?"

"Will you send someone to check on her?"

"Yes, but I need to know—?"

I hang up the phone and glance down at the roiling water.

I cock my arm, and hurl the phone into the river.

Chapter 12

There's something dignified about pouring your own coffee at a 7-Eleven. Cup? Pick your own cup. No one is going to ask you if you want a venti, or grande, or a supercalifragilisticexpialidocious. Cream? All the cream you want. Make it ninety percent cream, if you feel like it.

God, I'm tired.

I pay at the counter, take my coffee out to the truck, and settle in as I flip open the scrapbook.

The first page is the acceptance letter, congratulating Laura, and notifying her that she'll be living in Royce Hall. I flip to the next page, which is the photo of the girls in front of the dorm. There are roughly fifty of them, lined up in three rows. The first row is on one knee, the second is crouching, and the last is standing upright.

There she is—back row, third from the left. My eyes are instantly drawn to the red hair and blue eyes. She looks happy and excited. Again, I could only imagine the change from living with her mother in Thistleton, to going to college and meeting so many new pe—

Laura bleeding out on the floor of the warehouse.

The image is so vivid, I take a sharp inhalation of breath. I rub my eyes, trying to banish the image from my mind, and flip the page.

It's another group photo in front of a different dorm. There are fewer girls, so the camera is a little closer. Just as before, they're in rows. "Wilson Hall 2006!" it says at the bottom of the picture.

There's Laura, again, this time front and center. Her hair is shorter, and she looks slightly older. That first year of college does that to you, I guess.

I flip the page, and it's filled with photos of the girls moving into Wilson Hall. The following pages are filled with photos of Laura and her friends hanging out and going to parties.

Wait.

I flip back to the Royce Hall group photo. Next comes the Wilson Hall photo, and then pages and pages of Laura and the other girls of Wilson Hall.

Why aren't there any photos of Laura with the girls from Royce Hall?

I bring the scrapbook closer to my face and inspect the metal rings mounted to the spine that hold the pages. They're bent, ever so slightly. Someone has ripped out those pages.

That's it. Whatever I'm looking for is in those pages.

I've got to find someone who knew Laura at New Hampshire University.

I continue studying the photos. There are photos of Laura and her friends, and some of just Laura. I constantly go back and forth between these and the Wilson Hall photos. As I advance in the photos, I can see her circle of friends expanding. More guys start showing up, but I'm particularly drawn to one girl who begins to appear with more and more regularity. She has straight, long, brown hair and deep brown eyes. There are photos of her and Laura at parties, in addition to simple candid shots. Through the photos, I watch their friendship grow. There are movie ticket stubs pasted onto the pages, fliers for parties and concerts, and other memorabilia. They were best friends.

This is the person I need to talk to, to find out who has Murphy. All I need is her name.

I flip another page, and it brings me to an article cut from *The Wildcat*, New Hampshire University's student newspaper. The headline reads, "Student Legal Society Brings Challenge to New Parking Ordinances". Accompanying the article is a photo of a group of smartly dressed students. The girl I'm interested in is second from the end. The students' names are captioned under the photo.

"You're the one I have to find, Amy Winstead," I say aloud.

I pick up my phone, and pull up the browser. I'm worried that there might be too many Amy Winsteads and, sure enough, there are a few dozen in my initial search. I add "New Hampshire University" and "lawyer" to the search, and hit enter.

It returns the address and phone number for a law office in Montpelier. I tap the phone number on the webpage and my phone automatically dials the number.

It's getting late, so there's no surprise when my call goes to voicemail.

"You've reached the offices of Amy Winstead. Please leave your message after the tone, and it will be returned as soon as possible. You can also call back between our normal business hours. Thank you and have a wonderful day."

Beep.

"Hi, uh, my name is ..." I briefly toy with giving a fake name but decide to come clean. "Listen, my name is Jacob Reese. I wanted to speak to you about a mutual acquaintance—Laura Aisling. I believe that you may have known her when you both attended New Hampshire University. If you could give me a call back, I'd really appreciate it. It's, uh ... It's important. Thank you."

I leave my number, hang up, sit back in my seat, and roll my neck. Deep cracks emanate from my spine. I stare out the window to the setting sun. There's nothing more I can do today. I have to get some sleep.

I start the truck.

It's going to be a long drive back to The Hollows.

I'm facing the heavy steel door.
The pressure on my sh—

I startle myself awake.

My hands are gripping the steering wheel. It was only for a moment, but yeah, I was falling asleep while driving. I curse, clench my teeth, dial the heat up to full blast, and turn up the radio.

There's only twenty more miles to go, but this is the worst part of the trip. There's no stimulus to keep me awake. It's pitch black outside and the two-lane road just winds on and on through the unchanging forest.

"Just get home," I tell myself.

As a way to keep myself awake, I start thinking about what I'll say to Amy Winstead. I have the same problem that I thought I was going to have with Laura's mom—how can I ask questions without raising suspicions? I could tell her the truth that Laura and I dated for a while, but why would I be asking about their friendship? *I could tell her—*

—on my shoulder.
"*Jacob?*" a voice whispers.
Do not turn around. Do not turn ar—

—thumpthumpthumpthumpthump.

I open my eyes, and quickly turn the wheel to get the truck back into the lane.

"Dammit!"

I slap my face, hard. The sting gives me a temporary adrenaline rush.

I've only got a few more minutes to go. I'm almost home,

but already, the adrenaline rush has passed, and my breathing is slipping into a steady rhythm.

Out of the corner of my eye, I notice a light coming from the passenger seat.

It's the burner phone.

I quickly turn down the radio. I don't know how long the phone has been ringing. The number, like the number for the text message earlier, is blocked.

I quickly pick up the phone and answer.

All I hear from the other end is the sound of someone breathing.

I try to wait her out and make her speak first, but I can't take it anymore.

"Who are you?"

"The one who is going to take everything from you, just like you took everything from me," she whispers.

"What do you want?"

"I want you to understand. I want you to know what you took from me, and what I will do to make you pay. You left me in that room. You locked me in, and left me to rot."

"You're not her! You're not Laura!"

She giggles. "Did you have a good talk with Mother?"

Now, I'm wide awake. "You were watching?"

She doesn't answer.

"Listen to me," I say. "I don't know who you are but leave my dog alone. Give him back to me, and we'll—"

"Not until you understand."

"Understand what?!"

"What you took from me."

"You're not Laura! She's dead!"

She giggles, again. It's childish, and teasing, which makes it all the more ominous.

"You should really get that fixed," she says.

"What are you talking about? Get what fixed?"

205

"Your taillight."

The phone cuts out.

Blinding high beams suddenly fill my rearview mirror. I only have a second to brace for impact before the SUV slams into my bumper. The phone and scrapbook go flying. My chest thuds against the steering wheel. The truck lurches forward, and I fight for control of the wheel. No sooner am I able to correct the truck to keep it from going into the ditch, when the SUV slams into me, again. The truck fishtails, and I struggle to keep the wheel steady. I straighten out just as the SUV charges.

I'm still fighting the side-to-side motion. If the SUV hits me now, I'll go off the road. I stomp the gas to the floor, and the truck shoots forward. My burst of speed robs the SUV of full impact, and instead of ramming me to one side, it pushes me forward. The impact has smashed one of the headlights of the SUV, and I'm not as blinded as I was a moment ago.

I frantically glance from the road in front of me to the rearview mirror. The single fiery eye of the lone headlight begins to close the gap, setting up another impact. I'm outmatched. The SUV has more power, and a firmer center of gravity than the truck. It's about to slam into me when I jerk the wheel to the left, into the opposite lane, and tap the brake. The SUV misses, and pulls even with the truck. I yank the wheel back to the right, and use all of the truck's body to slam into the side of the SUV.

For a moment, I think I've hit her hard enough to push her off the road, but the SUV holds, and veers back in my direction. I pull the wheel hard, again, and our vehicles smash together. The sound of grinding and scraping metal fills the cabin. I glance at the SUV, but the tinted windows offer no glimpse inside. The truck is holding its own, but the SUV is going to win out.

Suddenly, the SUV brakes. I'm still accelerating and pulling right. The front half of the truck lurches out ahead of the SUV. I try to hit the brakes, but it's too late. I shoot forward into her path. The SUV revs its engine, and clips the back of the truck as I cut across the lane.

The truck goes into a spin. The SUV darts forward, accelerating into the night.

The trees and road rotate in front of me, illuminated by the headlights.

Then, I make the most instinctual and fatal of mistakes—I try to correct away from the spin.

It puts all of the momentum of the truck into a fight against the direction of the tires. I feel the truck come up on two wheels, and lean.

There's nothing I can do to stop it, now.

The truck is going to roll.

As the wheels leave the ground, the engine's RPMs spike in a high-pitched *whrrrr*. I scream as the world in front of me flips. There's a sickening crunch as the corner of the roof crashes against the asphalt, causing the truck to skip. It does a full rotation in the air, and slams back down, again. There's a *pop*, and my view is obscured by the airbag deploying. I roll one more time, and the truck lands on the driver's side. There's a sound like a thousand nails on a chalkboard, and sparks fly inches from my head as the truck slides along the road. The truck twists one last time as it goes down into the ditch, and lands on its roof.

Everything stops.

I'm hanging upside down, still strapped in by my seat belt. Already, I can feel the blood rushing to my head. I groan, and glance at the grass and trees through the hole where the windshield used to be.

Gingerly, I unclip my seat belt and collapse onto the roof of the cabin. Everything hurts. I'm covered in cuts and bruises, but I think I'm okay. I pull myself out through the window, ignoring the bits of glass that cut my hand, and slowly crawl away from the smoking wreckage. I come to rest in the cold mud by the side of the road and look back at the truck.

It's totaled.

I sink onto my back, look up at the stars, and catch my breath. It's all I can do.

My phone rings.

I reach into my pocket, but it's not there.

I pull myself up, and scramble back to the truck. Every movement hurts. My phone, along with the burner phone, is lying on the ceiling inside the cabin. I pick up both, put the burner in my pocket, and answer my phone.

"Hello?"

"Mr Reese?"

"Yes?"

"It's Amy Winstead. I'm returning your call."

"What?"

"Um, I'm Amy Winstead. You called—"

"Oh. Yeah, yeah. Right." I stand up, which causes me to grunt. "Look, thank you for returning my call, but now is not a good time."

"You said you were calling about Laura Aisling?"

"Yes, I was, but it's late. Can I call you back in the morning?"

"I'd like to know exactly what this is about."

"It's nothing, really—"

"Is this about her disappearance?"

"Yes, sort of, but like I said, this is not a good t—"

"Mr Reese, tell me what's going on. How did you know Laura?"

Her tone stops me in my tracks.

"Well, we dated for a few months. I knew her pretty well, but I'm trying to fill in some gaps. I'm trying to find out what happened while she was at New Hampshire University, and I was told you two were friends, so I wanted to talk, but, please, Ms Winstead, I really have to go—"

"Mr Reese?"

208

"Yes?" I answer. Why does she sound so pissed?

"You're telling me you knew her because you dated for a few months?"

"Yeah. So, I'm trying to—"

She scoffs. "Mr Reese, Laura and I dated for over a year."

Chapter 13

Amy and I are sitting on a park bench across from her law office in Montpelier.

"You look like shit," she says.

"Long night," I reply.

It was a long night.

After we arranged this meeting over the phone, I called Triple-A about the truck. It wasn't really a truck, anymore. It was scrap. I was shaken up, but thankfully, not permanently damaged.

When the tow truck arrived, he took one look at the pile of twisted metal lying in the ditch and said, "Gotta call the police."

"Do you really have to do that?" I asked.

"Gotta close down the road to pull 'er out. That requires the police." He looked at the truck, again. "What happened?"

"Swerved to miss a deer."

He let out a faint whistle. "Lucky deer."

The cops came out and blocked the road down to one lane. It proved an inconvenience to the three cars that passed in the hour it took to pull the remnants of the truck out of the ditch. I gave them the deer story, which they had no reason to doubt.

It was two o'clock by the time I collapsed into my bed for a night of restless dreams.

I picked up my Ford Focus from the rental company this morning and drove it to Montpelier for my one o'clock meeting with Amy Winstead.

She was waiting on the bench, just as we had discussed.

She's tall. Her hair is cropped shorter than in the photo I saw. Her features are sharper, and her countenance more serious. Her years in law school and practice are etched in her face.

"So," she begins, eyeing the cuts and bruises on my face and hands. "Why are you asking about Laura?"

"I'm trying to find out what happened to her."

"And how did you find me?"

"Laura kept a scrapbook from her time at New Hampshire University. I got my hands on it. There were a lot of photos of you."

She smiles, sadly. "Yeah. She loved taking photos. Wait. How did you get a hold of the scrapbook?"

"Her mother let me see it."

She raises a skeptical eyebrow. "Her mother let you see it?"

"Yeah."

"Well, at least now I *know* that you're a liar."

"Ms. Winstead—"

"Oh, for Christ's sake, just call me Amy."

"Okay. Look, you're right. I haven't been totally honest with you, or anybody, as of late, but something is happening, and it has to do with Laura. Whatever it is, it has to do with her time at New Hampshire University, and you were friends with her."

"Friends," she says in offended disbelief.

"I'm sorry. You said you were more? Please, tell me what happened."

She considers, and shrugs. "What do you want to know?"

"Everything."

She sits back against the bench, and looks out to the passing cars on State Street, which runs past the park. "We met during the second semester of our freshman year at a meeting of the Out Club. It was a sort of social support group for LGBT students.

211

Things were getting better, but it was still a tough time to be a student who was open about their sexuality."

"Laura was gay?"

She looks at me in disgust. "God, you really didn't know her, did you? No, she wasn't gay. She was bisexual. I mean, you said that you two dated, or was that a lie?"

"No, we dated, and yes, that was a stupid question. I didn't know. She never talked about it."

"Did you really meet her mom?"

"Yeah."

"Then you understand why she may have kept that to herself." She laughs under her breath. "I remember that just in case her mom ever showed up, she had this poster of Jesus hanging ov—"

"Over her bed."

She stops. Her expression softens. "Oh my God. You know about that?"

"I saw it in her room. She told me about it."

"That poster ..." she says, in that perfectly amused tone of someone speaking of a flaw in someone they love.

The light in her face at being able to speak to someone who knew Laura is radiant. It's clear she loved Laura in a way I couldn't comprehend.

"So, like I said, we met at the Outs. That's what we called it. I watched her walk into the room. She was really nervous and very shy. She was also really upset. She looked like she was about to start crying. I introduced myself, and took her aside. We just talked. We talked for hours. She told me about her home, and the town she came from. She told me that she was bisexual, and how she had hidden it from her mother her whole life. She was in a lot of pain. I was lucky. I had the one thing every kid like us needs growing up."

"What's that?"

"Parents who loved me, supported me, accepted me, and knew way before I did that I was different. Laura didn't have any of

212

that. We developed a friendship. She'd come to the club meetings. We'd hang out. I'd introduce her to my friends. Things kept going, and before either one of us knew it, we were dating." She smiles. "I fell in love with her ... She was beautiful, and it was amazing to watch this whole new world open up for her. She talked about how, for the first time, she felt alive. It was amazing to watch her be herself." Amy pulls back and stares down at the sidewalk. "Sorry. I don't know how much of this you want to hear."

"As much as you're comfortable telling me."

"Well, one night, it happened. We started sleeping together. I asked her if she had ever been with another woman, and she was a little cagey about it. She said once, but that it had been a mistake. It was like she felt guilty for it, but I told her that some hookups are mistakes ... We kept seeing each other. She started helping at the Out Club, but she was still in a lot of pain because she lived in constant fear of her mother. I told her that she needed to come clean and tell her mother who she really was. That freaked her out. She said that there was no way, and that her mother would pull her out of the school.

"We left it at that. Over the summer, we stayed in touch. We emailed, but no phone calls or text messages because her mom paid the bills and might see it. I was living in Colorado, so there was no way to see each other. Those were the three longest months of my life ... That first day back on campus, we saw each other outside her dorm, ran to one another, and kissed like we—"

Her speech fades but her smile grows.

"We had held hands in public before, but that was the first time we kissed and didn't care if the world saw us. We picked up right where we left off. It was wonderful. We almost got caught though, one night about a month after we got back."

"By whom?"

"Who else? Her mom. She paid one of her surprise visits. We were fooling around in her room when she knocked. We barely had time to get ourselves together before she opened the door.

Laura introduced me as her friend. Her mother said that I could join them for dinner. I went along because I wanted to be there for Laura. I wanted her to tell her mother who I really was. We walked to this Mexican restaurant, and the whole way there, Mrs Aisling kept telling Laura to be careful of boys and their sinful ways, but to be on the lookout for a good, Christian man. She asked Laura if she was going to church. She also asked me if I was going to church, and asked if I had been saved. I wanted to shout at her.

"When we got to the restaurant, Mrs Aisling was offended when the server asked if she would like to have a margarita. When the food came, she made us hold hands and she prayed …" Amy suddenly turns to me. "Look, I've prayed with people before. There are people in my life—friends and colleagues—who are religious, and they are some of the most wonderful, caring people you will ever meet. I love them, and they love me. When we pray together, it's about love. For Mrs Aisling, her prayer was all about sin. To her, punishment for sin was God's love. I knew right then and there that Laura was right. She could never tell her. She had to wait it out until she could simply get away. That's what she wanted to do. We even talked about it—about what we would do once we finished school …"

Amy's voice cracks and her eyes glisten. "Listen … I'm married. I love my wife. We have a son. My life is wonderful, but sometimes, and I've never told anyone this, but sometimes at night, when I'm lying in bed next to my wife, I think about Laura more than I should …" She waits for her nerves steady. "We continued to see each other. We even became more open about our relationship. I asked her if she was really bisexual or if she was gay, but she said, no, she was attracted to men, too."

"Did that bother you?"

"No. All I cared about was that she cared for me. She even told me that she loved me. That was one of the best days of my life … Then, one night, it just started to fall apart."

"What happened?"

"We were out at dinner. We were sitting on the patio, which was next to the street. Our table was right by the rail, and this girl comes up and starts talking to Laura. She's asking Laura all these questions about why she won't talk to her, and asking who I was. It was crazy. Laura tried to calm her down, but she wasn't having any of it. She ends up screaming at Laura, asking how Laura could do this to her, and saying that she's going to tell Laura's mother.

"I was stunned. Laura tried to get her to go, but she kept at it, about how they should be together, how they make up one person. Real crazy shit. I finally convinced Laura that we should go. The restaurant let us leave out a side door because that crazy bitch was waiting for us out front. I found out later that the restaurant ended up calling the police. We got back to my place and Laura was shaking like a leaf. I asked her who the hell that was, and she told me … It was that first girl that she hooked up with—the one she called a 'mistake.'"

"Who was she?"

"Her freshman year roommate."

"Laura hooked up with her?"

Amy nods. "They hooked up the second week of school. Laura said that she had been fighting her feelings towards women her whole life, and when she got to New Hampshire University, she felt free. It was just a thing. A chance to explore, and it only happened a few times." Amy looks at me. "You went to college, right?"

"Yeah."

"Proud of every hookup you had there?"

"Absolutely not."

"For Laura, she couldn't have picked anyone worse."

I'm struggling to process everything I've heard. "So, Laura's roommate was gay?"

"I have no idea. I suppose so, but more than anything, she was crazy. She was obsessed with Laura. Kept saying that they were in love. Laura tried to reason with her, but ended up moving out after the first semester. That's when she and I met. I realized that this was why she always wanted to go back to my place, and that she wasn't just worried about being found out. She was worried about her. I urged her to go to the campus police, but she thought that they would tell her mother.

"Laura wasn't the same after that. She was always paranoid. I tried to get her some help, but she wouldn't hear of it. We kept seeing each other. It started to get a little better, but then there was that night. *The* night … It was getting close to Christmas, and we were at my apartment. We were cuddling on the couch, staring at this little plastic Christmas tree we bought at Walmart. There was a knock on the door. I opened it, and there was Mrs Aisling. I'll never forget the anger in that woman's eyes. She looked at me, and then at her daughter, and she knew. We didn't have to say a thing."

"How did she find you?"

"How do you think?"

"The roommate?"

Amy shrugs. "Mrs Aisling told Laura to come with her. She said she was taking her out of school. I tried to argue with her, but Mrs Aisling screamed at me, 'You're not taking my daughter to Hell with you!' Laura tried to speak, but her mother cut her off with a look. I told her not to go, but she did. She walked right out the door. I—" Her voice catches and the tears start, anew. "Laura was so scared, and I felt so helpless. Before she walked away, her mother looked at me and said, 'Don't ever speak to my daughter, again.'"

I'm speechless. I'm weighing everything I know about Laura against what I've just heard, and it hits me—this is what she was trying to tell me in the weeks leading up to that night in the warehouse. She was trying to tell me about all of this, and I was too self-absorbed to listen.

Amy wipes her eyes and steadies her voice.

"Anything else, Mr Reese? My lunch break is almost over."

"Did you try to contact Laura after that?"

"Of course, I did, but her mother took her phone away. She wouldn't even let Laura out of the house. She didn't have a computer for email. I was worried sick."

"Why didn't Laura run away?"

"Where would she go? She didn't have a place of her own, or money, or a job. I would have let her stay at my place, but her mother would have found us. About a month later, I finally got an email from her. She said that her mother was enrolling her in a Christian college, and that this was her good-bye. She was writing it from the local library. She said that she loved me, and maybe somewhere down the road, we'd see each other, again. I wrote back, pleading with her to let me help. I even said that I would run away with her."

"What did she say?"

"She wrote back that there would probably be more mistakes … She meant it as a joke, but it hurt."

"What happened then?"

"I went after her roommate."

"Are you serious?"

Her eyes flare with intensity. "Oh, yeah. When I got that last email, I snapped. I found out which dorm she was in and her room number. I got inside the dorm and was ready to kick her ass. I found her room and pounded on the door, and this short, scrawny girl answered. I looked past her into the room, and there was stuff only on one side. The girl asked me what I wanted. I asked her where her roommate is and she said 'gone'. I asked when she's coming back, and she said, 'Never, thank God.' She said the girl's parents had come, and taken all of her stuff the week before. Apparently, she had some sort of mental breakdown. It had to have been about Laura leaving the school. Her parents pulled her out. The roommate said she had gone crazy. Now, she had the room to herself. She said she heard her parents talking about putting her in Sacred Heart. Know what that is?"

"Yeah," I reply.

Anyone who grew up in the area has heard of Sacred Heart. It's an old psychiatric hospital—the stuff of Halloween legends.

Amy sighs, and sits back. "After that, it was over. I missed Laura. I was still in love with her, but every day, it hurt a little less. I tried to move on … That is until the day I heard she was missing. It opened up every wound. I went to the cops, and told them about the roommate. Even mentioned that I thought the mother was messed up. They said they followed up on everything, but nothing came of it."

No. Nothing would come of it because I had covered my tracks, a fact I was not proud of.

"I have to get back. I've got a meeting," she says. "Any more questions?"

"Two."

"Fire away."

"This roommate, did she and Laura have any sort of physical resemblance?"

Amy sits up. Her face hardens. "Why?"

"I need to know."

"Tell me why you asked that."

"She looked a little bit like Laura, didn't she?"

Her silence is an affirmative answer.

"Fine. Yes. It was a weird coincidence, but they had a passing resemblance, except for the hair and eyes. I think that's why she was spouting that weird shit about them being one person."

A passing resemblance is all that had been needed to trick my mind into thinking I had seen Laura, but it was this woman. That's who I saw at the Halloween celebration. That's why she looked like she was the correct age. That's who Mrs Sherman had seen outside the cottage. That's who has Murphy.

"Last question—what was her roommate's name?"

218

"Rachel. Rachel Smith."

My face drops. "No … No … Please tell me her last name isn't Smith."

"Yeah. It's Smith."

I look around the park. "Shit."

"Is that a problem?"

"Yeah."

"Why?"

*

Because there are thousands of Smiths in the tri-state area.

I'm sitting in the rental car, staring at the search results on my phone.

Even working on the assumption that Rachel Smith and her family lived within relative driving distance of Sacred Heart, I'm still in the hundreds, and no specific hit for a Rachel Smith.

I drop the phone onto the passenger seat in disgust. Up until this point, I've been lucky. I got the license plate from a photo, and Rachel had made the mistake of wearing that old hat with the logo when she recruited Veronica. I had caught a string of breaks, but now those breaks were at an end.

I'm not going to be able to find Rachel Smith with standard internet sleuthing. There's only one place where I know they'll have her name and address, and there's no way that they're going to give them to me.

I have to somehow break into a mental institution.

Chapter 14

I think I've got it.

I've been working on my story the entire drive here. I was feeling confident, but now, sitting in the parking lot and looking up at the massive Victorian brick structure, my confidence is starting to crack.

The building is part of a complex that sits on top of a hill, overlooking Plymouth Valley.

I've heard so much about this place from my childhood. It had been an insane asylum for over a hundred years. There are horror stories about its past, when treatments for mental disorders were in their barbaric infancy. One of the buildings had housed a tuberculosis ward. You can find disturbing, black-and-white photos online of rows of beds in expansive rooms, and nurses leading lobotomized patients down hallways. It's the stuff of nightmares, and even though I said you *can* find them online, I don't recommend that you do.

All the stories were made even more mythic by the fact that it sits alone on a hill. I can only assume it was situated here so people wouldn't have to be constantly reminded of the suffering that took place inside. It had closed in the 1980s due to budget cuts and was abandoned for a time. That's when the squatters moved in. One of the rumors was that when the facility closed down, they simply let the patients out, and some stayed in the tunnels below ground that connected the buildings. I don't know if I believe that. It reopened around 2000. In my research, I found out that only the main building was in use, but there were negotiations to open the other buildings, and use them as research facilities.

As I approach the front doors, my confidence cracks even further. The website said that visiting hours were from ten a.m. to five p.m. It's four o'clock. I could have waited until tomorrow and worked on my story some more, but I wouldn't get any sleep tonight. With that added fatigue, I'd have a harder time keeping my story straight, no matter how hard I worked on it. Also, I'd do nothing tonight except think about Murphy.

The doors slide open without making a sound. I step into the lobby and am greeted by that hospital smell—a mix of antiseptic, plastic, and that unknown ingredient that makes it all so unpleasant.

Standing in the modern-looking lobby, you'd have no idea that the building was over a hundred years old.

There's an unattended reception desk in front of me. Behind the desk is a windowed room, where I can see a woman reading from a file and talking on a phone. To the left and right are heavy, keycard entry doors with small rectangular windows, through which I can see long hallways.

I step over to the desk.

The woman in the office looks up. She smiles at me and mouths, "One moment."

I nod politely and she goes back to her conversation.

I scan the desk and my eyes rest on a sign-in sheet sitting on the ledge.

Shit.

To get through the doors, I'll have to sign in. If I sign in, she's going to check my ID. I won't be able to use a fake name. There's

221

nothing I can do about it. One step at a time, and the first step is to get through that door.

The woman hangs up the phone, and steps through the office door into the reception area, behind the desk.

"Can I help you?" she asks.

Her expression shifts a bit as she notices the small cuts and bruises on my face from the accident.

I do my best to look apologetic, and a little embarrassed.

"Hi. My name is Jacob Reese. I was wondering if I could, ummm— I have an uncle who has dementia and, uh, well, he needs to be put in a facility. My cousin and I are looking at different places, and I was wondering if I could take a quick look around and possibly speak to someone."

"Oh, I'm very sorry to hear that, Mr Reese. I'm Dr Cavanaugh. I'm the Chief Administrator of Sacred Heart."

"Hi," I say, shaking her hand.

What is the Chief Administrator doing manning the front desk at a place like this?

She's eyeing the cuts and bruises again.

Perfect.

"Yeah. My uncle had an 'incident' when he didn't recognize me yesterday. That was kind of the last straw," I say with a sad smile.

She buys it without hesitation. "I see. Who is your uncle's primary physician?"

"Dr Williamson over in Burlington."

Her brow creases. "Dr Williamson?"

"Yeah."

"I'm pretty familiar with all the physicians on the board in Burlington, and I'm afraid I've never heard of him."

Double shit.

"He's fairly new. He moved from Newport not too long ago."

"I see."

"We haven't been too happy with him, and my uncle has started to deteriorate rapidly. My cousin has been the one dealing with it and he can't do it alone, anymore."

"What type of dementia is it?"

"I'm sorry?"

"What classification of dementia does your uncle have? Is it Alzheimer's? Vascular? DLB?"

I helplessly shrug and shake my head. "I'm not entirely sure. My cousin would know. I came in from out of town to help sort things out."

"Do you know what medications he's taking?"

"I don't. This whole thing has been happening really fast. I can find out, but right now, we're just checking out different facilities."

That seems to placate her. I do look like someone who's had a pretty rough couple of days.

"I was hoping for a quick tour," I say.

To my horror, she shakes her head.

"I'm sorry, but that's impossible. Before we could do that, we would have to speak with his current physician to determine if Sacred Heart is the best fit for him. It's state law. We have to make sure we have the resources to take care of him, and that he's not a danger to our staff or other patients."

The disappointment in my face is genuine.

"I'm sorry," she says. "I know these things are incredibly difficult and painful, but the law—"

"I get it. I really do," I say in a pleading tone. "It's just … I mean, you're right. It is really tough. It's tough on my cousin and his family. I know it's the rules, but … I'm … I'm trying to help him out. I have to go back home, tomorrow. Please, I just want to see the place so that I can tell him it's an option. If we do select Sacred Heart, you can do the interview with Dr Williamson, and if you decide it's not the right fit for my uncle, then that will be that. I'm just trying to cut out a step."

She's wavering. "It's … It's a patient privacy concern. That's why—"

"And I understand. I do. Even a quick, five-minute tour would be incredibly helpful …"

All I need is to get through the door. I don't know what I'll do then, but it's a bridge I'll cross when and if I get there, and I have to get there.

She's still thinking it over.

I go for the ultimate sympathy tactic—bluffing.

I shake my head in resignation. "I'm trying to help out my cousin. I mean, you know how tough it is—not knowing if the next minute is going to be a good one or a bad one, the depression when you realize that your parent doesn't know who you are. But if you can't do it, it's okay. I completely understand."

She looks me over one last time from top to bottom, sighs, and gives me a conspiratorial smile.

"Do you promise this will be our little secret?"

"Of course," I answer with a slight delay as I can't believe it worked.

"I'm not going to have you sign in, for obvious reasons, but I do need to see your ID."

"Absolutely," I say, taking out my wallet, and handing her my driver's license.

She studies it.

Christ, I'm glad I didn't give her a fake name.

"Five minutes," she says, handing it back to me.

"Oh my God. Thank you so much."

"Remember," she says with a wink. "Our secret."

I tap my nose, playing along. Her laugh lets me know it's the right move.

"Follow me, please," she says, and leads me to the door.

She takes out her keycard and waves it over a sensor mounted on the wall. The door buzzes, and she pulls it open.

"After you."

"Thanks," I say, stepping through the door.

The hospital smell intensifies. The hallway stretches for what appears to be miles. Doors line both sides. There are a handful of patients in the hall. Most are accompanied by orderlies. The patients are easily distinguishable by their red robes and slippers. Occasionally, there is the sound of a raised voice from somewhere down the hall.

"This is our main wing. All our patients are on this floor. We're in talks to hopefully expand and utilize other buildings."

"I read something about that."

"Really? How familiar are you with Sacred Heart?" she asks as we begin walking.

"I grew up about an hour away from here, so I knew of it. Not much more than the campfire story stuff, though. It was the place you dared your friends to go."

"Yeah. We're working hard to turn that image around. We're getting some of the best doctors and staff in the tri-state area."

"I'm sorry. I didn't mean to speak badly of the place. It's only what I knew of it before yesterday."

"I totally understand. It's not the best reputation, so thank you for not giving up on us for that. In a few more years, this will be one of the top facilities in the northeast. We just need a little more time."

I glance into some of the rooms as we pass and notice that a lot are empty.

"It's still an incredible building," I say.

"The history is fascinating. There's a records room downstairs and the files go back decades."

Bingo.

"Speaking of which," she continues, "if you want to leave me your uncle's primary physician's number after we're done, I can contact him, and we can start that process."

"Sure. I'll get it from my brother."

She turns to me, momentarily puzzled. "I thought it was your cousin."

Triple shit.

Since the moment she mentioned it, my mind has been obsessed with forming a plan to get into the records room, and I haven't been paying as much attention as needed to keep my story straight.

"It is," I say. "Sorry. I haven't had much sleep."

She gives me an understanding smile and continues walking.

I inwardly curse.

"We have a pharmacy on site. We also use the latest in speech and cognitive therapy. I know you said you didn't know your uncle's medications, but do you know if his physician was employing any sort of therapy."

"Uh, no, sorry."

This time, she doesn't give me a consoling smile—only a sideways glance.

I've got to get away from her and find the records room in the basement.

We pass a short connecting hall. Halfway down is a woman sitting in a wheelchair across from a janitor's closet. There's a stairwell at the other end. That's it. That's where I need to get.

"—records from your uncle's physician."

My head is still turned towards the hallway as we pass, and I don't even realize she's speaking to me.

"Mr Reese?"

"Hmm?" I turn to look at her.

"The records? From your uncle's physician."

I don't know what the question was, but I just assume she's asking for my fictitious uncle's medical records.

"Sure. I'll call Dr Williams for you and get them to you as soon as I can."

Her brow creases for a split second like she's frustrated.

She motions to an open door.

"Let me show you one of the rooms."

I follow her.

The room is small—maybe twenty feet by twenty. There's an

empty bed against the wall with monitors and some equipment resting on mobile metal trays. The frosted window lets in muted sunlight and is reinforced to keep it from breaking.

"These are our individual rooms, like the kind your uncle would be staying in, depending on his condition."

I'm not even paying attention. I don't know how much of the tour is left. My mind is racing for any excuse to leave her side. Should I tell her that I was so intrigued by the records room that I would love to check it out? No, that's stupid. She's not going to—

"—has Alzheimer's?"

Again, I'm snapped out of it, completely unaware of the question.

"What?"

"You said your uncle has Alzheimer's?"

"Uh, yeah."

This time, there's no compassionate smile. She looks like she's concerned. I'm still trying to figure out how to get away from her.

I nervously glance about the room.

"What's your uncle's name?" she asks.

"I'm sorry?"

"Your uncle. What's his name?"

"Uh, Doug." I feel like I've answered fast enough, but something is wrong.

"And your brother's name?"

"Anthony."

Oh, fuck. Fuck, fuck, fuck.

"I thought it was your cousin."

"It is. I have a brother. His name is Anthony."

"And your cousin's name?"

"Mark."

"What's your uncle's name, again?"

I have absolutely forgotten the answer I gave a moment ago. "Dav—I mean, Doug."

FUCK!

It feels like the temperature of the room has dropped ten degrees, due to her stare.

"Mr Reese, why are you lying to me?"

"I'm not lying—"

"A moment ago, you called his physician Dr Williams, but back at reception, it was Dr Williamson. You also said you didn't know what classification of dementia your uncle had, but now you say he has Alzheimer's. You don't know his medications, or if he's doing any therapy. And, you can't seem to keep your brother or your cousin straight … Why are you lying?"

I meet her stare but can't speak.

That's it. She's had enough. Up until now, I've been worried about getting information about Rachel Smith, but I never realized that if I failed, not only would I not get the information, I could also be in serious trouble.

Her stare hardens.

"Well, the tour is over. I need you to come with me back to reception," she says, walking towards the door, while keeping an eye on me.

I don't move. If I go out those doors, Rachel has the upper hand.

"Let's go … Now."

I have no idea what I'm doing, but remain rooted to the floor.

She nods. "Okay. If that's the way you want to do this."

She steps into the hallway and calls out, "Rory? Michael? Can you come here, please?"

She turns back to me and stands there with her arms folded, blocking the door.

Moments later, two mountainous orderlies appear behind her.

"Mr Reese, these are two of my best orderlies: Rory and Michael. Gentlemen, this is Mr Reese, and he's in the building illegally."

They join her in glaring at me.

"Mr Reese," Dr Cavanaugh continues, "you are in a world

of trouble. You are going to tell me why you lied to get in here or Michael and Rory are going to quietly escort you from the building."

The "quietly" was a command. She doesn't want a scene. She doesn't want me to draw attention and I instantly know why. I've found my leverage.

"I promise you; I won't be quiet. I'll make sure everyone in this building knows I was here."

There it is.

That blink that tells me her command backfired.

"Then I will just have to call the police," she counters.

"Be my guest."

The blink, again. Her body tenses. I've called her bluff. No way is she going to call the police and I know why.

Out of options, she decides to take the risk.

"Rory, Michael; get this man out of my building."

Seemingly itching for a fight, they step around her and move towards me.

"You can't call the cops because you'll be shut down," I say, backpedaling so I have time to get my words out before they're on top of me. "If you kick me out, I'll make a scene and call the cops from the parking lot. I'll tell them that you let me in. Sacred Heart will close."

I keep my eyes on her as Rory and Michael approach.

I think it's Rory who gets the first hand on me, and he knows how to restrain someone. In a movement seemingly too quick for someone so big, he has one of my arms behind my back and his tree trunk of a bicep across my chest. I'm totally immobilized. He tightens his grip, crushing my lungs.

As the air races out, I'm able to wheeze, "Or this can all go away ..."

*

"Sit down," Dr Cavanaugh says.

It's more of a civilized demand than a polite request.

I sit in the chair in front of her desk in the office behind the reception area. Rory and Michael stand by the door, slightly more relaxed, because I complied with Dr Cavanaugh's request to accompany them silently to the office.

Dr Cavanaugh walks around the desk and lowers herself into her own chair.

"Now, Mr Reese, you want to tell me what this is all about?"

I nod to Rory and Michael. "They should probably wait outside."

"Not a chance," Michael says.

"We'll keep the blinds open. They can stand by the door. They see something you don't like; they can charge in here and beat the shit out of me … but I'm doing this for you, Dr Cavanaugh."

She considers and nods to them.

Reluctantly, they step outside and close the door, but peer through the glass, watching us intently.

I turn back to her. "Listen, I'm really sorry about this. I truly am."

"Mr Reese, I was trying to help you. That's what we do here. I've run this facility for ten years. These patients need Sacred Heart and you're threatening to shut us down because I was trying to help you."

"I know. What I did was shitty. I fully admit that."

"So … why?"

"Because I need something, and yes, if I don't get it, I'll have to tell the authorities that you let me in, illegally. The medical board will come down hard on this place. It'll cause all types of problems. Problems you probably can't afford. You're strained enough, as is, right? Why else would the Head Administrator be manning the front desk? The worst of it is, you'll be fired, and I'm assuming Sacred Heart can't survive without you. But I promise, this can all go away."

"You promise?" she scoffs.

I nod.

I hate this. I hate the pain I'm causing and if there was some other way, I would take it, but there's not.

She sighs. "What do you want?"

"I need to see the records of a former patient."

She processes my request with an offended look. "Why?"

"I can't tell you that."

"Then, no."

"It's the only way."

"I can't do that. We have to protect our patient's priv—"

"You can protect the well-being of every patient in this building. I'm not going to print anything or take anything with me. There'll be no evidence I was here ... just let me see the file. That's it."

For the first time since she sat down, she looks away from me in disgust. Finally, she shakes her head. Her shoulders slump. She reaches over and taps some keys on her computer.

"What's the patient's name?" she asks.

I shake my head. "No. You can't know who it is. I want you to pull up whatever program you use to access your records. I'll do the search while you stand over here."

She sits back in hopeless frustration. "I can't have you pulling up records about our patients."

"Ten seconds. That's all I ask. After I look at the file, I'm going to walk out that door and you'll never see or hear from me, again. Sacred Heart stays open, and it's like none of this ever happened. If you ever think I broke this agreement, you've seen my ID. You know my name. You know where I live. Call the cops. Simple as that."

She stares at the top of the desk, then stands up and goes to the window. She gives the worried Rory and Michael a reassuring nod and pulls down the blinds. She turns back to me and motions to the computer.

"Get it over with."

I get up and go behind the desk.

She waits with her arms folded.

The program on the screen is pretty straightforward. There's the logo for Sacred Heart and two search fields: one to search by patient name and one to search for by case number.

I type "Rachel Smith" into the first search field.

The result is instantaneous. On the cover page is her name, date of admission, and attending physician. I scroll down. There are scanned handwritten notes, as well as pages of transcribed notes. I continue to scroll down, catching snippets like "obsession", "limerence", "highly intelligent", "readmitted", "fixation", "self-mutilation", and more.

"Your ten seconds are up, Mr Reese."

I ignore her and keep scrolling. There are so many pages.

"Mr Reese?"

Finally, I reach the page I've been searching for; the release report. It's dated a few months ago.

Rachel Smith
Born 8/17/87
Admitted for Suspicion of Relationship Obsessive Compulsive
Disorder + Limerence.
Released to custody of parents William and Kelly Smith
1148 Kingsbrook Road, Maidstone, Vermont.
Approved by Dr Brian Nguyen

Dr Cavanaugh steps forward. "Mr Reese?"

"Done," I say, and click 'back' on screen, which returns me to the program's home screen. My last act is to quickly go to the file menu, highlight the 'search recent' option, right click, and click on 'clear all'.

Dr Cavanaugh comes around the desk.

I hold up my hands and step away from the computer.

Immediately, she goes to the file menu and pulls up the 'search recent', trying to find who I was looking for, but it's gone.

I walk over to the blinds. Rory and Michael are still there, about to spring into action, but I hold up my hands.

I look back at her. "No one knows what happened. You'll never hear from me, again … And for what it's worth, I am really sorry."

She stares at me in disbelief.

"Mr Reese, I don't care how sorry you are."

She's right.

There's no use trying to defend myself.

I go out the office door, past Rory and Michael, through the main doors, and into the biting cold.

Chapter 15

I push the envelope of safety for the entire ride to Maidstone. Night is falling, and the cars on the road are starting to thin. I'm getting closer. I can feel it.

Maidstone is a small town that sits near the border with New Hampshire. The sign by the road welcomes me to the town, and announces a population of two thousand, two hundred and twenty-seven. Below that reads, "+1 now that you're here!" There is no downtown, or any sign of a town, for that matter—just scatterings of buildings.

I follow my GPS down roads that twist and turn through the trees. Occasionally, a gravel driveway pops out of the woods, connecting to the road.

The GPS announces that my destination is up ahead. The only possible option is a red mailbox sitting at the end of a seemingly random driveway reaching out of the forest. I turn into the drive and can see lights burning amongst the trees. I roll forward, and just as the view of the road is obstructed by the trees behind me, the house comes into view. It's a split-level with gray siding and a red roof. All the lights in the house are on. It would be charming if I weren't so on edge. There's a detached garage next to the house. The door of the garage is up and I can see a Chevy Malibu inside.

I park the car in front of the garage. I'm having déjà vu from my trip to Laura's mother's house in Thistleton. I remember the wind whipping against the side of the house, but here in the woods, it's total silence. There's no chirping of insects or call of birds from the forest. It's too cold.

I walk to the porch and look through the window, into the living room. The lamps on the end tables next to the couch are on. There's a painting of a ship at sea above the mantel of the fireplace. There's a television in the corner, but aside from the lights being on, there's no signs of life.

I go to the front door. I'm about to press the illuminated doorbell button, but stop when I see the door is slightly open.

I knock, and gently push it in.

"Hello? Is anyone h—?"

As the door opens, the smell washes over me. I know that smell. I know it from the basement of a warehouse. My eyes burn with tears. I turn and wretch. Had I anything in my stomach, it would have come up. I move away from the door, lean on the porch railing, and take in large gulps of air. I can still taste it in my throat and nose—the smell of rot and decay.

A horrible thought takes hold—Murphy.

I press my sleeve over my mouth, take a few deep breaths, and step through the door. My heart is pounding in my chest. Even though I'm taking short, shallow breaths with my sleeve over my mouth, the stench is still overpowering. To the left is a set of stairs that lead to the second floor. The living room is on my right. Straight ahead is the kitchen. Through the kitchen opening, I can see a window looking out at the forest. In front of the window is a table, upon which rests a piece of paper. I slowly walk into the kitchen. I make as little noise as possible, and dart my eyes from left to right, remaining alert for any sudden movements.

The kitchen is spotless. The counters are bare. The sinks are empty. There's no sign of the source of the smell.

I keep my sleeve pressed over my mouth as I take the piece of paper from the table.

> *I watched you walk into that place and I came here. I've had to speed up my plan. I don't know how you found me, but if you found that place, then you finally know. You understand everything. My parents tried to stop me from doing what's right. They're upstairs, asleep. You know what you took from Laura and I. Now, you understand what you've done, and what I'll do to make it right. You killed us, and left us in that room. I've brought Murphy home. He's waiting, and it's time for you to sleep.*
>
> —*R&L*

I race out of the house. I'm not going to check on her parents. I'll take her word that they are "asleep" upstairs.

*

The drive home should have taken an hour. I cover it in thirty minutes. I have no regard for speed limits or double lines. The burner phone sits on the passenger seat. I keep willing it to ring.

I reach the edge of my driveway and swing the car in at a dangerous clip. All the lights in the house and cottage are off. I skid the car to a stop next to the porch, grab the burner phone, and leap out. I vault the porch steps, practically kick in the front door, and throw on the lights.

"Murphy!"

I race through the house, hitting all the lights, and frantically shouting Murphy's name. I do a complete circuit, and wind up back in the living room. Every room has been searched, every light is on. There's no sign of him or Rachel. I go to the windows and scan the trees.

The burner phone rings in my hand. I quickly answer.

"I played your stupid game! I know who you are, Rachel! You said you brought him home."

"I did bring him home," she whispers.

A light in the cottage comes on.

"It's time to sleep."

Chapter 16

I step out onto the porch in a daze, and stare at the cottage. The light spills through the open front door and onto the porch, but the curtains are drawn.

It's waiting like a spider in a web.

I take out my phone and dial.

"Nine-one-one, what is your emergency?"

"My name is Jacob Reese. I'm at 213 Normandy Lane. There's a woman here who is mentally unstable. I need the police."

"Where is she, now?"

"There's a cottage on the property. She's in there."

"Do you know who the woman is?"

"Yes."

"Where are you?"

"I'm outside."

"Is she threatening you?"

"Yes."

"Does she have a weapon?"

From inside the cottage, I hear a plaintive bark.

"Sir?"

"I have to go."

"Sir, I need you to stay on the line with me. I'm sending police and an ambulance. Do not try to—"

I hang up the phone, and begin walking.

The gravel of the driveway under my feet sounds a million miles away.

I walk past the fire pit and onto the porch. The open door looks like a glowing portal.

I step through.

Rachel.

She's standing in the middle of the living room, dressed in her Little Red Riding Hood costume. Murphy sits by her side. With one hand, she's holding his collar. In the other hand, she has a gun, pointed at his head.

She's smiling at me, not in triumph, but in a creepy, sweet "I-told-you-so" manner.

Murphy looks okay, but he's scared. He doesn't understand the gun, but he can sense that it's not a toy. Murphy yaps at the sight of me, and tries to move. She holds him in place.

'Please, Murphy,' I mentally plead. 'Be a bad dog, for once. Bite her. Attack!'

I know he won't, because I've trained him so well.

"Hello, Jacob," she says, eyes glistening in the soft glow of the lamps.

I hold up my hands. "I'm here. Let him go."

She keeps the gun pointed at his ear. Murphy's big brown eyes look from me to her in confusion. Her smile widens. "You took everything from us. Why shouldn't I take everything from you?"

"Because the dog has nothing to do with this. You have some warped view of fairness, but he did nothing to you."

She considers my words, and then nods to the corner of the room.

"Stand over there," she says.

"Let him go first."

She presses the gun more firmly against his ear.

239

"Okay!" I shout. "Okay …"

Still facing her, I step sideways into the corner, making any escape through the front door impossible before she got off a shot.

"There," I say, coming to a stop. "Let him go."

She hesitates, enjoying my panic. Again, she presses the gun to Murphy's ear.

"Rachel, let him go, now!"

She smiles, and releases his collar.

Murphy instantly darts out the front door, and begins barking in the yard.

Rachel points the gun at me.

The hair, the scar, the contacts. She looks so much like Laura, it's uncanny. Her peaceful gaze makes it terrifying.

"Rachel, put the gun down."

"You have to pay for what you did to us."

"Rachel, there was no you and Laura."

"I loved her. I loved her more than anyone, and she loved me. We were going to be happy. I would make her understand that, and you took it away." Her voice is calm but forceful.

"It was a mistake, Rachel."

"You have to pay. You have to sleep."

"Rachel, stop! Your parents—"

"They didn't want me to make it right!" she snaps, causing me to start. Her calm demeanor has cracked and is replaced with simmering rage. "After they took me from school, they tried to make me forget Laura, but they didn't understand. They kept me there for over a year. They didn't understand. I played along with the doctors so they would let me out. After you killed Laura, they sent me back to *that place*—that hospital. I was there for years, and you … You were free. When I got out, I wanted to make it right. I *had* to make it right. My parents didn't want me to make it right. They said they were going to send me back to *that place*, again. I couldn't let that happen. Not again. I had to make it right—for Laura."

240

Just like in that warehouse, when Reggie was pointing a gun at me, I'm looking for any opportunity, any sliver of a chance to act, but she's too far away for me to make a move for the gun. She's also too close to miss. I have to keep her talking.

"Rachel, it's okay. We can—"

"It's not okay! When you sleep, it will be okay! You killed us!"

"You're not Laura!" It was my turn to snap, but it only enrages her more.

"We were the same! We were one person, and you killed her!"

"Rachel, I didn't kill her."

"You did! You shot her! You killed us!"

I hold up my hands, pleading with her. "No, Rachel, listen, I didn't—!"

"Stop lying!"

"Rache—!"

"STOP!"

Something starts clicking in my head. How does she—?

"You can't lie to me," she says, trembling with anger. "You shot and killed us. You sat there on the ground, with the gun in your hand, and watched us die."

My head is spinning. Something doesn't add up.

"You have to understand what you did. You have to take respon-sibility. You have to admit that you shot us, and then sat there on the ground, and watched us d—!"

It clicks.

"How did you know that?" I ask.

My question throws her. I'm not angry. I'm not panicked. I'm not thinking of the gun or Murphy. It's a simple, sincere question.

She stares at me, while keeping the gun aimed at my chest, but doesn't answer.

"How did you know that?" I ask, again.

She continues to stare.

Anger starts to creep into my veins. "How did you know that I *sat there on the ground*, with the gun in my hand, and watched her die? I've never told anyone about that. So, how could you possibly know?"

She's still smiling.

"There's only one way you could know that …"

Everything aligns. Everything makes sense.

"You were there," I whisper. "You were at the warehouse, that night … You were the reason she needed to talk to me. It was you. She was trying to warn me that you were out. You were the reason she was at the warehouse, looking for me … She was trying to get away from you … You were there …"

Rachel shakes her head. "I only wanted to talk to her. I was going to show her that we could be happy. I followed her there, and she ran inside. I parked in the road, and was walking up when I heard the shot. I hid, and then I saw *you*," she spits, "standing over us with the gun. You sat down, and watched us die." Tears begin spilling down her cheeks. "You could have saved us. You could have gotten help, but you didn't. You shot us, and watched us die. After you left, I went inside to find her, and I found that door, in the basement. I knew. That's where you put us. You left us in that room to rot!"

"Rachel, I need you to listen to me very carefully, okay? I didn't shoot Laura."

Her eyes flash with anger. "You're lying!"

"I'm not," I reply, as calmly as I can, "and I can show you."

She blinks.

"I went to the warehouse to meet a guy named Reggie. He was a bad person who tried to kill me. We were in the warehouse, and he shot me. The bullet went through me, it went through my side, and hit Laura."

I don't know if she believes me, but I can see the first signs of doubt in the quiver of her lips, and the trembling of the gun.

"I'm going to lift up my shirt, okay?"

She doesn't answer, only waits.

Very deliberately, keeping my hands in view, I slowly take a hold of my shirt, and pull it upwards. I twist slightly to show her the matching scars on my side.

"Here," I say, speaking very slowly. "That's where the bullet went in, and there's where the bullet came out. Reggie shot Laura, and I killed Reggie. I hit him with a pipe, and killed him. You never saw him, because he was hidden. I took the gun from his hand, just in case he was still alive, and I went to Laura. That's when you saw us. Afterwards, I put them in that room because I—I didn't know what else to do, but that's what you saw. I didn't shoot Laura."

She's wavering. The certainty is gone. "No … No … You killed us."

"Rachel, look at me, okay? Look right here," I say, pointing to my eyes. "I didn't shoot Laura."

Her trembling becomes worse. Her lips are shaking. The tears are pouring from her eyes and make a light *pat-pat* as they land on the floor.

"You're lying! You shot us!"

"*Her!* I didn't shoot *her!*" I snap. "You're not Laura! Don't you get it?! You made her go there, that night. You scared her so much, she ran to that warehouse to get away from you! It's your fault, too, dammit! I didn't kill her! I just didn't sa— I didn't save her." I can't stop the words before they leave my mouth.

She stares at me. Fear and revulsion begin to take hold.

"No …" she quietly pleads.

"You're the reason she came looking for me that night, and I didn't shoot her."

The gun lowers slightly. Her mouth twists in agony.

I see it happen.

I watch as her broken mind sees clarity, recognizing that she shares some of the responsibility for Laura's death. Her heart

243

breaks right in front of me. She keeps the gun pointed in my direction, but doubles over, as if she's going to vomit.

"No … No!" she cries, and lets out a blood-curdling scream. Her body is racked with sobs. "Laura … Oh God … Laura …"

I could make a grab at the gun, but there's a couple of feet between us, and she still has it pointed in my direction. If I make a dash for it, she could panic and pull the trigger.

My slight hesitation ruins any chance I may have had.

She straightens up and continues speaking through her choked sobs.

"Oh my God … Laura … My parents … What did I do?"

"Rachel, listen to me."

My voice brings her back. She steadies the gun, but her face is still a mask of pain and anguish.

"It will be okay," I tell her. "The police are on their way. Just put the gun down. We'll get you help."

She looks at the floor in thought, and then looks back up at me. "No … No. They'll say I'm crazy, and send me back to *that place*. That's not fair. It's not fair to my parents or Laura. Someone has to pay." She chokes on the words. "I have to pay."

"It's okay, Rachel. It will be all right."

She shakes her head. "No … it won't."

She glances at the ground one more time.

Now. I have to move, now.

"You said the police are on their way?" she asks, eyes still on the floor.

"Yes. The lady said the police are on their way with an ambulance. They'll be able to help you."

I steady myself on the balls of my feet.

This is it.

I shift my weight forward and prepare to—

She looks up.

Her expression freezes me in place. She has an angelic smile, as if she's had an epiphany.

"I know," she says, her smile breaking through her tears. "I know how to make it right. I'm to blame. I played a part in Laura's death. And there's my parents. I have to pay for what I did."

"Rachel, you don't—"

"But you're right, too … You didn't save her."

My heart stops.

Her pain has completely disappeared. She's calm, peaceful, and self-assured. "But do you know what? You saved yourself. I didn't think you could, but you did. You saved yourself, and you saved Murphy. And you showed me that I have to be fair."

I can't speak.

"You said the police and an ambulance were on their way?" she asks.

"… Yes."

She shakes her head at me like she can't believe how perfect it all is. "I'm going to show you mercy, Jacob Reese. You didn't save her, but I'm going to show you mercy."

"That's great, Rachel. Thank you. Now can you please—?"

"I'm going to show you mercy by giving you what you took from Laura."

I blink.

"What do you mean? What are you going to give me that I took from Laura?"

"You took away Laura's chance to live, but I'm going to give you one. That's how you pay; I'm going to give you a chance."

With tears in her eyes, and a benevolent smile, she aims the gun slightly lower …

And fires.

I collapse onto the floor in a ball, clutching my stomach. It feels like I've been hit with a sledgehammer. The pain is so intense, I want to scream. I want to wail like a child, but all I can manage are strained grunts through clenched teeth. Rachel is talking, but my ears are ringing, and her voice sounds like it's reaching me under-water. I'm vaguely aware of Murphy barking outside. I make the mistake of looking down at my hands. I pull them away from my stomach. They're covered in blood. My blood. I go back to pressing them against the wound, trying to hold my life inside of me.

I roll onto my side, still curled into a ball, and look outwards. Rachel's feet are within arm's length. The sledgehammer pain in my stomach morphs to include the sensation of a white-hot poker being driven through my gut. My eyes are bulging and every muscle is straining. The ringing in my ears is fading. I can hear Murphy outside, and Rachel's voice finally comes through clearly.

"—all of this, and you're right. I only wanted to be fair. So, I need to pay. I have to pay for what I did … and it's time for me to sleep."

I raise my head and look at her feet.

There's a silence.

The gun fires.

It clatters to the floor next to her feet.

Rachel falls.

Her body offers no resistance as it collapses. Her head hits the floor, her face in my direction. Her eyes are open. They still have that angelic look. Her mouth holds that serene smile. Slowly, her facial features go slack as her muscles relax. Her eyes remain open but the smile fades. Blood begins to seep out from under her head. It inches across the floor towards me.

I turn away, and press myself tighter into a ball.

Every twitch sends bolts of pain through my body.

Murphy's still barking.

My hands feel warm. I need to slow the bleeding.

I don't think the bullet went through. I think it's still in—
FUCK!

The pain is blinding. I'm still grunting, even though every grunt causes my stomach to contract, which brings a horrible flash of pain, which causes me to grunt, again, starting the cycle over.

The bleeding. I need to slow the bleeding. I think the bullet is still in me. I can use gravity.

I twist myself and roll onto my back. I let loose a scream, which brings more pain, and clamp down on my stomach.

Murphy's barking pauses, then grows more frantic than before.

Being on my back should help slow the blood loss. I press harder with my hands.

I start crying.

This is indescrib— I hear them.

Sirens, approaching fast.

Murphy continues barking.

Good boy, Lassie. Tell them that Timmy is in the well.

I almost laugh, but grunt, which snaps my mind back into focus.

I'm going into shock. The pain is lessening.

I have to stay here.

I have to keep my eyes open.

The sirens are growing louder.

Hurry. Please, God. Please! Hurry!

Keep your eyes open! Focus on the ceiling. Keep staring at *the—*

—heavy steel door. There's a pressure on my shoulder.

"Jacob?" a voice whispers.

I turn.

It's Laura.

We're standing in the warehouse. The music from the—

—STAY HERE!

I can see faint red, blue, and yellow lights playing across the ceiling. They're getting brighter. The sirens are growing louder.

Hurry. Please.

I just need to hold on. I just need to focus. Focus on the pain. Keep your *eyes—*

—music box fills the warehouse. There are pinpoints of light over-head like stars. All around us, moving through the piles of rotting

wooden pallets, people are dancing, waltzing to the music. I catch a glimpse of my parents dancing together. I see Reggie dancing with Rachel. Two of the dancing figures don't have faces. Somehow, I know they are Rachel's parents. Everyone is elegantly spinning to chimes of the music box.

Laura smiles at me and holds out her hand. "May I have this—?"

—KEEP YOUR EYES OPEN!

I press on my stomach, knowing the agony it will cause, but the flash of torture keeps my mind in the present.

DON'T DANCE!

I can hear the cars in the driveway, outside.

The sirens cut off but the lights continue to play across the ceiling and the walls.

I can do this. I can do this. I just have to keep my eyes open. Hurry.

I hear voices. Loud voices. They're at the door. Heavy footsteps. They're coming towards me. They're in the room.

Hurry!

I just need to keep my eyes open!

HURRY! *PLE—*

Chapter 17

I hate this heart monitor.

I know that's a weird thing to say because it's reminding me that I'm still alive, but after four days of relentless, methodical beeping, it's driving me crazy.

Four days. That's how long I've been awake. I've been in this hospital for eight days, but I was out for the first four.

I remember being shot. I remember lying on the floor of the cottage. I remember the sounds of the footsteps and voices coming towards me, but that's it.

Then, it was all dreams and oblivion.

I wandered around all the places from my life: my childhood, Laura's dorm, Mattie's house, the warehouse, my parents' funeral, The Hollows. Everywhere I went, I was the last person on Earth, haunting my own memories. Every place was quiet, except for the occasional random voice from somewhere in the distance. Some of them I recognized: Laura, Sandy, my father, Rachel. Others were alien, forceful voices shouting things I couldn't understand.

Finally, after feeling as though I had wandered for years, I ended up in the cottage, standing over the first and only person I encountered on my travels: myself, bleeding out on the cottage floor. Then, everything went black.

I could have stayed there. Enveloped in nothing, but then I started to hear this rhythmic sound from somewhere in the distant darkness. It grew louder and louder and the blackness around me grew lighter and lighter.

That's when I opened my eyes.

The first thing I saw and heard was the heart monitor.

The light in the hospital room was blinding. There was a mask over my nose and mouth and a tube going down my throat. I panicked and tried to move, but my body wouldn't respond. I could only slightly shift my weight, which caused me to be nauseous.

"It's okay. You're okay, Jacob," the doctor said in a soothing tone from my bedside. "I'm Dr Jensen. This is Nurse Hemmings." He nodded to the middle-aged nurse on the other side of the bed and continued, "It's best if you don't try to move, okay?"

The panic subsided. I realized that I must have been drugged up to my eyeballs.

Dr Jensen held up a small whiteboard and placed it on the bed at my side. He then took out a marker. "Now, I don't want you to try to talk but we do need to communicate a little, okay?"

I lightly nodded.

He put the marker in my hand, which I realized I had some control over, and placed it on the whiteboard.

"Do you remember what happened?" he asked.

I ignored his question and wrote 'Murphy' in a comical looping script because my fingers only slightly followed my brain's commands.

"He's fine," Dr Jensen said. "He's with your friend, Sandy. She's keeping an eye on him."

A flood of relief swept over me.

"Do you remember being shot?"

'Yes', I wrote.

Dr Jensen proceeded to explain to me that the bullet had been a wrecking ball to my guts. Those are my words, not his. I lost a lot of blood and almost cashed out in the ambulance on the way to the hospital. They operated on me for almost sixteen hours to repair the damage and it had been touch and go the whole time. They were finally able to stabilize me but had to put me into a medically induced coma, hence my around the world travels.

They removed the tube two days ago. I'm still on a drip for my nutrients and I've been told that I'm off solid foods for a while. For four days, I've been lying on this bed with nothing to do but think and turn over every moment that led me here. After a few hours, you just accept the catheter and the bedpan and the sponge baths and the constant blood draws and the overly enthusiastic 'How We Doin'?s' from the nurse. She's nice, don't get me wrong, but I'm not in the mood.

I know the police are going to want to talk to me. As soon as they took out the tube, it was only a matter of time. I still can't really move, but I am starting to talk, even if it is barely above a whisper.

I'm alive.

I fought my way here. I convinced Rachel to let Murphy go. I convinced her that I didn't kill Laura, but I did play a part in her death, and for that, she gave me a chance, and I beat it. It could have easily gone the other way. Rachel made a decision and let the chips fall where they may … and I beat it. I got my life back.

But now, I have a choice to make and I've done nothing but turn it over in my mind for the past four days because it's going to determine what *type* of life I'm going to get back.

When the police come to talk to me, I can do one of two things.

I can tell them everything: Laura, Mattie, Reggie, Rachel, all of it. I can come clean and finally get this off my chest. I don't know what comes after that, but I could stop hiding. I could stop looking over my shoulder. The nightmares would stop. The downside would be jail. I don't know for how long. I did kill Reggie. That would have to come out. Maybe I could argue it was self-defense. I have no idea if it would work. I don't want to go to jail. Not at all. The thought of being locked up for an indeterminate amount of time for whatever they charge me with terrifies me, but this would all be over, and not just for me. Mrs Aisling and Amy could start to move on, too.

Which brings me to my other option: I can keep going.

There's nothing that really ties me to Rachel or Laura or Reggie. I can plead ignorance. I don't think Veronica or the rental car guy would want to get involved. They probably won't even hear of this. Maybe Amy would, but that's a risk I have to take. I also don't think Mrs Aisling is a very reliable witness. I can lie all over again and say Rachel was a crazy woman who thought I killed Laura. They'll have the records and I don't think Dr Cavanaugh would tell them about my visit. They also have Rachel's dead parents. I can be one of her victims who just got lucky.

Once it all blows over, I can rebuild my life, leave The Hollows, and maybe start another coffee shop in some other perfect New England town, but the doubt would always be there. What if Rachel left a clue? What if I'm wrong and there is something to connect me to everything? How much worse would it be when they put the handcuffs on me then, rather than if I confess, now? But what if I can keep going, get through this, and it'll all be over? But how would I know it was really over? The answer is that I won't. I'll be free, but the guilt and the nightmares will continue, and the looks over my shoulder might be more frequent.

It's all I can think about in between the sponge baths, ice-chip lunches, and the incessant beeping of this fucking heart monitor. Yes, my heart is beating but it's a constant reminder that the time to make a decision is running out.

*

I know.

I know the moment Dr Jensen walks through the door two days later that the time has come.

252

As he steps in, he tries to open it only enough to get through so that I won't see into the hallway, but of course I do, and there they are. Two of them, wearing suits and serious demeanors.

"Good morning, Jacob," Dr Jensen says, closing the door behind him. "How are we feeling, today?"

I want to ask, 'Who's we?' but instead give him the truth. "A little better."

My voice is slightly stronger than yesterday, and the pain is a little duller.

"Good, good," he says and hesitates. "Listen, there are some men here to see you. They're detectives. They'd like to ask you some questions. I said I would ask you if you're feeling up to it. You can say 'no' and I'll send them away. I personally don't think it's best for you, right now, but it's your call. Do you want to talk to them?"

"It's okay," I answer.

I don't need any more time. I've made my decision. Let's get this show on the road.

Dr Jensen lightly shakes his head in resignation before turning and going back to the door. He opens it as I attempt to sit up a little more in the bed, which hurts like hell.

The two guys step into the room. One's got a tight crew cut and carries himself in a way that screams ex-military. The other is balding and heavyset with bloodshot eyes. They take up positions at the foot of the bed and wait for Dr Jensen to leave.

"Five minutes," Dr Jensen says, sternly. "That's all you get, for now." He then turns to me. "If there's any trouble, simply ring for the nurse," he says with a nod to the button mounted to the railing of the bed. He gives one last look to the detectives as he walks past them and steps into the hall.

The detectives wait until the door closes and then look at me. I can't tell if they suspect or pity me. Ex-military guy is a stone and even Old Bleary Eyes is inscrutable.

"Mr Reese," Ex-military begins. "I'm Detective McDougall.

This is Detective Simmons." Old Bleary Eyes dips his chin. "We know that this has been an incredible ordeal for you, but we'd like to ask you some questions. Is that okay with you?"

I lightly nod.

Detective McDougall takes out a notepad and a pen. He clicks the end, which brings out the point, and poises it over the paper. "First off, can you tell us what happened?"

I glance back and forth between them.

I look at the tip of Detective McDougall's expectant pen, waiting for my answer.

I take a breath … and begin.

Acknowledgements

From the moment I was sitting on the bed of a wonderful Airbnb in Portland, Maine, on my birthday with the guestbook in my hand, and had an idea, to this moment of you holding it in your hands, a lot of blood, sweat, tears, coffee, and ink went into *Dark Hollows*. Sure, it's my name on the cover, but it doesn't happen without the help of a lot of people.

Thank you, Mom, Dad, Amanda, and Stephanie, for all your love and support and asking for more pages. Thank you, Victoria Skurnick at the Levine Greenberg Rostan Literary Agency for your hard work. Thank you, Deborah Griffith, for catching all those phrases and word slips. Thank you, Olivia Hernandez, for helping me find my way through the woods.

And finally, a huge thanks to Abigail Fenton and the entire team at HQ and HarperCollins. You saw *Dark Hollows* for what it was and your passion, support, and guidance were everything a debut author could dream of. Thank you. Thank you. Thank you.

Thank you for reading *Dark Hollows*!

I hope you had as much fun reading *Dark Hollows* as I had writing it. If you did enjoy it, please give it a rating and a review. I can't tell you how far it goes in helping others find it. I've seen it myself and have discovered so many amazing authors and their work by reading their reviews. So, please, let people know what you think. They'll appreciate it, and so will I!

Happy reading!

Dear Reader,

We hope you enjoyed reading this book. If you did, we'd be so appreciative if you left a review. It really helps us and the author to bring more books like this to you.

Here at HQ Digital we are dedicated to publishing fiction that will keep you turning the pages into the early hours. Don't want to miss a thing? To find out more about our books, promotions, discover exclusive content and enter competitions you can keep in touch in the following ways:

JOIN OUR COMMUNITY:

Sign up to our new email newsletter: po.st/HQSignUp

Read our new blog www.hqstories.co.uk

🐦 *: https://twitter.com/HQDigitalUK*

📘 *: www.facebook.com/HQStories*

BUDDING WRITER?

We're also looking for authors to join the HQ Digital family! Please submit your manuscript to:

HQDigital@harpercollins.co.uk

Thanks for reading, from the HQ Digital team

DIGITAL
H Q

If you enjoyed *Dark Hollows*, then why not try another gripping thriller from HQ Digital?